Praise for *The Last Sailor*

"There is real life in Sarah Anne Johnson's new book, and genuine family drama too, all grounded in an authoritative evocation of old Cape Cod's waterways, marshes, and waterfront towns. *The Last Sailor* is memorable, clearly seen, and deeply felt."
—Jon Clinch, author of *Marley* and *Finn*

"A prose gem, the sentences moving with stately grace and clarity. I won't soon forget Nathaniel Boyd and the people around him."
—Richard Bausch, winner of the Rea Award for the Short Story

"*The Last Sailor* is a gripping, insightful story of loneliness, love, land, and sea, written with plainspoken grace."
—Heidi Jon Schmidt, author of *The House on Oyster Creek* (NAL)

"The prose in this book is clear as water, which makes sense as this is a water book, where everything unfolds beside or on the sea, or in that liminal space of a salt marsh, which is the source of all life. Johnson deftly charts the way anger and grief can thread through generations, poisoning the days until by some act of grace redemption is found. I loved my time in this world."
—Nick Flynn, author of *This Is the Night Our House Will Catch Fire*

Also by Sarah Anne Johnson

The Lightkeeper's Wife

The
LAST
SAILOR

a novel

SARAH ANNE JOHNSON

Published by Sourcebooks Landmark, an imprint of Sourcebooks.
P.O. Box 4410, Naperville, Illinois 60567-4410
(630) 961-3900
sourcebooks.com

Library of Congress Cataloging-in-Publication Data
Names: Johnson, Sarah Anne, author.
Title: Last sailor / Sarah Johnson.
Description: Naperville, IL : Sourcebooks Landmark, [2020]
Identifiers: LCCN 2019052856 | (trade paperback)
Subjects: LCSH: Domestic fiction.
Classification: LCC PS3610.O3765 L37 2020 | DDC 813/.6--dc23

LC record available at https://lccn.loc.gov/2019052856

Printed and bound in Canada.
MBP 10 9 8 7 6 5 4 3 2 1

For Gregg

I

1

S UNLIGHT PENETRATED THE FLAT EXPANSE OF CAPE COD BAY, EXPOS-
ing glittering schools of minnows and tentacles of green seaweed
drifting in the current. The windless August air was an oppression that
drove Nathaniel's hand into the cool seawater. Linen knickers stuck to
his legs with sweat and salt as he lay across the wooden seat, flicking the
fishing line with his finger to see if he'd gotten a bite. No fish since this
morning. No fish until the tide turned to run along the shore. Then he'd
take the trouble to rebait his hook and fish in earnest.

He liked being out on the boat. He wanted to be left alone. For ten
years, he'd achieved a comfortable solitude on the salt marsh, over two
miles from the harbor, until events conspired to bring him back into the
orbit of people he'd once held dear.

He eyed the ragged shore, where seagrass held the shape of weeks
and months and years of wind and the rocks of the jetty stuck out like
two dark thumbs to mark the harbor. He could see the mackerel boats
unloading at the pier, their sails listless in the still air.

When the fishing line grew taut, he raised himself slowly so as not
to shift the boat and disturb the water beneath. He began to reel the fish
in, feeling him fighting on the other end. The trick was to just let him
swim it out. Nathaniel squinted down into the murky depths, inching
the line a little at a time until he saw the shadow moving in desperate
circles, and only then did he jerk the line up. The hook set firm, and he

pulled the fish alongside the boat. A good one, thick around the gills with a fine rainbow sheen. Once in the boat, the fish flailed miserably. Nathaniel whacked him with the sawed-off end of an oar, and then the fish lay limp in the bilge where the seawater would keep him fresh.

Nathaniel rowed toward the jetty, working with a slow motion, letting the boat find its own momentum. The masts of a schooner came into view, then the jetty rocks, slabs of granite stacked like rubble. He rowed alongside them, the slap of the water ringing in his ears, the smell of brine and dried seaweed and broken clamshells with the meat picked clean overwhelming his nostrils. The tide shifted beneath him and swept his boat into the harbor. Familiar sounds struck him, the business of the docks: the creak and strain of a yardarm lifting crates, the clomp of horses pulling wagon carts, and seagulls squawking their comments on the entire scene as if they were the last and final word, angels speaking divinity.

He didn't look toward his father's house on the hill, but he knew his father was there, same as the schooners with their multiple masts and sails like wings and the fishermen scuffing along the gravel in their boots, the horses eating from feed sacks, and men loading crates of cod onto wagons. His father would be at the window, gazing over the fish-drying racks, eyeing the ice shack and the salt barrels, counting the number of fishing vessels, and tallying up the money pouring into the harbor on a Wednesday afternoon.

In 1898, the village of Yarmouth Port was growing, the harbor traffic increasing along with that growth. There were five or six schooners at a time, some from as far away as Gloucester, nearly seventy miles north. The boats moored in the harbor or tied up to the dock and handed crates of fish to a line of men who passed them down until they reached the ice wagon that transported the fish to the railway, where they were shipped to Boston and sold on the state market by Butler Fishing Company. Nathaniel tried not to think about Meredith Butler, but she was always there, like a breeze in the back of his mind. Since she'd married Theo Butler and become part of a wealthy family, he'd tried to let his thoughts of her drift out on the running tide.

All this harbor business went on with such rote familiarity that nobody thought about the boats and wagons and trains that took one fish from the sea and got it into the hands of the person who would eat it. Industry was booming, and Nathaniel's father was profiting by buying and selling land or renting to sailors and tenant farmers. Still, Yarmouth Port was one small cog in the larger wheel, and most of the inhabitants remained happily unaware of their role in the nation's growth. Local folks were consumed with building houses and ships, setting up law firms, dry-goods stores, blacksmith shops, haberdasheries—all the makings of a proper town.

Nathaniel wanted none of it. He'd moved to the marsh ten years ago, at nineteen, after losing his youngest brother, Jacob. The boy had been twelve years old, and he'd believed in Nathaniel the way only a younger brother can believe.

Nathaniel rowed the boat hard onto the beach where Elliot Kelly kept his traps and sat working his fingers in the netting that flowed over his thighs.

"Catch anything?" Eli said, his voice syrupy and languorous.

Nathaniel bent and slid two fingers into the bass's gills to lift it.

"Oughta keep you out of the poorhouse for now."

"Yep."

Nathaniel slid the oars beneath the seats and climbed from the boat. At five feet eleven inches tall, he was a man of sinewy strength, his features sculpted from physical work. Thick waves of sun-streaked brown hair hung loose about his shoulders and hid his gray eyes, ringed red and heavy at times. The hollow look of them spoke to something deeper than physical need, but he admitted no want, no desire. Angular cheeks and thick red lips and the prominent forehead and the firm line of his jaw made for a face that people looked at twice.

Nobody noticed the tiny scar on the edge of his upper lip where he'd caught a fish hook as a boy. His younger brother Phinneas, or Finn, had been the brave one who cut the hook with wire cutters that they kept in the fishing box. It was Finn who pulled the metal through Nathaniel's lip and used his own hands to stop the bleeding. The scar wasn't bad. It reminded Nathaniel of a good time between him and Finn, and that was worth something.

Nathaniel spotted a thick piece of twine on the ground. He ran it through the bass's gills, then carried the fish with the twine like the handle on a lady's bag. He walked the flat dirt road, past O'Shea's Restaurant and the sailmaker, keeping his head down, his eyes to himself. He turned away from a woman with a basket of flowers walking toward the harbor as if he hadn't seen her. He didn't want to say hello or be acknowledged in return. He wanted to blend into the landscape like a fish or a flower or a cloud.

In the back of Finn's fish shop, Davey Sampson stood at the wooden cutting block, running a knife along the underside of a flounder. He worked with the precision of a man, though he couldn't have been fifteen years old. He didn't look up, as if making eye contact would demonstrate a weakness he didn't want to reveal; he fought the stigma of his age with a bravado that belied his skinny arms.

Nathaniel went to the front of the shop and watched Finn pass a package across the counter to a local woman. The slope of his shoulders were like two mounds of worry gathered up around his neck.

When the woman was gone, Finn said, "I told you not to come in here when I have customers. Next time, I won't pay you."

Nathaniel nodded and handed the fish over to Finn.

"I mean it," Finn said. He turned and cast his eyes down. They were brown, like their father's eyes, always disgusted with everything they found disappointing in this world. He went to the cashbox and ran his fingers through some coins and over a single dollar bill until he decided the amount he wanted to pay and handed it over.

Nathaniel stuffed the money in his pants pocket. No sense counting it. The price was not negotiable.

"Father wants to see you," Finn said.

"I'll see him when we get back from Boston."

"He insists. Just go see him."

Nathaniel stood in the doorway, watching his brother rearrange a row of fluke on the ice tray. Finn worked as if work could save him. Their father had instilled in his boys the notion that a man's value in the world was directly linked to the value of his bank account, and satisfaction was found by taking in the sweep of one's land. While Nathaniel had rejected their father's way of life, Finn wanted to be just like him. Their father knew how to talk to other men about business so that people buying property from him couldn't help feeling they were getting a deal.

His confidence, his forthright approach, had influenced Finn, but he couldn't manage to emulate his father's integrity in his dealings with customers and the fishing captains. When he purchased fish, he tried to bring the asking price down. He made it sound like he needed to get a pound of fish for a nickel less if he was to sell it for any profit at all, as if he could negotiate the price based on some aspect of the local economy that the fishermen didn't understand. But they understood, and they knew to avoid him. Only Nathaniel and the Garrison brothers sold fish to him because they would not be bullied. Since they provided a wide range of fish—everything from flounder and mackerel to cod and swordfish—Finn was able to stock his shop.

Nathaniel hadn't seen his father in over six months, not since the man had come down to the harbor himself to visit his sons. "When are we leaving for Boston?"

"I told you already," Finn said. "Two days. Just meet me at the train, and try to wear something suitable for meeting my client, would you?" Finn shook his head as if his brother was something he could shake off. "Now, take the fish to Davey," Finn said, his voice curt, abrupt.

Nathaniel did as he was told. He laid the fish across the table and patted the full body. Then he left Davey to his work.

Outside the shop, the sun cast an eerie light across the docks. Dusk always caught in Nathaniel's throat. He remembered his mother, Helen, striking the ship's bell attached by the back door before she called for her sons. *Nathaniel! Finn! Dinner!* It was memory that persisted, right in the heart of him.

Nathaniel was tired from rowing now. He wanted to get away from the world of the harbor, his brother, and his father's request, but the trip to Boston weighed on his mind. He and Finn would travel by train to the city, where they would meet Edwin George from the boatyard. Edwin had a schooner he needed delivered back to Yarmouth Port, and he'd asked Finn to skipper the boat. While Finn had jumped at the chance to make money and have a good sail, Nathaniel hesitated. He hadn't been on a boat with Finn in ten years, not since the accident that took their younger brother, Jacob. It would be an easy sail, but nonetheless, he felt a combination of anticipation and grief that he could only quell by retreating into his world on the marsh.

He walked the wharf road, past sickly sweet smelling rows of grapevines, willow trees that bent over the road, and a few houses perched across the street from the marsh. When a familiar stray dog climbed out from behind a stone wall to greet him, Nathaniel stopped and scratched him under the chin. "Rascal, where you been?" Sometimes the dog followed him home for dinner and maybe a night beneath a roof, but he was as wild as a deer and just as independent.

Near the end of the road, Nathaniel took a left and found the path that led through briars and brush into the marsh. Rascal followed him through seagrasses washed flat by the tides and dried in the wind and the sun so they were soft beneath his feet. The smells of clay and salt and the fetid odor of rotting brush, the swish of grasses in the breeze that came in off the bay, and the gray evening light were his home.

They hurried along the path toward the island. Feeling the miles in his legs, Nathaniel moved through the fecund odors of wild grapes. A fox dashed into the woods. Nathaniel made out the copper-red body with black around the head, furtive in the light of late afternoon. Rascal ran after him, and Nathaniel knew that was the last he'd see of the dog today. Nathaniel imagined the fox's sense of smell leading it along the trail of a smaller animal that was itself instinctively chasing another odor that had to do with nuts or noncarnivorous sustenance. A flock of geese swooped low to the ground as if to claim it. Nathaniel looked up when he heard their loud, nasal complaints on their way to the fields where they pecked at the earth.

A world of instinct driven by unknowable forces confronted him every day, and he found reassurance in the fact that the fox knew to stay hidden in the daylight, and the geese knew where to find sustenance. Nathaniel wanted to survive on instinct alone. That was why he'd moved out to the marsh—to live outdoors and on his own, without the distraction of working for his father or fishing on a schooner with a bunch of other men. He was his own man, and that was something his father couldn't understand.

As he neared the island, nothing more than an outcrop of beech trees and scrub pine, bayberry bushes and briars, he stepped beneath a canopy of branches. He'd built the shack at the center of the island where even the highest tides couldn't reach. Only twelve feet by twelve feet, the shack held enough room to live in and had for a long time. Grass poked through the floorboards in spring and rotted beneath in fall, then the clean smell of frozen ground surrounded him all winter.

The structure had a strong foundation of stones he'd carried from the woods on the other side of Wharf Road. He'd survived many storms on this island, snow and gales and one hurricane. He knew how to barricade himself in. The shack was braced with logs. He'd placed the gray, weatherworn boards with precision and double-filled the walls with sea hay for insulation.

Nathaniel couldn't remember when he first thought of living outdoors. He supposed the idea had been with him since he was a boy, making fires from flint rock, sleeping with his brothers in a fort they'd built with a lean-to woven from branches and covered with a canvas tarp. Only fishing for what he needed to eat, growing turnips, building his own shelter—these things pulled at a primitive longing.

But moving to the marsh as an adult had been more than a response to that longing. It had been a desire for comfort and the kind of ease he could only find living outside. There was a purity in the marsh, a simple rhythm to each day that soothed Nathaniel, and he clung to that rhythm as a wall against loss. On the marsh, he didn't recall Jacob's footsteps on the stairs or expect him at the breakfast table. He didn't hear his father crying in the night. Nathaniel could live with the loss because he wasn't constantly confronted with his brother's absence, but still there were days when he didn't leave the shack, when he curled around a blanket and held his pillow to his stomach. At those times, no amount of sun on his body or wind or fish in his boat could soothe him.

When the tide reached the high-water mark twice a day, the island was separated from the rest of the town, and this, too, gave him comfort. Since he'd first moved out here, a new life had taken shape inside him. Each day passed in the same simple way—hearing the birds squawk, waking at sunrise, fishing and eating, then sleeping alone. His body became a gauge for weather—rain from the northeast, a southwesterly wind, clear skies and the ocean flat calm. He would row into the harbor and lose himself in fishing, and one day would follow after another.

Inside the shack, he blinked against the wafting dark. He reached for a shirt on the back of a chair and pulled it on over his bare skin. There was a daguerreotype of their mother in a small wooden frame nailed to the wall by the door. She'd died giving birth to Jacob. Nathaniel gently touched the picture with two fingers whenever he left the shack. Jacob's captain's hat hung on a peg by the door. He was seven years old when Nathaniel gave him the blue hat with a black leather visor and gold trim. The boy had refused to take it off, and from where he rode in the front of the rowboat, he had looked like a little figurehead leading them toward the bay.

Jacob wore his hat on the boat, at dinner, to church, where he was forced to hold it in his lap during services. He took it off to sleep and kept it on the table by his bed so that he could put it on first thing in the morning. Nathaniel knew that Jacob loved the hat because Nathaniel gave it to him and because the hat meant he was a captain, and he felt seen as more than a little boy. When Jacob stopped wearing the hat as he got older, Nathaniel had felt a pang of sadness.

Jacob would have loved the shack—helping his brother lay the foundation, hammering boards into walls. More than that, he would have loved sleeping within those walls, far from their father's house in an imagined wilderness, for that was how it was. Over two miles across the marsh could feel like a world away.

Nathaniel pumped some water into a tin cup and drank it down, then went inside and cast about for something to eat. The bread, hard from sitting on the table, filled his mouth with a feeling like salt caked to his tongue. The money he stuffed in a jar on the shelf. He couldn't afford to pay for much beyond the necessities he needed to survive. Like the salt beef he reached for on top of the cabinet. He unwrapped the piece of cloth and shaved a slice of meat straight into his mouth as he watched the last streaks of light across the floor. He let his weight fall back on the bed, his mind lost to the dark and the quiet of the day. Fish leapt in his dreams until Nathaniel also was in the water, and there was young Jacob drifting just beyond his reach, the fish glistening while Nathaniel kicked hard toward his brother. But for all his kicking, he didn't move an inch, and Jacob drifted farther away, and the fish, they didn't notice a thing.

2

A T DAWN, THE BIRDS COMPLAINED ABOUT THE MORNING AS IF they were the ones having bad dreams. Nathaniel rolled out of bed and thought about his father, how every time they spoke, his father tried to convince him to come in off the marsh, move into the family home, and find something to do with himself besides row on the bay. It was a useless conversation, and Nathaniel was tired of it. He pulled on a shirt, drank a cup of water, and glanced around the shack for anything he might need, but his needs came from a place inside himself that he didn't want to acknowledge. He followed the path off the island, passing over the miles of open marsh, then through cattails that grew taller than him near the road.

When he heard wagon wheels, a horse's steady clomp, and whistling out of tune, he knew it was Max Ballard. Max slowed his wagon in a clatter of boards knocking, and Nathaniel swung himself up and rode in the back of the wagon toward the harbor, the morning making itself known with a pale light that would turn hot within the hour.

They rode the half mile to the village, past the shops and fish shacks, to O'Shea's Restaurant, where Nathaniel slid off the wagon. "Get something to eat, would ya? You look like a rail." Max handed Nathaniel a nickel, but Nathaniel shoved his hands down into his pockets.

"Go ahead," Max said. "I had a good week at the farm." Nathaniel turned his back and started to walk away, then Max said, "Fine, you can bring me a nice big bass when you have one."

Nathaniel reached for the coin.

The restaurant's name had been written with rope and tacked onto a weathered board. On the front porch, two half barrels that had once been planted with herbs were now used as spittoons. The smell of grease pulled Nathaniel inside. He entered like a ghost, walking along the front window, away from the gatherings of fishermen talking about the tide and their catches. Nobody looked at him, and this was how he liked it. The people in town had learned to leave him alone. Years ago, they had looked at him with compassion—the young man who'd lost his brother—but now they looked away, accustomed to his silence and his life on the edge of the town.

There were old buoys hanging from the beams, quarter boards on the walls with names like *Marie Celeste*, *Zephyr*, and *Silas Fish*. A wooden oar hung over the doorway. Behind the counter hung a likeness of Ephram O'Shea. The picture was as much as Mrs. O'Shea would see of her husband again, but she carried on uncomplainingly without him, as did several of the wives in town who'd lost their husbands to the sea.

Nathaniel turned his gaze to the front window, where three little boys ran past carrying a minnow trap. Their scrawny arms and legs, their dirty feet—Nathaniel thought of his brothers, then tried not to. The boys pushed and shoved each other, fighting over the trap. The oldest boy spread the two younger ones apart until they stopped arguing. Then he let the smallest boy take the trap and run with it.

Not a lot of children came down to the harbor. Boys sometimes came

on their own, but girls only came with their mothers to buy fish or visit
their fathers on the schooners. There was a noted lack of women on the
pier, especially at this early hour. Nathaniel thought of his own mother,
how she'd let him and Finn stay down at the harbor until dinnertime.
"I don't know what you boys get up to down there, but if it's trouble, I'll
hear about it."

Once he gave the waitress his order, Nathaniel watched the sails go
up along the docks so that the boats looked like birds, ready for flight.
The *Spritefly* shoved off, the sails rounding out with wind and pulling
the schooner along. He wanted to shake loose the knot that tightened
his stomach. He was anxious about seeing his father and anxious about
their trip. Well, he decided, he could get the visit to his father over with
first; then he wouldn't have to dread it all the way to Boston and back
across the bay. When the waitress slid a plate in front of him, he waited
for her to leave, poked at the eggs for a few minutes, then left a good tip
before he disappeared out the door.

———∿∿∿———

Nathaniel walked up the steep slant of the driveway from the harbor
road. At the top of the hill, the house rose like an apparition. Two stories
of white-shingled success. He kept his head down as he walked toward
it, trying to think of what to say. The drive wound along the hillside and
up to the house. Nathaniel took his time going around back to get a look
at the bay from up high. He'd rather be down in it than up on this hill.
His father acted as if he'd created the view himself, when all he'd done
was build a house high enough to see the wide expanse of water.

When his father called from the office window, his baritone voice
pulled Nathaniel from the comfort of his own thoughts.

"Come in and talk to your old man."

Nathaniel stepped into the kitchen through the side door and leaned against the counter where he'd made eggs and toast as a boy. It was like stepping back into his boyhood, his brothers' voices mumbled and distant, contained in the air that had once smelled of their mother's soap, her shortbread cookies, and mint from the garden. He felt that time stretched to hold this moment and all the moments that had come before, the moments spent with his brothers fighting over the crispiest piece of toast or the biggest piece of chicken.

"Hungry?" his father asked. Since Nathaniel had last seen his father six months ago, the man had gained a round paunch. His neck was thicker, his chin doubled. He'd always been an active man, and Nathaniel wondered at the unfamiliar shape of him, but he shifted his attention to the table where he'd eaten with his brothers. It looked the same, water-marked from sweating glasses and hot mugs. He knew every swirl of grain and each crack in the curly maple, and it existed like a captured moment. This was where they had eaten dinner the night before the accident.

He followed his father into the front parlor where he'd pulled a reading chair up to an open window, the *Yarmouth Reporter* folded on a side table.

"Come on, sit." His father waved a hand toward the settee, the polished leather cast with sunlight that streamed through the tall windows. Nathaniel didn't like being in the house. "It's like pulling teeth getting you here, Son."

The smell of oiled leather and pipe tobacco made Nathaniel claustrophobic, as did the mahogany furniture and blue upholstery with floral stitching, the high bookcases filled with books whose bindings remained uncreased. There was no place for Nathaniel here, not since

Jacob died. He couldn't recall his brother's face or the sound of his voice, only the feeling of being with him. The portrait of him on the far wall didn't conjure his presence the way his bedroom—unchanged since the accident—did, or standing in the hallway between their rooms, remembering their excited voices the night before the trip.

Nathaniel sat on the settee, but he was restless, and his eyes cast about the room.

"It does a man good to see his sons. Your brother never comes up here unless he wants something."

"He has responsibilities—the shop and the children."

"Yes, I know," Nathaniel Boyd Sr. said, but his eyes said, *Still. I'm his father.*

"So why did you ask me here, Father?"

"I know you're not one for small talk, so I'll get right to the point. It's time for you to come into business with me. You're my oldest son. It's your birthright." His father paused to make sure that Nathaniel was hearing him. "I'll give you five acres. You'll first learn to manage the rental business. We have those twenty-three parcels of land that I rent out."

"I know about them, Father. What does that have to do with me?"

"I want you to work with the tenants, find a way to help them improve their farming so that I can increase their rent. I think you'd be good at it, Son. You'll learn to survey the wooded lots and calculate the value of the timber as well."

The fact that his father thought he would come to work for him made Nathaniel feel completely unseen. Unable to contain the volley of his anger, he crossed the room and leaned over his father's collection of surveyor's tools. Each one was a precision instrument used to calculate his land, land that held him captive like the sea captivated his boys.

Nathaniel turned to his father and looked into the man's face, at the creases in the corner of his eyes and the wrinkles in his forehead. "What makes you think I want to work for you when I have a life somewhere else?"

"A life?"

"What about Finn?" Nathaniel said. "He's proven himself, and he wants it."

"Finn's ambition is impulsive. He wants too much, too soon. And he's not interested in the land business anymore."

But Nathaniel knew his father's reasons were deeper than that. Even as a boy, the more Finn tried to please him, the harder Nathaniel Sr. pushed him away, as if there was something inherently wrong in his middle son, something he couldn't tolerate and wouldn't foster.

With his sturdy shoulders and formidable paunch, his father stood as if to fortify his argument. He walked to the window where he surveyed the harbor and the extent of his land. "It's been ten years. You've had enough time to put the accident behind you. Your brother's built a business and given me grandchildren. I want to give you the opportunity to do the same."

He tried to look Nathaniel in the eye, but his gaze shifted around the room and landed somewhere out the window over Nathaniel's right shoulder. Nathaniel knew that his father was deeply ashamed of him. He hid it under the guise of wanting to take care of Nathaniel, but he really wanted to take care of his own reputation. Here he was, a prominent landowner, connected with the most successful men on Cape Cod—politicians, judges, officers of the law, doctors—men who made the laws as well as enforced them, men who drove the biggest business deals and earned the most money, and his own son couldn't pick himself up and face the world.

"You're ashamed," Nathaniel said.

"You would be, too."

Nathaniel stared into his father's eyes, into the brown glassy glow of them, then turned to go.

3

NATHANIEL DIDN'T PACK A BAG. NOT A WALLET OR A SATCHEL. HE carried nothing on his way to the train this morning but the weight of his father's request, a weight he wanted to leave in Yarmouth Port. He watched for Finn, then spied him pacing by the ticket counter of the tiny train station, waving two tickets in his hand. Nathaniel picked up his pace to meet his brother.

"I knew you'd be late," Finn said. "The five thirty train's already boarding."

Nathaniel followed his brother onto the car closest to them, and they walked down the aisle until two seats were available near the back of the car. Nathaniel felt the tug of motion as the train started out of the station. He listened to the sound of the whistle that he often heard from down at the harbor. As they pulled out of Yarmouth Port and traveled toward Barnstable, his mind relaxed, and he turned to his brother. "I went to see Father," he said.

"I need to work." Finn scratched at his ledger with a sharp pencil. He bent over the book that he believed contained the answer to his future. Nathaniel had always known that Finn struggled with his numbers, and he watched him go up and down the columns of his ledger over and over again as they made their way off the Cape.

"Why do you bring that? What if it gets wet on the boat?"

"It's only a copy."

Nathaniel nodded, and they rode in silence until they reached Plymouth. Finn looked up from the ledger and tapped his pencil against the paper. "What's on your mind?"

"I told you. I went to see Father."

"I don't want to hear about it," Finn said. "Whatever happened is between you and him." Finn's eyes drifted back to the ledger, but Nathaniel persisted.

He glanced out the window at the wind-bent scrub pines that lined the railroad tracks. He watched the backs of houses, a woman hanging clothes on a line, a boy gliding high in the air on a swing, couples walking the path by the water's edge. When he felt himself thinking about Meredith's skirts blowing in the wind as she walked toward the water, he looked at his brother, who was lost in his own thoughts. "Whenever he calls me up to the house, he has some scheme for getting me in off the marsh. I'm tired of having to stick up for myself. He needs to accept my life the way it is."

Now Finn faced him full on. "You're kidding, right?"

"You're taking his side?"

"Nathaniel, you live in the marsh, one meal to the next. This trip will bring you the most money you've made in your life, and you probably won't spend it."

"What's your point?"

"You've been out there since Jacob died." Finn put his pencil down and gave Nathaniel his full attention. "When are you going to give it up, come in from there and try to make a life?"

"I don't want a life like yours, Finn. Kids and a wife, working all day in the shop. That's not for me. Even if Jacob hadn't died. Even if that accident had never happened, I'd live differently than you do."

Finn said, "I'm not going to be in that fish shop forever. You know that I'm saving money to buy a fleet of fishing boats, and I'm going to ask Father to invest in my business plan."

"I don't know which is worse, me expecting Father to accept my life or you thinking he'll invest money in your fleet."

"There's a chance—"

"Not really," Nathaniel said. "You know how he is about money."

"I've got a good plan for turning a profit. He'll want to invest once he sees the numbers." Finn went back to running his finger up and down columns of numbers in the book spread across his lap. Nathaniel had always known that Finn wanted to build a fishing fleet—he loved the sea and had spent years fishing as a young man. He hadn't wanted to open the fish shop, but his father wouldn't invest in a fleet until Finn had proven himself. That was why Finn constantly worked on his business proposal, with columns of numbers, expenses, projected profits. He reviewed the numbers over and over until he was sure that his plans added up. Finn hadn't needed their father to help him with the fish shop. He'd used his savings to pay rent and purchase stock from the fishermen to sell to the townsfolk who didn't want to get dirty negotiating with the fishermen on the docks.

Nathaniel wished their father would help Finn, buy him a single schooner to get him started, or at least support Finn's ideas, but their father had never been one to offer support beyond what he wanted his sons to do.

When Finn looked up from his ledgers, he reached below his seat for the satchel his wife had packed with lunch. Finn shared the sandwiches. Knowing that Nathaniel wouldn't bring anything for himself to eat, Elizabeth had made four turkey sandwiches with cheese and butter.

In Boston, exhaust drifted around the train, and Nathaniel watched the flow of passengers moving along the platform, in and around those waiting for the train back to the Cape.

"Come on, let's go," Finn said.

Nathaniel handed him the leather satchel he'd stashed beneath the seat in front of them. Finn slid his ledger inside, fastened the clasp, and shouldered the bag. He held it close to his body, as if it was full of the money he needed to buy his fishing fleet. But it was only a bag of paperwork that Finn couldn't let go of and that Nathaniel didn't understand. He followed Finn along the sidewalk, where they picked up a hansom cab that smelled of cigar smoke and musky cologne.

The driver led them along the waterfront toward Long Wharf. Fish delivery vehicles clogged the intersections, and the processing plants where the fish was filleted and salted for delivery lined the road. Nathaniel sat up tall to watch masts sticking up behind buildings, a familiar sight that he used to ground himself in the cacophony of human traffic. Soon they would be on the boat, and his leg would stop bouncing up and down with nerves.

Finn put his hand on Nathaniel's leg to stop the vibration. "We're almost there."

"I'm fine," Nathaniel said. Once they were out of the cab and searching the crowd for Edwin George, he felt a physical relief from his anxiety.

"There he is," Finn said, pointing toward the bow of a schooner docked in the middle of the fray. Nathaniel followed his brother, head focused on the ground where he watched Finn's feet leading them forward. Edwin stood on the bowsprit, a hand on the stays holding him steady.

"Edwin," Finn called, and Edwin swung his arm in a big wave.

Finn pushed through the crowd until they reached the schooner's gangway. He adjusted the bag on his shoulder and walked the ramp with renewed vigor. Nathaniel followed, his eyes on the rigging, the finely shined woodwork, the neatly coiled ropes.

Edwin must've noticed the path of Nathaniel's eye. He said, "I think you'll find her shipshape. She's called *Lilith*, after my youngest daughter. You'd best take good care of her, boys."

"Will do." Finn shook the man's hand, and Nathaniel did the same.

"You want to inspect her before you get underway?"

"I'll take a quick look," Finn said. "Nathaniel, will you check below for life preservers and extra lines?"

"You don't have to tell me what to look for," Nathaniel said.

"Just get moving. It's nearly ten fifteen, and I want to sail as close to noon as possible."

"That's pushing it, don't you think?" Edwin asked. "You'll need to plot your course and go over the boat."

"I've sailed this trip a dozen times," Finn said. "I could do it in my sleep."

"I'd prefer you didn't. I'd like to see my boat back in Yarmouth Port," Edwin said, smiling. "I know you've got this under control, Finn. I'll leave you boys to it." Edwin walked the gangway onto the pier and waved back at Finn and Nathaniel. "See you on the other side," he said, and he disappeared into the crowd.

The brothers stood for a moment in silence, looking into the distance at nothing. "Well, let's get to it," Finn said.

Nathaniel ducked as he took the steps down to the small rooms below deck. He found the roll of charts and unfurled the one of Massachusetts. The course they would sail from Boston to Yarmouth Port was a straight line, pending weather. Nathaniel placed the chart on the table and held down the corners with small glass weights. He traced the line of their course with the tip of his finger, as if he could reassure himself that the body of water they were about to cross was nothing more than a few inches on a map.

He counted the life preservers, checked the first-aid kit, recoiled extra ropes, and made sure the gas to the stove was turned off and safely stowed beneath the sink. Back on deck, he uncovered the compass and rubbed the glass dome with the sleeve of his shirt.

Finn walked back from the foremast, strutting as if his gait could ensure his control of the ship and the weather and the safety of their trip across the bay. He joined Nathaniel at the helm, where he unclipped the ropes that held the wheel steady.

"You're ready?" Nathaniel asked.

"Just let me think for a minute." Finn swung the wheel to and fro, feeling the glide of the rudder through the water.

Nathaniel sat on the transom and watched the crowd. He felt comfortable watching from this distance and within the confines of the schooner's rails. He didn't notice the girl until she spoke to him directly. She had strawberry-blond hair and freckles, plump cheeks and plump breasts, and a pretty little figure that made Nathaniel want to hide her. She seemed vulnerable, exposed, and he had to look away.

"Hey, mister," she said, but he ignored her. "Hey! Mister!" Nathaniel ignored her, but Finn came up from below and watched the girl waving toward them.

"What is it?" he said.

"I'm looking for a ride." When the brothers didn't respond, she said, "I'll pay you."

Finn looked her up and down, his hawk eyes scanning her body, which was mostly hidden beneath a long coat that looked too warm for the weather. She clutched a carpetbag close to her side. "Where to and how much?" he asked, thinking about the money as much as he thought about the girl.

"Where are you going?" the girl asked. She appeared to be considering not only her options but her destination and what she was willing to pay to get there.

"Yarmouth Port," Finn said. "On Cape Cod."

"I'm relocating, you see, and I need a comfortable place to get started."

"Yarmouth Port could very well be the place," Finn said, flirting now, but the girl wasn't put off.

"My name is Rachel." As she shook Finn's fish-stinking hand, she didn't turn from his gaze, which was amused now and curious. Nathaniel didn't want anyone else on the boat. Wasn't it enough that he'd agreed to make this trip in the first place? Now he was expected to make chitchat with some teenage girl?

Rachel came onboard, and Nathaniel nodded in her direction. "That's Nathaniel," Finn said. "You'll get used to him. I'll need fifty cents to get you across the bay."

"That's a lot."

"Cheaper than most," Finn said.

Rachel turned from the brothers and opened her carpetbag, her back hunched over as if to conceal her few belongings. She retrieved twelve one-dollar bills and handed them over to Finn, who turned them this way and that in his hand as if making sure the money was good.

Nathaniel went to the bow of the boat to cast off from the dock. "You're off," he said. As the bow of the boat swung from the dock, he raised the long jib, and the boat gently sailed into the harbor.

"Where do you want me?" Rachel asked.

"Right here, next to me," Finn said. "You know how to sail?"

"Not nearly." The girl didn't let go of her bag but held it firmly in her left hand, tucked tightly into her side.

"You can stash that below," Finn said.

"No, I'll hold on to it."

Finn shook his head and turned his attention to the boat. "Nathaniel, get that second jib up."

Nathaniel did as he was told. He hauled the sail and felt the solid weight of the boat lift as the canvas filled with wind and carried them from the safety of Boston Harbor.

4

Rachel watched Boston fall into the distance as they sailed away. The smoke from smokestacks, the sounds of carriages and the people, the outlines of tall buildings, all faded behind them. She stood by Finn, who placed each of her hands on a spoke of the wheel. He held his hands over hers, as if there was a danger she'd navigate them into trouble. She felt the gentle resistance of water against the rudder, the pull of the wheel that she had to counter by pushing up on one spoke and down on the other to turn the wheel and guide the ship closer to the wind.

Finn stood behind her, his arms wide so that he didn't appear to be hugging her, but he liked her. She could tell by the way he'd run his eyes up and down her body, the way he'd held her hand as she crossed onto the boat, and his eagerness to keep her near him. She didn't mind. He was handsome with dark hair and rugged features and a confident demeanor that she admired. When she was tired of steering the boat, she sat on the bulkhead over the cabin and let the wind blow through her hair.

Nathaniel was on the foredeck, avoiding her, she guessed. He'd barely looked at her, and he didn't seem interested in speaking to her, but it was okay. She had her ride away from Boston toward a town where no one would recognize her, and that was what she needed. She looked down at her feet where Finn had tied her bag to a cleat, making double knots to reassure her that it wouldn't get washed overboard. It held all her money in the world, and she would need it to make a new beginning.

She watched Finn steer the boat and glance toward his brother, then back at the compass. She didn't want either of them to know where she'd come from. She didn't want them to know how she had traveled south from Maine. She didn't want to talk about it, because then she would have to remember how her mother had left the family when Rachel was seven years old, leaving in her wake a rage that ricocheted from her father down to her older brother, Henry, then into Rachel and straight through her twin sister, Katherine, who drowned in the harbor in the middle of their eleventh winter.

Katherine had dreamed of traveling across the ocean they'd stared at every day from their bedroom window, left alone while their father fished or drank or debauched himself in multifarious ways. He showed up at home demanding a meal and slugging anyone who was too proud or too pissed off or simply too damn tired to take his bad temper and wait on him one more time. Rachel imagined Katherine walking into the frigid seawater as if it would carry her into her dreams of faraway places, but Katherine never made it out of Bath, Maine. Ike Flannery found her washed up on the beach, bloated and breathless as a cod brought up on a line and hammered into stillness. Rachel didn't see her sister dead, but she felt her dead as surely as if her right hand had been severed at the wrist, for that was where she always imagined Katherine, on her right as if attached by bone.

Katherine had been born first. Slow to make her way through the birth canal, she came out long and lean as if stretched during her trip into the world. After Katherine, Rachel popped out round and plump as a morning biscuit.

Rachel's decision to leave home had been sudden and had required courage she didn't know she possessed. The money in her bag wasn't hers, but she needed it if she was to get away from her father's rage and her memories of Katherine.

Her trip from Maine had been by boat. At seventeen, she reminded herself that she was the youngest of those onboard, mostly seamen traveling to meet up with the ship for their next voyage. Rachel stayed close to the captain's wife, Helena, a German with a knack for rummy and lust for sugar. Rachel refused the cookies Helena offered. She hadn't been able to eat more than sea biscuits and salt crackers since she'd been aboard. In the captain's quarters, they played cards until Helena had won all the buttons, and she said, "Don't worry, dear. Next time, you'll take the pot."

In Boston, Rachel left the ship with regret, for she'd grown fond of the captain's wife.

On the dock amid the rush, she'd stood motionless. She was a girl from nowhere Maine. Her cotton dress and faded skirts, a thin wool coat that dragged along the ground, frayed with travel—they were her mother's clothes, which had been worn by Katherine, then later by Rachel, who was too small for their length.

How many weeks had it been since the four walls of their house back in Maine pushed in on her while she braced herself for her father's return? When the door in the front room had finally slammed open, she'd stood back against the wall in the tiny kitchen, away from the jagged force of his rage.

"I'm making dinner, Father. Potatoes and onions, your favorite."

"No meat again, for chrissakes."

She hated everything about him, from his greasy black hair to the stubble on his chin to the smell of his sweat that filled the room.

"I've had a miserable day," he said, words slurred with liquor. He was covered in pine pitch from his job at Snow's Shipbuilders, where he caulked and tarred the seams in new schooners. It was grimy work, and he resented it. He stepped toward Rachel, and the grainy smell of alcohol hit her like a wall. She felt the violence in him, saw it in the taut muscles of his neck, in the veins on his temples, in his quaking arms. She stepped deeper into the kitchen, but he stumbled after her.

"No, please," she said, her voice strangled by desperation. "Papa, please."

He slapped her across the face, as if she was the source of his rage. He slapped her again, and she fell back against the wall. She didn't cry, but he was hurting her. More than her flesh, it was her spirit he pummeled. So spent was she with waiting every night for the first blow to land that her own rage burst into the light of day with each slap across her face.

Rachel picked up the tin plates and the shattered salt bowl. She kept quiet and swept while he poured himself a drink. Her brother, Henry, was useless. He shrank from her father by avoiding him completely. If it meant he couldn't eat dinner, then he went hungry. He was a coward who escaped into poetry, as if words could save him. Their father was never going to stop hitting, screaming, drinking his way through their lives.

They ate dinner in silence. Henry didn't join them, and their father didn't complain when he heard the scrape of Henry's chair in the upstairs room. More for him. He ate like an animal, shoveling food into his mouth and swallowing without chewing. He drank with the same gluttonous intent, as if to get the substance in and feel its effects as quickly as possible. Rachel realized that one day he could kill her, whether by the force of his blows or the slow erosion of her spirit, and she couldn't tolerate it anymore. That was when Henry had come to her with his plan.

The bookkeeper's office where he worked had a safe. He could help her get away, leave the safe open, and let her in the door. If she got out of town quickly enough, no one would know. The townsfolk would think she'd fled her father's rage. The man was notorious for picking fights in the pub and starting screaming matches with men at work for no reason other than the fact that he needed a drink. Rachel worried that Henry would get caught. The fact that someone had been able to get into the safe at all would tip off Henry's boss. He was putting himself at great risk, as was she by taking him up on his offer. "You'll have to leave, too," she'd told him, and he'd agreed. They'd split the money, and while Henry sailed north, Rachel headed south. Now here she was, sailing toward an unknown port with her carpetbag lashed to a cleat.

—✺—

When the wind picked up, Nathaniel came toward the bulkhead where she sat to take her aft. "I like it here," she told him, sitting on the deck with her back against the mast. She liked the feeling of the wind rushing over the boat, her hair blowing out from her bun, and the salt spray on her face. She liked the feeling of freedom and the sense that she was far away from the world she'd known before.

"You have to come aft. The wind's picking up, and I don't want you up here. It isn't safe." He held his hand down, and Rachel took it to haul herself up. When he steadied her shoulder to help her get her balance, she jerked away from him. She could find her balance just fine. She followed him along the windward rail, letting her legs sway with the waves as if she were a seasoned sailor.

Finn stood at the helm, his eyes on the compass, which he wiped off with the sleeve of his shirt. "You can stand here with me," he said.

"Can I navigate?" she asked.

"No." The word dropped like a stone, a thing she couldn't argue with. Nathaniel leaned back against the stern of the boat where the rail curved around. Rachel felt him watching her, not the way that Finn watched her but in a discreet and curious way. She wondered what he was thinking, but then she turned her mind to Finn pointing out the different sails, and she lost herself in the sound of his voice and the rhythm of the waves. She was glad to be moving quickly toward a destination far from home. She held onto the ship's wheel, firm enough to fight the boat as it pitched in the waves.

5

HOURS HAD PASSED SINCE THEY'D LEFT BOSTON, AND NOW Nathaniel watched the girl as she looked down into the ship's compass and tried to make sense of their heading. Finn placed a hand on her shoulder and tilted her away so that he could see the compass himself. "Southeast," he said. "An easy sail."

"But it's so windy."

"That's what makes it fast," he said. "Nathaniel, show her on the chart where we're going."

"That's okay," she said.

"Don't you want to know where you are?"

"I'm right here," she said.

"Yes, you are." Finn leaned in toward her, and Nathaniel shifted his attention to trimming the mainsail. He wrapped the mainsheet around a winch and hauled it in until the sail billowed with the heavy wind. He felt Rachel watching him. Whether she was curious about the sailing or about him, he didn't know. He went back to the aft rail and kept his eyes on the sails, which worked together like wings.

When Rachel joined him at the rail again, he didn't take his eyes from the sails. He wondered what had driven her to take this trip with two strange men to a town where she didn't know anyone. She must not have people of her own, he thought, or any prospects to speak of. If a young woman didn't have a marriage or a family, what were her options?

Work in service, he guessed. He didn't want to think about the other options, the women on the dock swinging their bustles toward the men, holding up the hems of their skirts to entice newly land-bound sailors.

"You're awfully quiet," Rachel said. "You don't like me?"

He looked at her then, and she looked away. She couldn't have been more than seventeen years old, the same age as Finn the last time Nathaniel had been on a boat with him. They'd been on a one-day trip intended to get Jacob accustomed to the boat. Then they planned to come ashore and rest before they went out to the fishing banks for a week. They were borrowing the *Sparrow* from the Garrison brothers to take Jacob to the fishing grounds for the first time. They'd fish for cod using nets hung from booms that swung over the boat. The brothers had promised Jacob since he was a small boy that they would take him when he turned twelve, and he was holding them to it.

The trip was for Jacob's birthday, but Nathaniel knew that for Finn, it was about something else. For years, Finn had tried to convince their father that he could succeed in a fishing enterprise. He wanted his father's funding, and this was a chance to prove himself. He'd been working on the Garrison brothers' schooner *Lancelot* since he was fourteen years old, making his own money, building his body, and filling his mind with dreams of starting his own fishing fleet. At seventeen, his body had taken the shape of his work. Nathaniel admired his younger brother for his clear-eyed focus and his ability to work.

Nathaniel also knew how Finn had resented Jacob. When their little brother was born, their universe had been interrupted. Their mother died three days after the birth, and this small creature took up all their father's attention. Even though they had a woman who cared for them, their father came home early from work most days. He barely said hello to Nathaniel and Finn before he went to hold the baby. Was it his match tip of red hair or his tiny fingers reaching out for something to grab? Nathaniel didn't know what his father saw in the boy. He only ached for his mother, but Finn was hurt without his father's attention. He took to sulking and going down to the harbor to watch the boats or pick fights with other boys.

"Go keep an eye on your brother," their father told Nathaniel. "Don't let him get into trouble down there."

Nathaniel complied, and when one day Finn picked a fight with a local boy—over what? A stolen marble? A cross word spoken?—and fists came out, Nathaniel tried to stop the fight. He grabbed at Finn's arms as Finn swung recklessly at the boy, smacking him in the eye, then the nose. When the boy still came at him, Finn picked up a board from the ground and swung it at the boy's ribs to knock the wind out of him. The boy cried for his mother. Tears and snot and blood.

"Baby," Finn said. "You're a baby, and now everyone knows it." He spoke through his heavy breathing, assessed his bruised hands. The group of children stood back. They looked at the boy on the ground, then looked at Finn in disbelief.

On their way home, Nathaniel and Finn were silent. Nathaniel tried to think of what to say to their father about the black and blue marks on his brother's hands and face. How would he explain his inability to stop the fight? Surely, he was to blame for his brother's wounds. When they reached the bottom of the lane, Finn stopped and bent over at the waist. He cried, slowly at first, then in gulping sobs that shook him until Nathaniel pulled him close and held him. They sat on the ground at the bottom of the driveway until Finn stopped crying, and then they remained, watching the afternoon fade until the sky was pink and the sun was an orange orb bleeding across the horizon.

"What'll we tell Father?" Finn asked.

"I'll talk to him." Nathaniel felt heavy with the weight of his responsibility. He hadn't been able to protect Finn from himself. He'd seen the look on Finn's face, his cold determination as he swung at the boy, and he wondered if he would ever be able to protect him.

—◦—

Nathaniel watched his brother steer the boat with one hand, gaze into the compass, then up at the sails. Finn lashed the wheel in position to keep the boat on course, then ran up to the bow to trim the jibs, letting each sheet out a bit, then reeling in until the sails filled with wind again. He worked from a squatting position, bent forward slightly in a prayerlike pose, as if this boat were his church, the sails his congregation. Nathaniel felt a moment of softness for him then, for all that he'd been and all that he'd become, in spite of losing Jacob, in spite of their father. Nathaniel joined him on the foredeck and bent down to take the jib line from him.

"I'll get this," Nathaniel said.

Finn handed the rope over and stood up. He patted his brother on the shoulder. Nathaniel nodded, pleased to see his brother in his element and not standing behind the counter at the fish shop. He watched Finn return to the helm. In spite of their accident so many years ago, Finn had proven himself a talented sailor. Feeling the pull of the rope, the tilt of the boat in the waves, and the wind billowing his shirt, Nathaniel experienced that old feeling of comfort with the workings of a schooner, a comfort he hadn't felt in a long time.

6

FINN FELT THE SWAY OF THE BOAT BENEATH HIM AND THE SALT spray in his face. This was when he felt most alive, as captain of a schooner on its way across Cape Cod Bay. He'd been sailing since he was a boy, then taken on the work of a fisherman to make the money that eventually helped him open his shop. He was in command of his life in the same way that he was in command of the boat. He glanced toward Rachel, her hair damp and plastered against her forehead, her coat flapping in the wind, which had turned and picked up from the northeast. Nathaniel worked trimming the sails, first the jibs, then the mainsail, then the jibs again, as if his efforts could stave off the squall taking shape on the horizon in dark swirls of air. In spite of the storm that took his brother, Finn wasn't afraid of anything at sea. He knew how to handle a boat, and he knew how to handle himself.

He pointed out their southeastern course on the compass, then pointed toward their destination. "We're on a beam reach now that the wind's shifted, and that'll take us across and straight home," he told the girl, who followed the line of his finger toward Yarmouth Port. She nodded her head, and he watched the line of her pert little nose, the freckles on her face speckled now with salt that had dried on her skin, then washed away in the ocean spray, then dried again. She was brave. He'd give her that.

While she stared into the distance, he placed a hand on her

shoulder and turned her toward Yarmouth Port. "There," he said, and
he could swear she leaned toward him. She paid attention to him and
took his competence for granted the way his wife no longer did. She'd
stopped noticing him when he came in the door after a long day at
the shop, stopped noticing him as he undressed by his side of the bed
and slid beneath the sheet. She was tired of his irritable moods, but he
didn't know how to pull himself out of it.

"Can I steer?" Rachel asked.

This time, he stood closer behind her, the front of his body against
her small back, and she didn't move away.

Once she tired of holding the wheel with its heavy pull, Finn took
over. Rachel walked to the foredeck and sat, leaning against the mast.
Nathaniel came back toward Finn, whether to get away from the girl
or rest after his attentions to the sails, Finn didn't know.

Nathaniel stood beside him and looked ahead toward Yarmouth
Port. He wiped the compass glass of mist and read their direction from
it as if his gaze could make them get home sooner. "I've been thinking about Father, about what he said." He spoke to break the silence
between them, a silence that contained his fears and Finn's certainty.
"I'm not going into business with him. I'm not coming in off the marsh."

"You told me this all ready."

"I know it."

"Well, he's not going to invest in my fleet if that makes you feel any
better."

"Why would it?"

"He disapproves of both of us, not just you." Finn had talked
Nathaniel into taking this trip—their father had bribed him into
it. A couple of weeks before they'd decided to go, Finn had visited
Nathaniel Sr. on the hill. His father was determined to get Nathaniel

to change his life. He spoke to Finn with force and a kind of desperation, as if he needed to save his oldest son.

"If you can get him off the damn marsh and onto that schooner, maybe he can face up to himself," their father said. "It wasn't his fault that Jacob drowned. If you can get him on that boat, maybe he can move on. Maybe he'll come in from whatever life he thinks he's living."

"I don't know, Father. He's very set in his ways."

"You get him out there, and I'll consider giving you the money you need for that first fishing boat."

Finn looked directly into his father's eyes. "Is that a promise?"

His father nodded, and Finn had gone to work on Nathaniel, promising him enough money to fix his shack and save for the winter when he couldn't fish and food was scarce. "You'll enjoy the trip, Nathaniel. It's something we can do together again. Like before."

"I'm not interested."

"We can't go on like this. We have no relationship."

"You want a relationship? Since when?"

"I'm tired of you coming into my shop just for the money." Nathaniel had stared past Finn out the front window of the shop. He didn't respond to Finn or seem to even hear him. "Then do it for the money," Finn said. "Do it to get out of this town for a day. Prove to yourself that you can still sail across the bay and survive."

When Nathaniel acquiesced, Finn was relieved. He told their father immediately. The fact that Nathaniel was going to get off the marsh, even for a day, made their father grateful to Finn, and that gratitude would get Finn the money he needed for his business venture.

Finn pushed Rachel away from the helm as the squall headed directly for them, even though they weren't far enough from home for him to worry. Still, he kept his eye on the moving clouds and fell to thinking about his conversation on the train with Nathaniel. Finn knew it was true that their father didn't approve of either of his sons. This trip was proof enough that their father set the standards and his boys had to live up to them.

Finn believed that even though he'd talked Nathaniel into this trip, his father might help him, but he would never love him. His experience had always been that their father preferred young Jacob, the miracle baby who'd survived their mother's death. He even looked like their mother with a spark of red hair on his tiny head and freckles across his nose and the tops of his cheeks. Finn couldn't help remembering that when they were kids—Jacob was only nine years old, Nathaniel sixteen, and Finn fourteen—Nathaniel Sr. had insisted that Finn work on his own to gain experience in the world, but Nathaniel got to take Jacob out to the marsh and the harbor. When Finn asked why Nathaniel didn't have to work, their father said, "Because he's watching Jacob."

Their father even took Jacob for a ride in the carriage to learn about timber, something he would never do with Finn, no matter how often he asked. That morning, before his father took Jacob off in the wagon, he had looked across the table at his brothers, but they didn't look up from their eggs.

Their father stood by the table, watching his sons and waiting for Jacob.

"You never take us, but you'll take him." Finn looked at his father and waited for a response, but none came. The man took Jacob by the hand to lead him out to the carriage. Finn watched them disappear through the back door. The door rattled shut, and Finn stood up from the table and paced before the kitchen counter. "Why doesn't he take us, Nathaniel?"

Nathaniel put his dishes in the sink and wiped his hands on the front of his pants. He stood by the window in only his trousers, barefoot, bare chested, always in as little clothing as possible during the summer months. Finn watched him stare out the window, then Nathaniel turned his face back to his brother. "Let's go out to the island," he said.

"I'm sick of that. We'll go fishing. We can sell our catch on the dock." Finn was all industry, always discontent with his brother's wanderings and his dreamy love of being outdoors with nothing to do but enjoy the sun on his back. "Come on," Finn said. He left his dishes on the table for Bea, the housekeeper, and dropped his dirty napkin onto his plate.

On the water, Nathaniel rowed while Finn set the fishing lines over the transom. They were jigging for bass, setting lines with lures and flicking the line to give the lures the look of a real fish underwater. When there was a tug on the line, Finn gave it a quick pull to hook the fish, then he let it swim itself out. Nathaniel slowed up on the oars while Finn reeled the fish in, hand over hand in a familiar rhythm.

"He's a good one," Finn said, pulling the fish aboard the boat. With the fish flapping in the bilge, Finn smacked him on the head with a mallet and set another line. Nathaniel took up the oars again. They fished until they had three big bass in the bow of the boat, then they headed back into the harbor.

On the dock, they sold the fish to Silas Fish Trading Co., and Finn divided the money into two equal parts.

When they got home, Jacob was sitting beside their father at the big desk in the study while his father guided the boy's hand down a row of numbers. Jacob looked up at his brothers from beneath the visor of his captain's hat. "Where you been?" he asked, his eyes alight with excitement.

"Fishing," Finn said. "We had a good catch. Sold three bass."

Their father looked up, then said, "Jacob, we're not done. Son, pay attention."

Finn shook his head and left the room. He didn't say anything to Nathaniel on his way out. He slammed his bedroom door and recounted the money on his bed, lined the six dimes and three pennies so that they were all facing in the same direction, then pulled out the canister from beneath his bed and added his earnings to his savings. To hell with his father's landowning business. He'd buy his own schooner one day and start a fleet. That would show the man what he was capable of once and for all.

He went down to his father's study where Nathaniel Sr. sat alone at his desk. Finn could hear Jacob and Nathaniel talking with Bea in the kitchen. It was near dinnertime, and he heard Bea was getting them to help set the table. Finn stood before his father, waiting for the man to look up, and when he didn't, Finn interrupted him. "Father," he said as if he were stepping into an abyss.

"Phinneas, I hear you've had a good day fishing. Good for you." Nathaniel Sr. placed his pen in the inkwell and blew across the columns of numbers in his ledger. He wore a white linen suit with a red tie even though he worked from home, had his shoes polished and his hair cut every week. Finn stared at his father, then at the numbers. He wanted to understand what they added up to, but his father knocked his fist twice on the desk and stood up. "What do you say we have our dinner?"

"I'd like to learn the ledgers, Father. If I'm to go into business for myself one day. Won't you teach me?"

"We've talked about this before, Son. You need to practice your numbers."

"I can do it if you show me." Finn put all his energy into standing up to his father, as if he could influence the man by sheer will.

"Well, all right. If you're that determined, I'll show you."

Finn sat beside his father at the desk while his father flipped open the ledger and began to explain the columns of numbers and what each row meant. Finn was taken with the orderly stacks of numbers. His eyes swooped over the page, then followed his father's fingers.

"These rows are for the type of expense, and the columns are for the month. So here we have the cost of surveying for January, February, and so on. You can add the column of numbers to get the total expenses for the month of January. Why don't you go ahead and give it a try."

Finn took the piece of paper that his father handed him, and he used a pencil to add one number to the next. As the numbers grew, he lost track, and their meaning slipped away from him. Was this the total costs of surveying, or the total of surveying and maintenance for January? What did this number here mean, the one with the comma? He was frustrated and afraid that his father would be angry with him if he made a mistake.

"Tell me what you've got," his father said, and Finn crumpled up the piece of paper and threw it across the desk.

"I've got nothing. That's what I've got." Finn pushed himself back from the desk and left the house through the front door, making sure to slam it hard. Outside, he went to the woodpile stacked against the side of the barn. His father chopped and stacked the wood on weekends as a form of relaxation. Finn took a log and threw it as hard as he could against an oak tree. When he hit the tree, he took another log, but this time, he missed.

"Why can't I do it?" he shouted, unsure if he meant hit the tree or figure the numbers. What difference did it make? No matter how he figured, it added up to failure. His mind was a riot, and he wanted to burn through the noise with the sheer force of his violence. He threw logs until he hit the tree more than he missed, then he started throwing logs on the ground, dismantling the woodpile until the ground was covered with logs. He wanted to tear his father down. Why couldn't he give Finn something to succeed at? His ankles turned as he crossed over the logs onto the grass. In the half light of dusk, he ran down the drive and across the road to the marsh. He knew his way without thinking about it, his body moving of its own accord, faster, faster, until his mind cleared and he was only motion, a stream of energy making its way toward the outcrop of trees that appeared as a shadow in the darkening air.

When he reached the clearing, he bent over to catch his breath. With a fire going and a canvas tarp spread on the ground beneath the lean-to, he thought about going home, but he couldn't get himself to stand up or douse the fire. He covered himself with the extra tarp and lay back, watching the night sky. He could navigate with a compass and a sextant. He knew his numbers well enough for that, and what he didn't know, he would learn. He was more determined than ever to work out his numbers so that he could buy a fishing boat of his own, start a fleet one day, and make something of himself, like his father had made something of himself.

—⁓—

Rachel called across the boat to Finn, pointing at the clouds to the northeast. "Don't worry about that," he said. He felt confident in his abilities to manage the boat, and he clung to this feeling as if it could save him. He eyed the squall that moved toward them with heavy wind and the beginnings of rain. "Nathaniel," he called, and he waved his brother back to the helm. "Time to tighten up the sails."

Nathaniel eyed the streaks of black cloud.

"Don't worry," Finn said. "We're almost there."

"I'm okay," Nathaniel said, and he went to work.

Finn watched his brother move with grace through his tasks. Between the two of them, they'd get this schooner and the girl to Yarmouth Port. Only a few hours until he guided the boat into the dock and Edwin George paid them in cash. It would be a good day's pay. Even Nathaniel couldn't argue with that.

7

O VER TEN YEARS AGO AND A DAY BEFORE THE BROTHERS' TRIP, Nathaniel hung from the top of the mast. The island appeared as a cloud of trees against the marsh. They were preparing for the practice run when Nathaniel swung around and gazed toward Sandy Neck, the barrier beach that separated the harbor from the wider expanse of bay beyond. He saw the length of the harbor road and the roofs of the ramshackle buildings that made up the harbor village, the docks and cod flakes, and the boys yelling as they threw pennies and dove from pilings.

Below him, the curved gunwales of the schooner, the lines of the wood strapping that made up the decks, the bulwarks and cabins all looked far away. Nathaniel swung on the wooden seat attached to rope he'd fastened to a halyard. He'd hauled himself up to oil the block and tackle and make sure the lines ran free and clear. He had sailed on schooners with Finn. He knew the run of the halyards, the main sheets, and jibs. He understood how to navigate in the dark and how to manage the helm in rough seas. Jacob wanted to learn everything, and Nathaniel would teach him. He'd unfurl charts across the table and draw their course. He'd walk the boy through every rope and pulley on the forty-foot vessel.

He ran his oiled finger over the brass wheel of a pulley, then pulled the rope through until it didn't squeak. Satisfied that he'd cared for each bit of hardware atop the mast, he slowly lowered himself, the wide world receding as he came down onto the deck.

Jacob popped up from the cabin and watched Nathaniel unclip himself from the bosun's seat. "I want to try it," Jacob said. His red hair was cut to his scalp and glittered in the sun; his green eyes glinted.

"Not today. We've got work to do." Nathaniel worked with Jacob to recoil all the lines, stow gear belowdecks, and furl the sails so that they'd rise easily as they pulled away from the dock in the morning. It was nearly dark when Nathaniel glanced around the boat for something that needed tending, but the boat was in good order.

Nathaniel and Jacob walked the dock toward the road.

"I want to go to the island," Jacob said. When Nathaniel didn't answer him, he said, "Please."

"It's late," Nathaniel said, and he led the boy toward home. At the bottom of the driveway, he sent Jacob up to the house, while he continued south along the harbor road toward Young's Boatyard. Only three schooners sat at dry dock for repairs, and *Atlantic* was the one he would climb aboard using a ladder that had been laid upon the ground. He wrestled the thing up so that it leaned against the gunnel. As he waited for Meredith, the sounds in the boatyard were muffled and strange, the hulls of the boats rising up like giant arcs, shadows in the dark. Nathaniel had played among the boats at dry dock as a boy, hiding behind the exposed keels, sneaking aboard to look for stray boat cushions or lengths of rope, anything he could take and use for his own. Footsteps broke the silence, and Meredith appeared as a shadow in the already dark air until she came into view, wrapped in a shawl and rushing toward him.

"I wasn't sure you'd come."

"Don't be foolish," she said, and she went right for the ladder, reached to grab an upper rung, and stepped her foot up. She climbed while Nathaniel held the ladder firmly against the boat, and once she was onboard, he followed.

Cushions lined the berth in the bow to make a neat little bed. They lay back and looked at the stars through the open hatch, and Nathaniel listened to the sound of their breathing in rhythm. He felt the length of her body alongside him, her warmth and her ease with him.

"We'll marry soon," he said. "We'll build our house and be alone in it, the two of us."

Meredith leaned over him and stroked his cheek. She unfastened the bun on the back of her head so that her hair fell down her back and over her shoulders, showering them in the rosewater smell of her soap.

He'd known Meredith since they were children attending the one-room schoolhouse at the top of the harbor road. Nathaniel skipped school as much as he attended, but he sat through class enough to notice that Meredith was quick with an answer to any question. It was clear that she did the reading. When they were fourteen years old, he'd been given the seat directly behind her. She often turned around and placed her cocked elbow on his desk to talk to him about class, but he didn't listen. He watched her pink mouth form words and the smooth line of her square jaw as she turned away from him. He watched the dark hairs on the back of her neck come loose from her carefully tied bun as the day went on.

"What do you do when you skip school, Nathaniel?" Class hadn't started yet, and she turned around to face him where he leaned back in his chair and absently fiddled with his pencil. "You're always on the marsh. I've seen you when I go to get fish with my mother. What do you do out there?"

"I'm not always out there. I go fishing, too."

"Take me sometime," she said, but it was more of a question, and the expectation in her eyes of an adventure appealed to him, and he considered her request for a minute.

"You mother wouldn't let you," he said.

"My mother doesn't know where I am all the time." She spoke coyly, then turned around and faced the teacher, who was standing up from her desk to begin class promptly at eight o'clock. Nathaniel regretted dismissing the girl, regretted the opportunity to get to know her.

At lunch, she approached him again. "You'd really decline a lady a walk through the marsh?"

"I'm going rowing this afternoon if you want to come."

"Yes," she said, her eyes gleaming.

Meredith had loved the boat, loved riding in the stern seat with Nathaniel's legs stretched toward her, his torso learning forward with each stroke. She talked about her family. He told her about his dream to build his own house and live off the land and the sea, and he felt himself opening up to her in a way that he didn't talk to other people. Was it the wind across the water that relaxed them into their conversation or the sun warm on their faces that eased them into each other's company, or was it something about her? He didn't know, but he couldn't stop telling her about his brothers—Finn's ambitions and Jacob learning everything that was put in front of him.

"Finn comes to school, though," Meredith said.

"He wants to go into business. He needs to get an education in order to please my father."

"And you don't care."

Nathaniel shrugged his shoulders and kept rowing. The afternoon was cool and cloudless. The bay reflected the blue of the sky, and the horizon appeared as a seam between two shades of blue, similar and distinct, and Nathaniel pointed for Meredith to see. She gazed and nodded and leaned her face back to feel the sun. He knew that day that he would marry her. When she climbed out of the boat, she stood on shore and brushed sand from the bottom of her dress, then looked up at him with such openness in her face that he felt his heart warm, and he wanted her. He would want her for the rest of his life. They courted for three years before they were physically intimate, and last year, when they turned eighteen, he proposed to her. He gave her his mother's engagement ring, which she liked to drag along his spine so that the diamond scratched his skin. It felt harsh and romantic and like a love he could never lose.

After they made love that night, Nathaniel held Meredith against his chest. He traced the outline of her mouth to memorize her lips, pressed his palm to her cheek, and held each of her ears in his fingers so that he could recall the shape when he imagined her from the deck of the *Sparrow*, because surely he would be thinking of her as he gazed across the boat, past his brothers and toward the coast of Cape Cod.

"You'll have fun on your trip," Meredith said. She nestled in closer to his body, and he pulled her against him, holding her against the time they would be apart, which no matter how brief, always felt like a lifetime. Soon he would be a married man with a wife to protect and a house to build on the land his father had given him to get started. Each of the boys got a five-acre plot, and he would put his to work as soon as they returned from their practice run and their week at sea. He nudged Meredith then to suggest they get themselves ready to leave. She groaned as she rolled away from him.

"I hate this part," she said.

They dressed in the dark and descended the ladder. Nathaniel watched Meredith weave her way among the boats until she disappeared, then he started for home. His body hummed with the feeling of Meredith moving on top of him, and he only wanted to see her again.

8

O N THE *LILITH* WITH FINN AND RACHEL, NATHANIEL WORKED the mainsail sheet, letting the sail out with a gust of wind, then reeling it in again once the gust passed. He worked the rope in his hands, grateful for the calluses he'd built up from rowing. The muscles in his arms and in his back vibrated. His legs braced against the bulwark, muscles taut. His body hummed with the rhythm of his work.

As the boat heeled over in the waves, water crashed over the upper rail. Nathaniel was soaked, and he cleated the mainsheet so that he could go get Rachel off the foredeck. He held onto the handrails on the cabin and worked his way forward until he reached her where she leaned against the mast.

"You need to come back. The squall."

"What's a squall anyways?"

"Nothing to worry about. You just can't stay here."

Rachel ignored his hand when he reached down to help her up. "I like it here," she said. Then she pushed his hand away and stood with one hand braced against the mast, her legs accommodating the sway of the boat. With the sleeve of her coat, she wiped the salt spray from her face, blinked her eyes, and glared into him, as if it were his fault that she couldn't ride the storm out head on. She walked ahead of Nathaniel toward the back of the boat, where Finn stood manning the helm. "Your brother wants me back here, but I was fine right where I was."

Finn pointed toward the clouds on the horizon, the streaks swirling down that were rain. "You stand here, close to me. I'll watch out for you."

"I'm going to keep her back here," Nathaniel said. "Where she can't slip on the deck."

"I'm fine," Rachel said, reaching for the wheel, but Finn nudged her hand away.

"If the weather gets rough, I want you to hold on to this railing or go belowdecks where it's safe."

"I'll stifle down there." Rachel stood close to him, eyeing the bad weather, then turning toward Yarmouth Port.

"Then hold on to the railing."

The rain started slowly at first, gentle drops tapping the deck. Nathaniel went below and returned with a rain jacket for the girl. The coat was too big for her and heavier than her own, but it would protect her from the chill of the wind, cooler now and stronger as it blew across the deck.

Nathaniel was worried now. They should've turned around when they saw the squall coming toward them. He'd known in his gut that they wouldn't make landfall before it hit them dead on, and now that they were in the thick of it, he felt his heart shudder with images of the last storm he'd sailed in. He held on to the rail, then ducked when a wave came over the boat. He stepped closer toward his brother and the girl. Each step was an effort to push away the past, but with the rain in his face, his clothing soaked and stuck to his skin, the past was on him as if time had collapsed and he was back on the *Sparrow* with his brothers those ten years ago, Jacob pointing at rain on the horizon, streaks of gray that hung down from the clouds like dark jellyfish. The gray cover of clouds had drifted in heavy and dark, but it wasn't until they reached the middle of Cape Cod Bay that the rain started all at once, like a line they crossed. Jacob fetched the foul-weather gear from below, and the boys pulled on their oilskins and fastened their hats beneath their chins.

When a wave caught the *Lilith*, it pushed the boat over and dragged Nathaniel from his memories of that last day with Jacob.

Rachel grabbed the rail as the sails reached down toward the water. The rain pattered against them. It ran along the decks and washed over their feet. The wind blew across the middle of the boat, and the full sails carried them swiftly toward Yarmouth Port. As the clouds descended, they rode the waves, feeling the sea beneath the boat like a benevolent hand. Not until the sky cracked open and lightning struck in the distance did they feel the force of the storm.

Nathaniel watched Rachel where she stood by Finn, holding on to the railing. Her coat snapping in the wind made her look like a bird who could fly away.

"Rachel," he said. "You should go below. It'll be safer."

"I'm fine right here," she said, flashing her green eyes at him as if she dared him to make her move. She stood with her back erect, her hands clamped on the rail. Her legs swayed with the boat's motion through the waves. She reminded him of Jacob, standing beside Finn with no fear, trusting the brothers' command of the schooner.

"Finn, we need to shorten sail now that the storm is on us. It'll slow us down."

"No way. We're making good progress through the waves. You don't have to worry."

Nathaniel nodded and went back to the mainsheet, where at least he had some control. It was only a squall, not the full force of a nor'easter, he told himself, letting the sail out, then hauling it in again, letting it out, and hauling it in. He could see his brothers on the deck of the schooner all that time ago as clearly as he saw Finn and Rachel leaning into each other as if the storm empowered a flirtatious dance between them.

Nathaniel wanted to be back on the marsh, where the simple routine of his days helped him keep memory at bay, but the past washed over him like waves over the railing.

—⁓—

Onboard the *Sparrow*, he'd called out to Jacob to hold on as the first wave broke over the bow of the schooner and splashed against the sail. When the next wave filled the sail with water, he had let the mainsail run free until it billowed in the wind and emptied out, then he hauled it in, using the winch. He hauled as fast as he could so that they didn't get tossed about in the sea, but it was useless. The sea battered the boat with heavy knocks that shook the masts.

Jacob looked from one brother to the other to see how he should feel as a wave came across the side of the boat and drenched the three of them. Water ran across the deck and pooled over the scuppers. The brothers were cold now and shivering. A gust of wind tore the jib loose so that it snapped hard enough to hurt somebody. It threw the schooner off course, and Finn cursed. "Goddammit, Nathaniel, would you get that under control?"

Nathaniel crawled along the windward rail. The rope that held the sail in place whipped back and forth. He watched it until he felt its rhythm, then he reached his hand out and grabbed it. The rope tore at his hand, but he held on and pulled the sail in while Finn got the boat on course again.

"We should shorten sail," Nathaniel said. "There's too much wind for the boat to handle."

"We need to sail as fast as we can. The storm will batter us if we don't get in."

"That's rubbish, Finn. We need to play it safe, slow things down." They shouted back and forth over the sound of wind and rain spattering the decks.

"We'll not shorten sail," Finn said.

"Finn. Goddammit, listen to me!" Nathaniel yelled at his brother, but Finn was resolute, and he was in charge, so Nathaniel backed off.

The boat rode low in the water on a beam reach, the wind across the middle of the deck, so that the boat hit the waves broadside and took on water over the windward rail. It was Jacob's job to keep the compass glass free of water. He wiped it over and over with a rag to keep it from beading with raindrops and sweat so that Finn could read it. The visibility was not more than fifty yards in any direction, but they knew from the chart and from experience that they were no more than half a mile off Sandy Neck.

Jacob stood over the compass, teeth chattering, stomping his feet into the deck, then patting his hands together to warm himself. He wiped the compass again and looked to Finn for approval.

"We'll be there soon," Finn said.

Then there was a sound like thunder, a rumble that came from belowdecks and slowed the schooner in its course. The boat dragged with the weight of water pouring in around the bow. Nathaniel raced to free the halyards so that the sails let loose and the boat headed up into the wind where it would drift and not place further pressure on the cracked hull. The sails snapped. The boom swung across the boat.

"Watch your head!" Nathaniel yelled. "We need to get the sails down."

"No," Finn said. "We need them to keep us on course."

"The wind will drive us over," Nathaniel argued. "Drop sail!"

"I'll not do it. I'm the captain, Nathaniel. Man your station and do as I say!"

Jacob held on to the railing along the bulwark. "Don't let go," Nathaniel said. "You hold on no matter what."

Nathaniel climbed down the hatchway to inspect the damage belowdecks, but once he reached the cabin, he was up to his neck in water. He looked around for anything he might want to save, but he only wanted to save his brothers. He sloshed through the water toward the life vests. When the boat tilted in the waves, Nathaniel braced himself by placing a hand against the roof of the cabin, which was nearly at a right angle to the sea. He took a deep breath and dove beneath the surface where foam stirred up sand and formed a cloudy murk. He kicked until he went down to the rack where the vests were stored, but the schooner lurched, and the wall hit him in the head. He kicked himself toward the surface and looked around to get his bearings. The boat had tipped over more. He took another breath and dove. He kicked himself down, following the roof to the hull of the ship. He held his breath a few more seconds, just a few more, but then his lungs expelled a burst of air, and he had to float himself up to the surface.

The cabin was nearly full of water now, and he pulled himself onto the deck where Finn and Jacob waited. "Where are the life vests?" Finn shouted. "We need the life vests, Nathaniel."

"I can't get to them," Nathaniel said.

The tide had carried them a little closer to Sandy Neck. They could see the lighthouse at the end of the sand spit from where they stood in water up to their knees. When the main mast snapped at the top and the sail collapsed into the water like a worn-out doll, they panicked.

The canvas sail filled with water, and the schooner began to tip. Parts of the hull broke apart in the waves. Nathaniel stood behind Jacob with his hands clasped to the rail on the bulwark, forming a kind of wall between the boy and the sea.

Finn reached for a coiled rope and untied the ends so that he could stretch it out between the three of them. The rain lashed the boat; the sea tossed it like a broken toy. Finn tied three consecutive loops so if they held onto the rope, it could keep them together. Each holding a loop, the boys lowered themselves into the bay. They kicked themselves free of the boat and swam toward broken bits of wood. They found broken boards that could support their weight, and Finn passed the first one to Jacob, then found one for himself. They lined up three in a row with Finn in the front, Jacob in the middle, and Nathaniel in the rear. Finn began to kick toward the lighthouse at the end of Sandy Neck, and his brothers followed him, one after the other, up and over the waves. From a distance, they would've appeared as three bobbing buoys marking the channel home.

9

WAVES BATTERED THE *LILITH*, AND RACHEL HELD ON TO THE railing. Finn looked up at the sail, then turned the boat slightly to head off the wind and take pressure off the boat. "We're in the thick of it!" Nathaniel yelled above the sound of the wind flapping the sails, ropes creaking, and the masts straining.

"It'll pass," Finn said. "Don't worry about it."

Finn grabbed Rachel and pulled her closer to the helm, but she struggled away from him and held on to the rail beside Nathaniel. She tilted her head back and let the rain wash over her face, then turned to face the wind.

Nathaniel heard the sound of wood tearing apart, and then the boat veered off course. It was the foremast, cracked and tilting in the wind. The jib fell to the decks, ropes ran through pulleys, and the wind made a balloon of the fallen canvas sail.

"Get that sail!" Finn shouted over the sound of the rain. He veered into the wind to slow the boat's motion while Nathaniel ran forward to get the jib down.

Nathaniel stuffed the sail into a bag and ducked from the freed rope whipping past until he was able to grab one end and tie it off on a cleat. The top of the foremast had fallen into the sea but dragged alongside the boat by the metal stays that had held it in place. It was nothing like the nor'easter that had pummeled the *Sparrow*. A squall was a smaller storm with less wind and rain—nothing like the storm that had taken Jacob. For this, Nathaniel was relieved. He pulled on the metal stays that held the foremast dragging in the water, pulled until he had the wooden spar securely onboard and fastened to the rail where it wouldn't roll around and do damage. Satisfied that the sails, the ropes, and the foremast were stowed safely, Nathaniel walked aft, holding on to the handrails along the bulwark with each step. His wet clothes clung to his body. His hair hung in his eyes, dripping in rivulets down his face, but he was okay. They were okay.

At the helm, he told Finn that all was in order, then he joined Rachel where she stood holding on to the wooden handrail, occasionally leaning around the bulwark to check on her bag. She smiled at him and tilted her head back again to receive the rain on her face like a blessing. She let go of the rail and held her arms wide open in the wind, and at that moment, a huge wave broke over the windward side of the boat. Finn ducked behind the wheel to avoid the velocity of water, but Rachel slid down the deck. As fast as Nathaniel reached down for her, she was gone.

"She's over!" Nathaniel screamed at Finn. He raced to get the lifesaving ring, tied a free rope to the ring, then fastened it to a cleat on deck. "I can't see her. I'm going in!" Nathaniel didn't even look toward his brother as he yelled. The wind could've carried his voice away, but he didn't care. He held one arm through the life ring and scanned the water for Rachel. There was no sign of her. He leapt over the side of the boat and into the water. When he came up spitting seawater, he saw that Finn had sailed into the wind and let loose the sails so that the boat drifted near the spot where Rachel had fallen overboard.

Nathaniel searched along the surface of the water for her arms waving, her head bobbing—any sign of her at all—but there was nothing. He swam as far as the rope tied to the boat would allow, then he stretched in every direction. It wasn't until he swam toward the bow of the boat that he saw her, one hand raised, her head rising and falling, rising and falling. He kicked toward her as hard as he could, but the boat was drifting away from her and carrying him along with it. She was so close. He saw her on the rise of a wave, then she was gone. He panicked, let go of the life ring, and swam toward her. The only thing that mattered to him in that moment was getting her safely onboard the *Lilith*, but the waves lifted and dropped him, lifted and dropped, and he couldn't get sight of her.

—ᴠᴠ—

Nathaniel waited for the sight of Jacob's head and the narrow width of his shoulders to pop up with his kickboard, but when another giant swell washed over them, Jacob didn't show up. Nathaniel pulled himself forward on the rope to where Jacob should be, hand over fist, until he reached the empty loop. He searched the surface of the water for his brother, but there was only the floating board. Blood coursed through his body in a rush that made a sound in his ears, a near buzzing—or was that his fear?

"Jacob!" he yelled when he saw the top of his brother's head pop up. The boy was gasping. He looked at Nathaniel and waved to signal that he was all right. Nathaniel kept his eye on him, watched him disappear in the trough of a wave, then pop up again on each crest, disappear and pop up. He looked toward Sandy Neck where he could make out a small house near the lighthouse. They were getting closer. When he turned to watch Jacob again, he waited for him to surface. *One, two, three…six.* He swam up to where the boy had been swimming with his kickboard, but the kickboard drifted with no sign of Jacob.

Nathaniel dove beneath the waves where a foamy wash clouded his view. When he didn't see his brother, he swam lower until he couldn't hold his breath, and his body burst toward the surface. He took another deep breath and dove, looking in every direction, but there was no sign of Jacob. Then he was there, drifting toward the bottom, his white shirt billowing and filling with water. Nathaniel kicked toward his brother and extended his arms until he almost had him. When he caught the edge of the boy's shirt, he held fast with his fist and tried to pull him closer, but the weight of the water made him too heavy to move. He was sinking, his face blank, eyes closed. Nathaniel used the edge of the shirt to pull the boy around, but Nathaniel's chest burst open, and he took in a mouthful of water. He coughed, and against every thought in his mind, his body reached for the surface while his brother sank toward the bottom.

—*vvv*—

Nathaniel surfaced for a deep breath of air, then dove down until he saw Rachel. She was only five feet below the surface of the water, drifting, facedown, arms outstretched. He swam underwater, kicking hard, using his arms like wings to fan himself forward, until he grabbed one corner of the jacket and reeled her in. He pulled her by one arm toward the surface until they both popped out of the water. Rachel coughed, but her head tilted to one side. A gash of about four inches crossed from her right temple up into her hair, and blood washed over her face. She was breathing, though. Finn steered the boat toward them, and when he was near enough, he threw the life ring toward them. Nathaniel swam with the girl under his arm. He took hold of the life ring with his free arm and held fast while Finn reeled them in. The storm was letting up a bit as they made their way toward the boat. Once they were close, Finn dropped a rope ladder over the side.

"She's unconscious!" Nathaniel yelled.

The wind was easing off, and he heard Finn clearly when he said, "I'll get the harness." Nathaniel held the ladder with one arm and Rachel with the other until Finn lowered a line with the bosun's harness on it. Nathaniel had to let go of the ladder to fasten the canvas straps around Rachel. He treaded water, his breath coming hard, as he slid the strap under her arms and cinched it at her chest where the rope ran up to the deck. Finn stood, ready.

"Haul away!" Nathaniel's voice rasped, and he yelled again. "Go ahead, Finn."

Finn wound the rope around a belaying pin and pulled, one long tug after another, while Nathaniel climbed the ladder with Rachel pressed against the front of his body, arms around his neck. He carried her up, up. When she opened her eyes, she startled and looked to Nathaniel. "I've got you," he said. When they reached the deck, Finn bent down to grab Rachel by the harness, but she swatted his hand away. She wouldn't let go of Nathaniel.

"I'm going to climb over the rail," he said, speaking into her ear so that she could hear him in the rain. "Then I'll pull you onboard."

Rachel nodded, but she didn't let go of his shoulders. He peeled her fingers loose, then placed each of her hands on the ladder so that she hung by her harness, clinging to the boat. She watched him swing himself onto the boat. "Nathaniel!"

"I'm right here," he said. While Finn hauled her in, Nathaniel reached down for her and pulled her onto the deck, where she promptly passed out again. He felt for her pulse, listened for her breathing, which moved in ragged rhythm with the rise and fall of her chest. It was the gash on her forehead that he worried about. He tore off the frayed bottom of his shirt and blotted around the wound. He pressed hard to stop the bleeding, but it didn't stop. He took his shirt off and tore strips from it to make a bandage around her head.

"Get us in," Nathaniel said.

Finn reeled in the mainsail and manned the helm. The one big sail was enough to get them home, and Nathaniel trusted his brother to get them there. "It wasn't your fault," Nathaniel said. "We didn't see the squall, and she was horsing around."

"Okay," Finn said.

"Really, it wasn't," Nathaniel told him, and he held the girl's head in his lap as Sandy Neck came into view. "We're almost there, Rachel. We'll get you to the doctor. You don't have to worry."

Nathaniel blotted at the blood as it seeped through the bandages and trickled down her face. Still, she was here, breathing and alive. He took a deep breath and tried not to worry as the boat made progress through the waves. There was Yarmouth Port in the distance, his father's house on the hill.

When they'd been rescued after the wreck of the *Sparrow*, the shore had been lined with folks from town, waiting as if the fate of the *Sparrow* was a harbinger of their own family members' fates. Nathaniel had watched his father at the edge of the dock, leaning forward as if urging their boat closer. When the rescue schooner finally drifted in and tied at the dock, Nathaniel Sr. stood back and waited for his sons. There was a lot of talk, thank-yous to the rescuing captain and words among the crew that he could not make out.

Their father pulled Nathaniel to him and hugged him, then Finn. He made sure to hold Finn and squeeze him and pat him on the back. He looked toward the cabin door, waiting for Jacob to appear. The boys watched him, heads down, then Nathaniel Sr. fixed his eyes on their faces. He didn't want to understand what he saw so clearly etched in the hard lines of Nathaniel's forehead. He turned from the boys, held the palm of his hand to his forehead, and stood for a moment, silent.

When he turned back to face them, he spoke in a voice that was strained and stoic. "You're freezing. We'll get you some fresh blankets."

"Jacob..." Nathaniel said, his voice breaking. "We lost him." Nathaniel nearly lost his breath, but his father placed a hand on his back as he huddled with Finn. Finn, for the first time, didn't say a word. They stood motionless on the dock, as if one step away from where Jacob had drowned would be a step into a life without him, and not one of them could face that yet. Nathaniel Sr. let out a gasp of breath that became a sob. He didn't want his boys to see him like this. He clenched his teeth hard and pushed a hand into his mouth to hush himself.

People gathered around them like an incoming tide, then they receded, then they circled them again. No one knew what to do, what to say. Max Ballard stepped forward and wrapped the boys in dry blankets.

There was much talk on the dock about the wreck.

Right off Sandy Neck.

So close, they were almost home.

Such good sailors.

People tried to overhear the family talking as Maxwell guided Nathaniel Sr. and the boys to his wagon. He helped Nathaniel Sr. up each step onto the wagon seat and then set a box on the ground so that the boys could step into the back of the wagon.

He clicked at the horse and started off for the grim ride home. Nathaniel continually turned his head back toward the water.

"Son," his father said, and Nathaniel put his head down and sobbed.

Nathaniel knew that explanations were in order, but he didn't deliver the facts until they got home, cold, clear facts: the unexpected storm raced them toward the harbor; the tide drove the schooner onto the shoals; the waves cracked the hull; they decided to swim for shore. The rest of the story would come out in pieces over the days and weeks to follow.

The top spar that snapped on a reckless jibe that sent the boom flying across the boat until the sail filled and swung them away from the oncoming wind.

He didn't want to think about this, but every day, his mind went over the events. He blamed himself because he lost sight of Jacob, and then when it mattered, he couldn't swim down to save him. He could've tried harder to hold on to his brother, a few more seconds without air, just one more minute, and he could've gotten him to the surface.

In the weeks after losing Jacob, Nathaniel took long walks and went over and over each detail of the accident in his mind to try to figure if there was something he could have changed. He had inspected those cracked seams and deemed them ready to go. So had the Garrison brothers and Finn, but Finn was too eager and couldn't be trusted, so it had been Nathaniel's judgment that mattered in the end. Then there was the fact that he hadn't been able to reach the life vests. Maybe if he'd stowed them closer, maybe if he'd made them more accessible. But the worst thing had been having the edge of his brother's shirt in his fist and not being able to hold his breath long enough to pull Jacob to the surface.

That was where he had ultimately failed. His weakness followed him around in the dark. His scolding self never let up. When he went home, he thought he heard Jacob on the stairs or waiting in the yard for Nathaniel to finish his breakfast so they could get down to the rowboat.

There were Jacob's boots worn on the instep from the way his ankles turned in. There was his shirt thrown on the floor in the hallway. His bedroom smelled like rank feet and salt and the particular odor of him, and Nathaniel could barely stand in the doorway without a powerful grief taking hold of him. At dinner, Jacob's empty chair was like an accusation.

At night, Nathaniel woke to his father's angry outbursts: a side table and lamp flipped over onto the floor, a prized crystal bowl smashed against the wall. Nathaniel believed his father's anger was directed at him, and he understood. He wished his father would lash out at him and Finn, scream hateful words and blame them for their recklessness. The sounds of calamity from downstairs didn't bother him. It was his father's broken sobbing at night after they had all gone to bed that annihilated him in the dark, a grief that matched his own.

10

THEY PULLED INTO THE DOCK IN YARMOUTH PORT, BUT NATHANIEL didn't stand up for fear of disturbing the girl. Finn said, "Jesus Christ, Father's waiting. He's going to be angry."

"Or afraid," Nathaniel said. "The storm…"

Their father walked across the gangway onto the *Lilith*. "What have you let happen here, Finn? I made a simple request. Get your brother off the marsh and onto the boat. Make him do something productive, and you not only wreck Edwin George's boat, but you got someone injured." Their father removed his hat and held it in front of his chest. He wiped his brow with a monogrammed handkerchief. "And who's this godforsaken girl?"

"It was a squall, Father. There was no way to predict it."

"What do you mean, you talked him into getting me off the marsh?" Nathaniel looked to Finn for some explanation. He thought Finn had wanted to be with him, to repair some past pain and estrangement. Ah, it had been a ploy all along, his father and brother conspiring against him.

Finn didn't speak, nor did their father. Nathaniel lifted the girl into his arms. When Rachel opened her eyes, she cried, "My bag. I need my bag."

"I'll bring it to her later," Finn said.

"No, I need my bag."

Nathaniel heard the nervous breathing beneath Rachel's words, but he ignored her and walked across the gangway past his father and up the harbor road toward the house.

"Son," his father called after him, but Nathaniel didn't turn from his forward motion. The girl leaned against his chest as he walked, and he watched her eyes close as she grew limp in his arms. She couldn't have weighed more than a hundred pounds, but he was tired from swimming and holding on to her in the waves. Still, he'd get her to his father's house and call for Dr. Howe. He carried her along the harbor road until he saw out of the corner of his eye Meredith Butler running across her yard. The sweep of her skirt caught in the wind as she watched him from thirty yards away. His breath caught in his throat. He wanted to turn away from her toward his father's house, but he didn't think he could carry Rachel up the hill, and the Butler house, which rose like a ship's hull from a vast, manicured lawn, was right on the harbor. The girl was bleeding through her bandages now. He stopped walking and gazed up at his father's house. When Rachel began to moan, the sound of her pain cut through him. He turned toward the Butler house.

As he crossed the yard, Meredith ran toward him and looked into the girl's face without slowing Nathaniel down. She looked just the same as she had ten years earlier at nineteen years old. He hadn't been this close to her since their last night in the dark at Young's Boatyard. He averted his gaze and focused on the girl.

"Who is she?" Meredith turned to Nathaniel for some response. He hoisted the girl up higher in his arms, then Meredith took him by the elbow to lead him to the house. "I called for Dr. Howe when I saw you through the spyglass. The blood..."

Nathaniel followed Meredith to the side door. He ducked the girl through the doorframe, then carried her along a short hallway to a sitting room where he laid her on the settee.

"Bring a glass of water and a cold cloth," Meredith said. Dot, one of the maids, disappeared toward the kitchen. The other maid, Rose, hovered around the girl, not sure what to do. Nathaniel stood back from Meredith as she held a cold cloth to Rachel's head, but he couldn't take his eyes from the spot where Meredith's thin fingers pressed the wound. He hadn't seen Meredith up close in so long, and her familiar warmth and sheer competency reminded him of who they had been. He gazed at the soft expression in her eyes and the deft way that she placed a hand under the girl's head to rearrange the pillows.

"There, that feels better now, doesn't it? It's going to hurt, but Dr. Howe is on his way."

Rachel opened her eyes wide, jade green with straw-colored flecks, hatch marks of brown around the pupil, and full of fear. "Where's my bag?"

"There, there. Don't worry. We're going to get you good as new." Meredith sat on the edge of the settee and held the girl's hand.

"I need my bag. I really need it. You don't understand."

"You'll get your bag. Don't you worry about a thing. You're in good hands here, dear."

Nathaniel removed himself to the far window, curtained against the light of day. He felt foolish standing around while Meredith cared for Rachel, but he didn't want to leave the girl—not broken like this. They'd never found his brother's body, but he'd imagined him washed ashore somewhere, mouth agape, clothes in tatters, a stranger standing over him. He didn't want to think about the condition of Jacob's body when he washed ashore. Instead, he hoped the stranger would take care of his brother—fold his arms over his chest, carry him up from the shore, and bury him in solid ground. He wanted to help Rachel, but he didn't know what to do.

When the doctor arrived, Nathaniel stood back from the girl. Dr. Howe was the only doctor for several towns, and he'd sorted out a good many broken bones and sicknesses over the years. He was a tall man, fat as a bear around the middle with strong legs and scrawny arms and a suit cut to fit his figure so that the buttons met in front in spite of his girth. His red face, splotched with veins, was beaded in a thin sheen of sweat, and he wore round spectacles that made his eyes look larger than they were.

Meredith dragged a heavy chair over to the settee, and Dr. Howe lowered his weight upon it, drew the stethoscope from his bag. His fingers eased the strips of Nathaniel's shirt from where they'd settled in Rachel's wound. The wound had stopped bleeding, and the doctor pressed his fingers around it to examine the depth and contusions. He opened the girl's eyes wide and looked into them. He felt her pulse, looked down her throat and in her ears. "What happened?"

"She's been passing out on and off since we pulled her from the water," Nathaniel said. He recalled the girl's stillness as she lay on the deck of the boat, skirts splayed, arms outcast. Now he noticed the constellation of freckles on her nose, her full lips and small mouth. He wanted to protect her from a world where accidents happened, and this feeling of wanting to protect her was old in him. He turned from the girl to look out the window at the sails along the harbor like low-flying clouds, puffy with air. He lingered because he wanted to know that she was okay, that she could heal and be well again.

"She's got a lot of bruising and a bad concussion. The losing consciousness concerns me. She could have internal damage, but we won't know for a few days, maybe a week. I can stitch her up, but she'll have to rest. She shouldn't get up or move around at all. She could be okay, but it's too early to tell."

"What do you mean?" Nathaniel asked.

"I mean she has to rest and recover herself before we can know anything for sure. She's young and healthy from the looks of it. Her chances of recovery are very good. It just depends on how hard she hit her head. Does she have someone to care for her?" Dr. Howe asked.

"She can stay here," Meredith said, and Dr. Howe nodded his approval. Nathaniel stepped out of the way of the doctor as he packed his bag and worked the heft of his body between the furniture and out of the room.

"Stay if you want to," Meredith said, looking into Nathaniel's eyes, then looking away. He couldn't bear the depth of her gaze, couldn't stand the sight of the dark hairs falling from the back of her bun and sticking to her neck or the way she rubbed her finger and thumb together when she was thinking—all of it made him remember their time together so long ago.

"I oughta go," he said.

"Not yet. Tell me what happened to her."

"She got quite a knock on the head, and she was underwater. I had to jump in to get her. She drifted in and out, but by the time we got her on the boat, she was totally unconscious. I wrapped her head as best as I could, then you saw me trying to get her to my father's house."

"You saved her," Meredith said, giving him a meaningful look that he wanted to get away from. "Do you know who she is?"

"We picked her up in Boston. She wanted a ride. It was strange. She didn't really care where she went. She was traveling and looking for work, so Finn agreed to take her with us."

When Rachel opened her eyes, she looked at Nathaniel with a piercing curiosity that made him turn away.

A knock on the front door startled the three of them. Meredith gave the girl one last look before she got up to answer the door. She came back with Finn, who carried his hat in one hand that hung by his side. His hair was covered in dry salt, his beard a day's growth like a shadow along his jaw.

"I came to check on Rachel," Finn said.

"She's in a very fragile state," Meredith said, standing before Rachel as if protecting her from an intruder. Nathaniel believed that Meredith wanted it to be just the two of them caring for the girl, Nathaniel and Meredith, like it used to be.

Finn shifted from one foot to the other and glanced toward the windows where dusk was settling over the marsh before he looked back at Rachel.

"Do you have my bag?" she asked.

"I forgot. I'll bring it tomorrow," he said. "You don't need to worry about it."

Rachel opened her mouth as if she was about to argue with Finn, then thought better of it. She glanced around the room, pressed her hand to her bandage, then closed her eyes. "I need my bag," she said.

"You'll get it. Stop worrying, would you? Now tell me, do you remember falling overboard?"

"I remember Nathaniel pulling me from the water," she said, her eyes darting as if searching for the bag.

"I manned the boat so that I wouldn't lose the two of you," Finn said. "It was a heavy squall." He looked from Nathaniel to Meredith as if for acknowledgment of the role he'd played in assuring Rachel's safety.

Rachel asked Nathaniel to come closer. She took his hand and squeezed, looked up from the couch into his face. He bent down to let her see him.

"You need rest," Meredith said, then looked over her shoulder at Finn.

Finn looked lost, then a hard scowl crossed his face. "I'll be seeing you," he said, and he found his own way out. Nathaniel followed him, but Finn was in full stride toward his shop, and Nathaniel knew better than to go after him.

—⁓—

Nathaniel headed across the marsh, grateful that the girl was in Meredith's good hands. Meredith would know how to take care of her, and the doctor would check in. Still, she was in danger. There was no way to know. He could only hope that she recovered. He didn't have to worry that he couldn't save her. He'd pulled her from the water, gotten her ashore. After losing Jacob, there had been no relief from his wondering, *Why did I survive and not Jacob?* He hadn't been able to face his father, because he blamed himself for not saving his brother. He was the oldest, and it was his job to protect them. He'd failed miserably, and he couldn't face the charitable stares and condolences of people in town. He couldn't stand the way they looked at him with pity.

When a storm came a few days after the accident that took his brother, he'd been relieved. He'd watched heavy clouds drift over the water and waited as if for exculpation. He'd dragged one of his father's mahogany chairs in front of the north-facing window so that he could monitor the storm on the horizon. He wanted to go back to that day on the boat, back to the part where they'd leapt into the water and Jacob had believed in them. That was the worst thing of all, Jacob's unwavering belief in his brothers. No matter how frightened he was, he'd always followed his brothers, who made him feel safe, no matter what.

The storm darkened, and Nathaniel wanted to feel the rain on his body, the wind beneath the boat. In the bedroom, he pulled on his old linen pants and headed out. His legs found their way to the harbor without him. All he had to do was follow his own mindless motion. When he reached his boat, he pulled the anchor from the sand and pushed the skiff into the water. Even in the dark of the storm, it was easy to follow the shadow of the jetty out into the bay, and his body fell into rhythm as if into himself.

When he turned to eye the weather over his shoulder, streaks of gray hung down from the dark clouds. He rowed toward it.

He hadn't anticipated the wind, which came before the storm, a slight lift at first, a resistance to his speed through the water. His shirt flapped around his body, his hair flew in his face, but he rowed into the challenge of it. Nothing would stop him as he raced to meet the storm. First the drizzle pecking at the back of his neck and tapping at the wooden seats of the skiff, a warmth running down the back of his shirt. The rain smelled fresh and clean, then there was the taste of the ocean in the back of his throat. He felt in control, as if the skiff were a part of him as it had been for so many years, a pure and true part of him.

The clouds came as a shadow over him; the drizzle became a hard rain that pummeled his back. He leaned his face forward to keep the water from his eyes. He blinked, but he couldn't see through the torrent. The skiff rose on the crest of each wave, then dropped with a thud, rose and then dropped. Nathaniel hadn't rowed in a storm like this before. As the wind picked up, he thought of turning for shore, but the cresting waves, the pummeling rain, freed him from his anguish. They consumed his attention and filled him with a rush of feeling he felt in his muscles and bones. Only a storm could obliterate him. Only a storm could carry him into some other part of himself, a part that could take control and manage the boat against the sea and the wind and the rain.

As he grew tired, his mind became more determined. He leaned forward with the oars, then drew them back against the weight of the waves. He refused to acknowledge the pain creeping up his back, the weakness in his arms. Instead, he focused on *stroke, stroke, stroke,* and he rode the rhythm of the waves as if they were like the beat of his own heart keeping him alive. The boat slammed harder, the thud that after a while racked Nathaniel's back. The sound of the waves against the hull, the thwack of the boat against the water, the rain splattering all around filled his head with a loud, rushing din until no one sound was distinguishable from the next. They all became a loud presence, like the presence of the bay, a wide and fathomless thing that would stay with him long after the storm.

After a while, he forgot where he was going. He was rowing into the storm, and now that he was in it, he felt consumed. He only wanted to stay in the heart of it. As the boat lifted on the crest of a wave, he braced his feet against the stern seat. The wind rushed beneath the hull and caught the boat like a sail so that it pushed the small skiff backward and launched Nathaniel into the water like a catapult. He held onto the oars until he thought they would pull his arms out at the shoulder sockets, then he let go and took flight. The water was warm, warmer than the rain, and he drifted down into it where he could see the shadow of the skiff at the surface. He kicked toward it. He wasn't afraid. He had nothing to lose. He broke through the surface of water and swam toward the boat where it was overturned in the waves. There must've been an air pocket beneath that kept the boat afloat. Nathaniel pulled himself toward the hull, but there was nothing to hold on to. He could only drape himself over the bottom like a washed-up clump of seaweed. He felt the rain on his back, the waves in his face. Wasn't this what he'd wanted? Oblivion?

It was Elliot Kelly who found him. Eli who'd seen him leave the harbor
and row toward the storm. Eli who knew enough to keep an eye out for
him. He'd let Nathaniel drift with the boat for a good long while before
he sailed his schooner up alongside him.

When Nathaniel lifted his head, he wasn't relieved, nor was he disappointed. He waited for Eli to throw the life ring.

Eli dragged him aboard, and Nathaniel fell onto the deck shaking.
The sun had gone down, and the wind had left him cold in the water.

"You want to bring that skiff in?" Eli asked.

Nathaniel eyed the boat and nodded, his face blank.

It was some work sailing alongside the skiff, righting her in the
water, and craning her onto the schooner with the winch that Eli used
to drag in lobster traps.

Eli tossed Nathaniel a wool sweater and set sail toward the harbor,
his long hair pulled back in a ponytail, his dark skin darker in the night.

"You done trying to kill yourself?" he asked.

"I wasn't—"

"You done?"

Nathaniel nodded.

That night, he slept for twelve hours, then woke to the confines of
his room. He felt stifled and only wanted to be outside. Downstairs,
he refused his father's questions and went to meet Meredith at the
boatyard, as they had planned two days ago. They stood at the bottom
of the ladder that leaned against the *Atlantic*. "I'm leaving," he said
before they had time to climb onto the boat.

"What do you mean, you're leaving?"

"I have to get out of here." He hesitated and considered the true meaning of his words—that he was giving up their life together—but loss was a wave that folded in on itself. Finally, he spoke. "I don't want to see you. I don't want to see anyone. I want to be alone."

"But you love me."

"I can't."

"Don't you love me, Nathaniel?" Meredith leaned in to his chest, but he couldn't lift his arms to console her. She sobbed into her hands, then wiped her hands on her dress, then sobbed again, as if her sobbing would change his mind. "But we have plans, a life, a whole world. How can you—?"

Nathaniel couldn't find the right words because there were no right words; he was numb. He walked her home, but she walked ahead of him, as if even now, the distance between them was too great to bridge. After dinner, Nathaniel took a bag of tools from the barn, a sack of salt fish, vegetables, and bread to get him started, and a change of clothes from the house. He knew where he was going. He wasn't coming back.

That was his last memory of Meredith, the last time he'd been in close proximity to her. He felt agitated after seeing her again, and he wanted to push away the feeling of sitting in the same room with her. The energy between them felt thick and unnerving. He wanted to stay away from it.

II

11

THE MORNING AFTER THEIR TRIP FROM BOSTON, NATHANIEL started a fire in the pit away from the shack. He sat back on his haunches and watched the fingers of flame reach skyward. When he heard an unnatural rustle in the bushes, he grew alert, focused. It could be Rascal, he thought, or a deer maybe, but it was Finn who walked out from behind the blueberry shrubs. "Jesus," he said, pushing branches out of his way. "I'll never understand why you live out here, Nathaniel."

"What are you doing here?"

"Father wants to see us."

"And you think I care about that?"

"I'm sorry I tricked you into sailing with me," Finn said. "Father promised me money for my fleet if I got you out on the boat. He thought it would help you get over whatever it is that keeps you out here."

"I like my life," Nathaniel said.

Finn glanced around the clearing, at the circle of stones. "So what was it like being at Meredith's house?"

"That was for the girl." Nathaniel thought about Meredith leaning over Rachel, her tenderness and concern.

"Still, that's a lot of the past popping up in your face, Nathaniel. You must think about it sometimes, even after ten years, losing Jacob, Meredith. Maybe you'll face facts. You can't live out here forever. What will happen to you when you're old and you have no money? What if you get sick or need help and there's nobody here to help you? You have to think of these things. You're too afraid to go back to life without Jacob, but you're without him anyways." Finn sat on an overturned stump that served as a stool. He looked at Nathaniel as if he were speaking a truth that his brother couldn't help but understand, when in fact, his words only angered Nathaniel and made him feel more alienated from Finn than he'd ever been.

"I know the facts," Nathaniel said.

"Like the fact that Meredith Butler has a husband with a lot of money, and she'd never pay attention to you. Not anymore."

"What did you come here for, Finn?"

"I want you to come up to see Father with me. He wants to talk to us about what happened out there. He's worried about his reputation and what Edwin George will think of him because his sons got caught in a storm. Again."

"We could've shortened sail," Nathaniel said. "We could've done better."

"We did well, Nathaniel. You always have to blame yourself. It was the wind, not us, that cracked the mast. It was the sea that knocked Rachel overboard, not us."

"What if I hadn't jumped overboard? We would've lost her."

"But we didn't."

"Still."

"Just come with me. Please."

Nathaniel agreed to go, not because Finn wanted him to but because their father would bother him until he heard an explanation of what happened in the squall.

—⁓—

Nathaniel Sr. called them into the house from his office window. "I'm in here," he said, and they followed the sound of his voice. "Come in. Sit down, boys."

Nathaniel waited for Finn to sit in front of his father's desk, then he took a chair off to the side.

"I want to know what happened out there."

"There's not a lot to know," Finn said. "The squall hit us dead on, regardless of how we tried to sail clear of it. I'm just glad we were able to save the boat."

"The mast cracked," their father said. "You call that saving the boat? And that girl…who is she, and what was she doing on that boat?"

"Her name is Rachel. She needed a ride, and she looked very vulnerable on the docks with all those men," Finn said. "We just wanted to help her."

"When I line up work for you, I expect you to carry out the task without compromising my relationships. This is an embarrassment for me. Do you understand that?"

Nathaniel watched the conversation, not sure why he was in the room at all. This was between Finn and their father.

"Nathaniel, what do you have to say in all this?"

"I'm not getting into it with you. You both tricked me into going, and now you can figure this out for yourselves. I don't care."

"That's no attitude to have. When I give you work, I expect you to take responsibility." Nathaniel Sr. waited for Nathaniel to respond, but Nathaniel didn't say a word. Their father turned his attention to Finn. "How am I supposed to support your fishing fleet when you can't even get a boat across the bay from Boston?"

"Father, that's not fair. I delivered the boat in spite of the storm."

Nathaniel wondered what would've happened if they'd shortened sail. He'd insisted, but Finn was the captain. Nathaniel wasn't going to protect his brother from their father's accusations. He wasn't sure that his father was wrong. And after Finn had tricked him into thinking they were going to be brothers again, he wasn't going to stick up for him.

Their father paced behind his desk, a solid mahogany piece of furniture that separated the brothers from him. "And you want money for your fleet?"

"Yes," Finn said. "I upheld my end of the bargain. You should hold up your end." Finn and their father both looked at Nathaniel for a reaction, but Nathaniel gave away nothing of his hurt feelings and anger.

"Well, bring your plans to me, and make sure they're goddamn good enough." Their father turned his back to them and faced out his tall window toward the bay. "That's all," he said, dismissing them.

12

THE WEIGHT OF THE COFFEE MUG IN HER HAND LET HER KNOW SHE was real. *I am here.* She thought of Finn coming to the door of her house, how she'd sent him away. She didn't want to admit it to herself, but she'd wanted to be alone with Nathaniel while Rachel slept. Sitting near him, talking about the girl or the weather or nothing at all, made her realize the fact that she no longer loved Theo. When had she stopped loving him? She didn't know.

Before they married, when Meredith was twenty-one and Theo twenty-six, the intensity of his attention had drawn her in. When he'd taken her sailing on the bay one morning early in their courtship, he explained to her how to raise the sail by pulling on the halyards and tying them off on the cleat. He showed off maneuvering the boat from the harbor, but in the open bay, he taught her to manage the mainsheet as they tacked into the wind and then headed off into a beam reach. The next time they went out, he let her take the tiller and explained to her the finer points of sail. The words filled her mind. *Ready about. Hard alee. Jibe. Jibe ho.* In the boat, they formed an intimacy through their connection to the wind. As Meredith called, "Ready about," and swung the tiller to leeward, they both ducked under the boom as it swung across the boat.

When she thought of Nathaniel during those early days of her courtship with Theo, she tried not to look across the marsh. When he'd moved out to the shack, his absence had become a constant source of pain for her. She tried not to think about the taste of his lips or the feeling of his pelvis pushing into her. The weight of his body haunted her, and she slept with pillows along the front of her torso for comfort. For weeks, she'd stayed in bed, claiming a headache or fever, demanding the doctor come to the house even though she had no real symptoms. She believed she would die. Her mother, Jane, ministered to her as if she had the flu—with cold compresses on her forehead, hot compresses on her joints, tablets of pain medicine—until she grew frustrated.

"Meredith, you can't lie around the house all day. You're as bad as him, removing yourself from your problems. You need to get up, do something. Stop wallowing in this heartbreak."

"You don't understand." Meredith lay her forearm over her eyes as if her pain was unbearable.

"I understand perfectly well." Her mother opened the shades and let some light into the room, but Meredith groaned and rolled toward the wall. "You're not a child, Meredith. You're a grown woman with a grown woman's problems. Now you need to get yourself out of that bed."

Meredith felt the covers ripped from the bed so that she was revealed lying there in her nightclothes. It was three o'clock in the afternoon, and she couldn't move.

"Up," her mother said, reaching for Meredith's hand, but Meredith sat on the edge of the bed as if putting her feet on the floor would be like stepping on hot coals. "Come on," her mother said. "We've got work to do."

But to Meredith, her future had become a blank slate. She lost herself in dusting, sweeping, scrubbing, until cleaning became a remedy to her broken heart.

When she met Theo two years later, she pushed her longing for Nathaniel down into a locked box within her heart that she swore she would never open. She directed her attention to this new man, his sunburnt, freckled arms, and his blond hair that tossed in the wind.

Theo's family was rich from selling the fleets' daily catch to larger interests in Boston. He would never allow her to work, and it took her a while to accept this. What would she do with her time? "You'll run the house and take care of me. We'll take care of each other," Theo said.

His fingernails were always clean. His skin, smooth as a woman's, had amazed Meredith when she first ran her fingertips along the underside of his palm. His only work had been behind a desk or among other men negotiating prices for fish or the cost of shipping a boatload of mackerel, cod, and bass to Boston. He wasn't handsome, but he was attractive in a way that had more to do with a stern air of competence and authority, as if he didn't need to touch the objects in a room but controlled them nonetheless. His pale-green eyes and small nose were offset by a strong jaw and broad shoulders that gave Meredith the feeling that he could stand up to life without flinching. He held his physical strength in check, but she knew it was there from the easy way he hauled up a sail and carried her onto shore one day in a fit of laughter. She'd felt the hardness of his arms and his unflinching back, and she let him carry her even though it was against her nature. While his prospects were good, it hadn't been money that attracted her to him but hope—hope that she could get over Nathaniel Boyd and make a new life for herself.

On her wedding night, when Theo had taken her to bed, his gentleness had disappointed her. She wanted to be ravaged, thrown back on the bed and rendered weak with passion, but he was careful, tentative, and she needed to reassure him that she wasn't hurt.

When she and Theo married, he'd joined his father's business. He was formal and polite with her and dressed in expensive suits with shining leather shoes polished to a fine sheen. As he became preoccupied with the daily work of expanding their operation, he grew distant, and Meredith spent more and more time on her own. She ran the house, which mostly ran on the hard work of two maids, Dot and Rose. But the maids stopped talking when she came into the room. They viewed her as an intrusion on their daily routines, and she felt like a guest in her own house, but it was her house and they were the maids, she told herself when she heard them giggling in the next room.

She left her coffee cup on the counter and walked into the yard with the spyglass. She liked the solid weight of it in her hands and adjusted the focus on the marsh that led to the harbor. She didn't want to look toward the island where Nathaniel lived, but there was the spyglass swinging in that direction, and there was Nathaniel, walking toward her. She waved and waited for him to approach. It was strange talking to him after so many years. When she'd first taken up residence in the Butler house, she'd watched Nathaniel rowing from the harbor, noticed him walking across the marsh, but over the years, she'd trained herself not to look for him. Her life was with Theo, and she couldn't cling to a dream that was no longer possible. Yet here he was, walking across her lawn.

When he reached her, they walked into the house. He was nervous and shy, and he turned away when he saw her scanning his face for some sign of feeling.

"Is it okay I'm here?" Nathaniel asked.

Meredith ignored the question beneath his question—*is it okay I'm here after all these years, after leaving you and disappearing into a different life from the one we planned?* Meredith kept her thoughts on the girl, since that was the only reason he could have come to her house. She didn't acknowledge their past or the awkward feelings between them.

She didn't acknowledge Theo or how angry he'd be that Nathaniel was in his house. Theo had been away for a few days in Boston. He didn't know about Rachel or Nathaniel bringing her to the house. What would he do when he found out? She didn't want to think about it.

"How's the girl?"

"She's in and out of awareness. I'm keeping a close eye on her. She hasn't said much when she's awake. Moaning sounds mostly. I've no idea where she's from or what brought her here. Do you?"

"No idea at all."

Meredith suddenly felt nervous having him in her house. Why had she invited him across her yard?

"What's the matter?" Nathaniel asked. He'd always been able to read her so well. Then, as if sensing her questions, he said, "I wanted to check on the girl. That's all."

"It's quite awkward, you know. If Theo came home—"

"I know. I'm sorry. I can leave," he said.

"Well, she's awake now, so maybe you can get her to talk. You can join us for breakfast if you like."

"But Theo?"

"He's out of town on business. He's always out of town." She sighed and led Nathaniel to the sitting room, where he waited in the doorway for the girl to recognize him. Rachel sat up on the settee drinking water from a teacup, her hands perched on each side of the cup as if she held a precious elixir. Her hair drooped, greasy and unwashed, and her head was bruised and swollen, but the straw-colored flecks of her eyes brightened in the morning light.

Meredith opened the drapes and lifted the windows to let some air into the room. Her full skirts rustled. Her bodice revealed her hourglass shape.

"You're here," Rachel said.

Nathaniel sat in a straight-backed chair but soon got up and turned toward the open window. He looked across the harbor toward his father's house on the hill, then at his brother's shop before he turned back toward Rachel with his full attention.

She leaned forward to place her cup on the table, winced, touched her fingers to her head.

"We'll get you some ice for that," Meredith said, and she directed the maid to bring the ice. She picked up her cup of tea and wrapped her fingers through the handle. Meredith caught Nathaniel's gaze for a moment—his piercing eyes and the way he could look right into her. Then they both looked at the girl, at her swollen face, at the pot of tea on the table, anywhere but at each other.

"I can't trouble you anymore," Rachel said.

"You'll have to trouble me for another five to seven days according to Dr. Howe. It's going to take a little time to heal and get your strength back. You've had a serious blow to your head."

"Will I be all right?"

"Yes," Meredith said. She didn't want the girl to waste her energy worrying. "You just need to take it easy for now."

"Thank you, Nathaniel, for coming to my rescue."

"He's an excellent swimmer," Meredith said.

Rose came in with the tray laden with breakfast. She cleared the coffee table before laying out eggs, ham, toast with apple butter, coffee and cream. Rachel pulled herself into a sitting position and leaned over the food.

"What brought you to Yarmouth Port?" Nathaniel asked. "Do you have family here on the Cape?"

Rachel's face grew tight, and she touched the tips of her fingers to her bandage as if she could ease the pain that resided there.

"Are you from Boston?" he asked. When she didn't answer, he said, "We only want to know you so that we can help you."

"You're awfully young to be on your own," Meredith said.

"I've been on my own a long time."

"I see," Meredith said. Rachel closed her eyes and drifted away from them, whether from her injury or to escape, Meredith didn't know. Her concern for the girl stirred some long-dormant part of her that had wanted to mother a child. She tried not to think about her inability to conceive with Theo, as if the love for Nathaniel that she'd buried in the locked box within her heart had kept Theo's child from coming into the world.

"I should go," Nathaniel said.

"I'll walk you out."

At the back door, he stepped outside, and she stood with the door held wide so that she could watch him go. "You'll come back?"

Nathaniel turned toward her. He looked confused, then he nodded and walked toward the harbor.

13

THREE DAYS SINCE THE ACCIDENT AND NATHANIEL WATCHED
Meredith's house, which appeared to be drifting in the fog. He'd
fished long into the dark. It was after eleven o'clock when he came
ashore with a small sea bass and a couple of codfish. He walked toward
the flickering candle that led to Meredith sitting late in the kitchen. She
had always been a difficult sleeper, waking to drink chamomile tea in
the middle of the night before she could go back to bed. It was strange
to be walking toward her now, and not so strange at all. He felt her
behind the dimly lit window as if she were a force pulling him closer.
He wanted to bring her the fish—that was what he told himself as he
stood in her yard, unable to move in any direction and so standing still
there, under the quarter moon on a clear night where the stars were
bright enough to pierce his heart.

The house was solid in the dark, the white clapboards soft with
moonlight. Shutters whispered complaints in the wind. This was her
house, the house where she changed from her dress into a nightie and
slept next to Theo Butler. It was nothing like the shack, where there was
no protection from the birds in the night or the wind or the smells of
the marsh. It was safe and quiet and time for him to leave, yet he stood
motionless.

When she opened the door to him, he was surprised.

"You're back," she said.

He felt caught, a trespasser, but when he saw the curious look on her face that turned to happiness, he forgot what he was thinking. "Just brought some fish," he said.

"Stay."

"I can't."

Her disappointment caught him off guard, and when she turned to go back into the house, he followed her. She led him to the kitchen where the candle had turned mostly to dripped wax, and she put the kettle on. He dropped himself into a chair.

Meredith served them coffee before she sat at the table with him. In the silence, Nathaniel wished he knew what to say.

The pale candlelight danced against the wall, and he watched the shapes. He couldn't explain his being there, but Meredith didn't seem to need an explanation. It was as if she'd been expecting him.

"Rachel falling... Did it make you think about Jacob?" Meredith asked. It was a bold question, and it hung heavily between them. Losing Jacob was the reason he'd left his life and Meredith and everything they'd dreamed together. He felt her wanting answers, and the questions on her face pulled at him.

Of course he'd thought about Jacob when he pulled Rachel from the water, but staying in every moment exactly as it came each day was the only way he could keep himself from those old memories. He had to feed himself, keep his shack sturdy in any kind of weather, and make money to keep his skiff in shape. But the needs of his daily life hardly kept him from grieving his brother and wrestling with his feelings of responsibility.

"I think about it when I look across the water toward the point," Meredith said. "The whole town gathered by the harbor. That helpless feeling of waiting has never left me." She looked into the tablecloth, at the floral pattern barely visible in the dim light.

She watched Nathaniel for signs of discomfort before she continued. He didn't want to talk to her like this, but her voice worked on him. The privacy of the kitchen felt like a place apart, real and not real. Their voices floated in the dark, and there was an undertow to the past that he wanted to swim clear of. Still, he felt himself begin to talk about the accident in the open light of Meredith's concern. "I could've held my breath longer, swam a little harder," he said. "That's what I tell myself. None of us wore life jackets. We were so young and sure of ourselves. We thought we could beat the storm to shore, but the storm tide on the shoals hit us from out of nowhere."

He looked at her then and remembered the night before the fishing trip, making love in the dry-docked schooner at Young's Boatyard, the plans they'd made. He'd loved her with his whole body, his whole mind. He lived with his heart full of her. Then he left. Sitting at her table, a sadness came over him, and he held back tears. He'd never thought that she could be the very thing to save him. Why was he thinking it now?

"Each year, there is less and less of him, and now I can't remember so simple a thing as the sound of his voice."

"You have to let him go."

"It was my fault. I lost him."

"It wasn't your fault." Meredith stirred her coffee. "I missed you desperately."

"But you met Theo. Your life didn't stop." He looked into her eyes for the first time in many years, and he saw behind her sadness the young woman he had known. He wanted to offer some comfort, but he had no words. He placed his hand over hers on the table, and she looked down into the rough terrain of his skin. With her free hand, she covered his, and then he stood to go.

"You'll come back?"

The vulnerability in her voice moved him. He wanted to reach a hand out and touch her shoulder, but he didn't move. "What about Theo?"

"He's always traveling for work or at the office or wherever it is he goes. He's never home anymore." She didn't try to hide the resentment in her voice.

Nathaniel felt her loneliness as sure as he felt his own. He was lonely at the thought of returning to the shack without her, and this disturbed him. He was never lonely, and this turn in him made him want to leave, if only to prove to himself that he didn't need her, but on his way out the door, he said, "I'll be back."

—⁓—

Nathaniel let two days pass before he crossed the marsh again to Meredith's house. He knew he shouldn't be in Theo Butler's house, but he told himself that Theo was never there, so it was okay. Meredith met him at the door in a light summer dress, pale yellow with pink rosebuds embroidered in the fabric, a white collar that brushed against her neck where he remembered the soft skin, and there was the tiny freckle by the dip between her collarbones. He never imagined that he'd see her again or feel her presence in a room. She led him down the hallway, the sway of her hips like a reminder of their younger selves.

They sat in the parlor where Rachel still lay on the couch asleep. He sat in a chair across from Meredith and listened to her voice, the timbre so familiar he could feel it in every thread of his being. "I think she's been asleep rather than unconscious, because she sat up to eat, and she's been snoring."

"That's a good sign," Nathaniel said.

"Would you like a snack? Maybe a sandwich?"

"No thank you."

Meredith talked to fill the space between them, filled with years of feeling that now hung in the room with a weight like humidity. Nathaniel didn't know how Meredith felt since he'd first removed himself to the shack. He didn't know her grief or regret, didn't know for how long she'd missed him. Instead of talking about how she felt, Meredith told him how she had been entertained in Boston and made a tour of Europe early in her marriage to Theo. She had been to New York to the theater, and Theo's father had taken a liking to her and spoiled her with a diamond necklace, which she only wore on the most special occasions at which he was in attendance. She couldn't play the piano or sing, but she could draw a little, and as she spoke of these things to Nathaniel, she recited them not as events that mattered in her life but as mere facts of her existence.

Nathaniel turned his attention to the girl. He was touched again by the girl's vulnerability, the way she lay with a blanket over her legs, the worried look on her face as she opened her eyes and looked around the room. Was she afraid of her injury, of the pain, or afraid of having to leave Meredith's care? He wanted to soothe her or distract her. He didn't know which.

"How are you doing?" Nathaniel asked.

Rachel touched her head in an absent way, as if testing her injury to see how much it hurt. It was clear to him that she wouldn't admit to her pain. "Meredith is taking good care of me, but I'm afraid I've overstayed my welcome."

"That's nonsense," Meredith said, placing her teacup on the table and biting into a chocolate cookie. As she spoke, the smell of her powder floated over him. He was stunned by the sheer extravagance of her hair as it fell from her bun and the steady gaze she fixed on him. Her pale skin, her delicate wrists and thin fingers made her attractive in a most feminine way. As she refastened the bun on the back of her neck, he smelled his own clean rainwater smell and was glad he'd taken the time to bathe and put on a clean shirt.

Nathaniel sipped his tea, trying to hold the delicate cup without breaking it. His hands felt crusty and callused from fishing and rowing the boat. He rubbed the fingers of his free hand together as if to smooth them, then wiped them on his pants.

"I'll be in the kitchen for a while with the maids. We've got to plan dinner for the week so they can do the shopping. Can you stay, Nathaniel?"

"Yeah, sure," he said, his eyes following Meredith as she left him alone with the girl. Rachel looked at him as if waiting for him to say something, but he didn't know what to say. In the silence, he couldn't help but wonder what had brought her to ask him and Finn for a ride to Yarmouth Port.

"I know what you're thinking," she said. "I can see it all over your face. You're quiet, but you're easy to read."

Nathaniel reached for a cookie, but he wasn't hungry, and he left it on his napkin.

"My life was no good where I came from. That's all I can say. Too many bad things happened, and everywhere I looked reminded me of something terrible. The only thing I could do was leave, get a different view on the world, you know?" Rachel looked at him as if he could save her from something more than a tumultuous sea.

Nathaniel nodded. "I do know."

When he finished his tea, he placed the cup gently on the coffee table and went to Meredith's west-facing window. This was her view, the vibrant green sweep of marsh that led out to the bay, the masts visible over the buildings at the harbor. In the distance, he saw Finn standing in the back door of his shop, surveying heaps of discarded crates and barrels of rubbish that would need to be burned.

Then as his eye tracked across the scene, he saw the tilted rocks of the jetty. He was reminded of the day before they'd lost Jacob. He'd taken Meredith out to the end of the jetty with his mother's engagement ring. His father had given it to him after his mother died—he was the oldest son, he should have it, his father told him. That morning, he and Meredith sat together at the end of the rocks, their feet dangling over the granite slabs as they watched the waves approach them, then recede, revealing the layers of seaweed and barnacles stuck to the rocks. "It's beautiful here," Meredith said, staring down, then turning to Nathaniel and kissing him on the lips.

Nathaniel fidgeted with how to approach her, what to say. "Meredith," he said, stammering a bit.

Meredith turned to him, concerned. "What is it? Is everything okay?"

"You know how much I love you."

"Yes," she said, brushing the hair from his eyes.

"And I want to spend my life with you."

"It sounds like there's a 'but' in there, Nathaniel."

"Quite the opposite." He pulled the ring from his pocket and held it before her on the end of his finger. "I want you to be my wife. I want for us to marry as soon as we can. I want to start our life together, to sleep in the same bed, and wake in the same house and grow old together."

Meredith wiped a tear from her eye.

"Is it okay?" Nathaniel asked.

"Yes, of course."

Nathaniel took her hand in his own and slid the ring on to her finger. The ring was too big, but it was a beautiful diamond surrounded by two rubies, her birthstone, that he'd had added. "We can get it resized," he said, and for now, he wound a piece of sea hay around the back of the band to steady it on Meredith's finger.

"I love it."

Standing in Meredith's house now, he tried not to look at her on his way to the door. He remembered Meredith's mother, Jane, on the day of their engagement, turning her daughter's finger this way and that to view the diamond at different angles.

"It was Nathaniel's mother's," Meredith said.

Jane kissed Nathaniel on the cheek and held him by the shoulder. "You'll be a good man for my Meredith, won't you, son?"

"Yes, ma'am. I plan on making her very happy."

"I'm already very happy," Meredith said.

Nathaniel turned from the window and approached Rachel where she lay on the couch. He wondered what terrible things had happened to drive her from her home. Her eyes were closed, her head rolled to one side. He pressed a hand to her forehead like Meredith had done, but he didn't know what he was feeling for. When the girl rustled awake, he pulled his hand away.

"What brought you here, Rachel, if you don't mind me asking."

"It's okay," she said. She pulled herself up on the pillows so that she faced him where he sat in the chair by the settee. "I don't mind telling you, but then you'll have to tell me something."

"Like what?"

"Like why you live out in the marsh. I've seen you walking out there, out that window there." Nathaniel turned toward where she pointed and nodded. The girl began to tell him about her father, the violence and the drinking. She told him about her mother leaving and her sister walking into the sea. While she spoke, Nathaniel remained silent, listening. "I couldn't take it anymore, having to brace myself for another smack. I saved enough money to get a boat to Boston, and I left one day while he was at work. Simple as that. I walked down to the harbor and got on a boat."

"That's very brave."

"Running away is never brave."

"Sure it is," Nathaniel said. "You left everything you've ever known."

"Now it's your turn."

Nathaniel told Rachel about the storm, about swimming after Jacob and not getting to him in time.

Rachel listened, then she blinked her eyes and seemed to be drifting. He was left to his vigil, watching over the girl and waiting for Meredith to return from the kitchen. It seemed she'd been gone forever and no time at all. He waited in the dusky light that filtered through the windows, waited for the girl to fall asleep.

14

FINN STOOD AT THE BUTLERS' FRONT DOOR AND BANGED THE BRASS knocker. He knew they were in there. He'd seen Nathaniel approach from across the marsh, just like everyone else in town had seen him. It was no secret. He carried Rachel's heavy bag in one hand, then shifted it to the other. It wasn't that he couldn't hold it but that he felt nervous standing there after the way they'd ignored him the other day.

When Meredith finally answered the door, he asked to see Rachel. "I've come to see how she's making out. Is she okay?"

"She's sleeping, Finn. She needs her rest."

"Can I talk to my brother, please?"

"Another time, perhaps?"

"You're not going to let me in?"

"It's just—"

"No, it's fine," he said. "Another time."

Finn walked toward the marsh with the full force of his legs and held his stride until he reached the back of the fish shop out of breath. He still had the carpetbag in his right hand, and he shook his head at his own forgetfulness. Then he thought, it serves her right. Still, he'd wanted to see Rachel, to hear her voice and remind her that he'd saved her, too. He dropped the bag at his feet, frustrated that he hadn't been allowed in the house. Then the thought occurred to him—what was so important about the bag? He bent over to open it. A mud-colored shawl, a white nightgown, a couple of undergarments. But the bag was heavy, so he flipped it over and dumped the contents onto the ground. That was when he saw the packages of bills wrapped in rubber bands. He figured it had to be over three hundred dollars, a huge amount by any standard. Where could she have gotten it? He quickly returned the money to the bag and pushed through the door of his shop. He stashed the bag in the closet in the back of his office where no one would find it.

He leaned over his desk where he'd written a business proposal for his fishing fleet. He flipped through pages lined with columns of numbers demonstrating expenses, projected profits, yearly incomes. He'd reviewed the numbers over and over until he was sure that his plans added up the way he wanted. He needed to be sure of his reasoning in order to strike the right chord with his father, but the money in the closet distracted him. What if he didn't return it? Where had she gotten it? He wanted to know, but he tried to shift his mind back to winning over his father, who seemed dead set on not helping him.

Frustrated and unable to focus, Finn stood and locked the door to the shop and walked toward the edge of the water. The fishing boats at anchor floated still in the windless air. The water was flat, not a ripple. No block and tackle clanged against a mast, no steady splash of water against the dock. Finn picked up a stone and skimmed it across the surface of the water, where it made tiny circles that shone in the moonlight. Where had Rachel come from? he wondered.

That money could help him buy a schooner to start his fleet. All he wanted to do was fish for cod, then buy a second boat with his profits and build from there, shipping fish to Boston to sell on the state market. He imagined sitting behind a mahogany desk in his own home looking over the water like his father—a house large enough for the children to each have their own bedroom, and a stable for horses. He believed that with a fishing fleet, he wouldn't have to argue prices with other fleet owners or stand there asking his customers the same questions day after day, smiling when he didn't want to. He felt his unhappiness with each pound of fish he handed across the counter. Even the steady ring of the cash register didn't console him. But he couldn't take the girl's money. Not without knowing where it came from.

He turned to walk up the harbor road toward home. The bustle of the town was a fact of the day, and he savored quiet nights like this when he left work late. He thought about Rachel resting across the marsh. He liked her, the curves of her body where they pressed out against her coat, the eager expression in her eyes when she saw the squall approaching them. She had an adventurous spirit, and this engaged him. He thought maybe she'd be willing to have an adventure with him. She liked him. He could tell. While he wanted to see her, he wasn't going to return to the Butler house. Not after the way he'd been treated, as if he was an outsider, when he was the one that got them in to shore safely. He blamed his brother for taking all the credit. If Nathaniel hadn't been at the Butlers', he would've been able to see the girl. Maybe now that he had her money, she'd pay attention to him again.

As he neared the road to his house, his thoughts shifted to his wife. Elizabeth had stopped offering him a glass of scotch, making him his favorite pot roast, and kissing him on the cheek when he came in the door after a long day at the shop. When she sat across the table from Finn, wiping Susie's mouth with the corner of a napkin or scolding Ezra, the oldest and the only boy, there was a distance that she seemed to nurture, a general lack of interest in him. No wonder he was drawn to the girl. She'd paid attention to him, flirted with him, and that was something gone right.

15

IT WAS LATE AFTERNOON WHEN RACHEL TRIED TO BRING MEREDITH into focus. She tried to hold on to Meredith's voice, but a weight, like sinking underwater, pulled her down, and she couldn't resist the relief of giving in. She closed her eyes and dropped into the hollows of unconsciousness. Rachel let go of the world for hours at a time, then woke to memories of her hands reaching into the safe, the dry feeling of the bills in her sweaty palms. She tried not to remember her fear walking to the harbor or the kindness of sailors who'd helped her onboard a southbound vessel, as if they'd seen for themselves the welts on her arms from her father's fevered grip. She tried not to think about her carpetbag left on the schooner, and instead, she reassured herself that Finn would bring it to her. He liked her; she knew that for sure.

The next time she woke, she felt the pain and remembered the sudden rush of cold water that slammed her onto the deck, then carried her into the bay. When she hit the teak deck, she heard a sound like the crack of a gun inside her skull, the sound of her head hitting rock. The sound reminded her of her father, who used to come home drunk and fumble through the cabinet for his pistol. She'd watched out the window where he swayed in the moonlight and fired shots at the old willow tree. She felt the soft couch beneath her, felt Meredith's watchful gaze, and she longed for sleep to remove the pain that traveled from her head throughout her body. When she closed her eyes, she saw her bones in yellow, illuminated with the diffuse light of her awareness, as if the crack on her skull resonated through her entire being. She groaned without intending to.

"What can I do?" Meredith asked.

I just want to sleep, but the words didn't come out. Meredith's worried expression held her like a warm light until she closed her eyes.

When Nathaniel appeared with the basin and bandages, he looked at Rachel with such distress in his eyes. There was a sadness in him that matched her own, and she wanted to know him.

He'd pulled her from the water.

He'd saved her.

"I'm going to clean your wound," Meredith said, wringing a cloth into the water. "You might have an infection. I need you to stay still." She removed the bandage from Rachel's head, then patted at the area where the stitches throbbed. "The doctor is on his way."

When Dr. Howe arrived, he pressed at the wound around the stitches. Rachel tried not to wince, but she felt pain in her body as if the injury had shaken her to her core. What was she doing here on this stranger's couch, in a town where she didn't know anyone? Had her life been so difficult that she would choose such an escape? The doctor leaned the heft of his body over her, placed a scalpel to the wound to test for infection.

"She's got a small area of infection," he said. "I can clean it, then rewrap the bandages. The fresh air will do her a world of good. Keep the windows open as much as you can."

When Rachel woke again, Meredith placed a hand on her shoulder.

"I'm right here," she said. "The doctor's gone, but he's taken very good care of you. Nothing to worry about."

"Where's Finn?"

"Finn?" Meredith asked. "Why—"

"My bag."

"He'll be back," Nathaniel said, and his quiet presence reassured her.

Meredith shifted herself in her seat, and Rachel felt safe in the warm glow of her care even though she was embarrassed by her need. She couldn't get up to fix food or bathe herself. She wanted to get out of the room with its embroidered draperies drawn across the windows. But Meredith was kind, and she sat with Rachel for hours at a time, telling her stories from her childhood. She watched Rachel with eyes full of compassion.

"I'll make you some tea," Meredith said.

"Don't trouble yourself," Rachel said.

Meredith leaned over to swipe a strand of hair from Rachel's face, her eyes searching for something to make right.

"You're very kind," Rachel said.

Was this rest, this feeling of repose in which she didn't have to worry about a plate thrown across the kitchen, an open palm across her face? The maid brought her meals, took away her chamber pot, and changed her blanket. Such ease as this Rachel had never known. She blinked against the light in the room. She was here in Meredith's house where time was suspended and the world stayed outside and far away.

16

BLACK EYES STARED HIM IN THE FACE FIRST THING IN THE MORNING. Hot, rank breath on him. It was that damn dog come back to bother him? Nathaniel reached an arm over the bed and scratched the thing on the back, then pushed him away. He was skin and bones this time. The dog lay on the floor and sighed, settling into his breathing, and it eased Nathaniel to hear him there, stretching to find his comfort along the floorboards.

"Rascal," he said and reached down for the dog. "You want something to eat?"

Nathaniel didn't want to get out of bed. He rolled over with his back to the dog and clutched the pillow to his chest. Birds sang in the trees by his shack. Their trilling cries pierced his waking mind until a restless unease took hold of him and forced him out of bed. It was the unease of sitting across the table from Meredith Butler, recalling the accident that had taken Jacob. Meredith's fragility in the earliest hours of morning had touched Nathaniel, and he didn't want to feel that she was home to him, but there she was, prying around the edges of his awareness with her voice like a balm to his grief. She tapped into a need he didn't know he had. He thought of the church dance they'd attended when they were young, before their first kiss, how she'd stepped in to him during the slow dances and let him hold her tightly around the waist.

The dog nudged Nathaniel's hand, concerned with his own needs.

"Yeah, I see you," he said to the dog, who danced around his legs and followed him outside to the pump where Nathaniel filled an old clay bowl with water and set it on the ground. He crouched and looked into the animal's face until the dog met his eyes. Rascal had a square head with a thick snout, brown and black all over. He was big across the shoulders with heavy legs and fat feet, but today his ribs rippled along his skin, and his face was thin. Nathaniel didn't know if the dog had ever had a home or where he roamed when he wasn't on the marsh, but he usually looked well fed. Nathaniel imagined Rascal attaching himself to some other sucker along the coast who was willing to feed him and offer him a friendly pat on the head.

The first time Nathaniel met Rascal had been in front of O'Shea's. The dog had been running his snout along the base of the windows, sniffing for something to eat. Nathaniel brought his plate outside and placed it on the porch where the dog ate the scraps in a few gulps. When the dog was done licking the plate clean, he stared at Nathaniel with his head cocked, as if Nathaniel could read his mind. Water. Of course. Nathaniel brought a bowl, and the dog drank and drank. After that, he followed Nathaniel back to his shack and spent the night, but in the morning, he was gone.

"Why do you keep coming back here?" Nathaniel asked the dog.

Inside, he boiled the turnips and carrots, which he shared with Rascal, but the dog needed meat.

"I know it, boy."

Nathaniel washed himself in well water and found a shirt less dirty. The dog followed him in and out of the shack, back and forth for no reason, until Nathaniel pulled the door shut behind him and started toward the harbor.

Along the trail, he threw a stick into the wide creek. He stopped to watch the dog take a running leap. Front legs outstretched, Rascal flew over the water until he splashed and swam after the stick. The damn dog looked happy. Nathaniel shook his head. Rascal galloped up the path and dropped the stick at Nathaniel's feet.

"Let's go," Nathaniel said.

At the harbor, he sat outside O'Shea's on the sagging porch, the bench tilting beneath him. Rascal lay at his feet. The morning was coming on muggy and hot, a physical weight on his skin. The dog panted wildly and scanned the air, taking in the smells of the nearby mackerel smacks, pipe smoke, and the musty smell of wood and damp earth rising up through the porch boards. Mrs. O'Shea brought the steak out on a chipped plate. "I'm not letting your dog eat off my good dishes," she said.

Nathaniel sliced the butt end of meat where the grizzle curled. He looked Rascal in the eye and held the steak forward, eyes staring into the dog, saying not yet. The dog leaned toward the meat, and Nathaniel tapped him on the snout until he backed off. He tried again, looking into the dog like it was a conversation they were having. Rascal didn't take the meat from his fingers until he nodded approval.

"You'll feed that dog, but you won't feed your own damn self," said Mrs. O'Shea.

"I'm eatin' this steak, aren't I?"

"Only because that dog's hungry," she said, tightening her apron strings. "How's that girl over at the Butlers'?"

"You heard? She's got some kind of a head injury. She's a strong girl, though."

"Does she have people here? A place to stay?" Nathaniel shook his head no. "I've got a room available upstairs." She turned the heft of her backside to Nathaniel on her way back into the restaurant.

Early morning brought the fishermen who had money in their

pockets. One after another they arrived, boots scraping the porch, to join the chorus of voices emanating from within. Nathaniel couldn't help judging each man by his reaction to the dog. Those who ignored the dog he considered uninteresting, but those who took a minute to crouch down and scratch Rascal behind the ears he smiled toward and asked what brought them to town, what boat they were sailing on, and where from. More than the dog, it was Meredith's voice that ran through him like water and opened him up until he felt free in a way he hadn't felt since before losing Jacob. A little bit of happiness, or something like it, skittered through him and allowed him to speak.

He sat with the sun on his face, the dog at his feet. When he heard Finn's wife, Elizabeth, call his name, he jerked himself up. The dark braid she usually wore down her back hung over her shoulder so that it dangled in front where he could see the crimson ribbon she'd woven through it. Her face was round and pale, her eyes downcast, preoccupied. She was always in a hurry, always going somewhere with a child in tow, a basket on her arm, or another child with its small legs wrapped around her waist. She had always appeared strong, both physically and with an unwavering internal drive that Nathaniel thought must help her manage Finn. "We were just bringing Finn his lunch. He forgot it this morning. He's always in such a rush," she said, holding Ezra by the hand. The boy squinted into the sun, and he swung one arm at his side while he gazed from side to side, taking in the sweep of the harbor activity. He wrestled his hand free from his mother as he stared at Nathaniel and the dog. Nathaniel tried to return the boy's curious gaze, but he couldn't withstand Ezra's wide-eyed scrutiny. The boy looked up to him as if he were a riddle that could be solved, his father's brother yet so unfamiliar. Ezra seemed mystified by a man who could live outside and go out in the boat whenever he wanted and run along the marsh and live outdoors. It was the stuff of dreams for a boy. He looked at the rope Nathaniel wore around his waist to hold up his trousers. "I like your belt," Ezra said.

"Yeah, it works." Nathaniel ran his hands along Rascal's slick coat, and when he saw the boy eyeing him again, he said, "You remember him? You can pet him."

Ezra looked up to his mother for her approval before he stepped cautiously toward the dog, who only wagged his tail and stuck his snout up under the boy's hand, which made Ezra giggle.

Elizabeth watched Rascal where he leaned against Nathaniel's legs, panting wildly in the heat. She held her braid in one hand and worried it between her fingers. She looked past the boats at the dock toward Sandy Neck in the distance, then back at Nathaniel. "Ezra here wants to learn how to row. Is that something you could teach him? Finn's so busy with the shop and—"

"I can't. I'm going out now to fish," he said with increasing unease. He didn't want to be responsible for the boy, not after what happened to Jacob. He couldn't bear it. Why would she would ask him to do this? They only spoke briefly if they ran into each other in town. They said hello or nodded in acknowledgment, but never had she approached him like this.

The boy stepped away from the dog, an embarrassed, hurt look on his face that he tried to hide by tucking his head into his shoulder and turning away.

"Thing is, Nathaniel, he looks up to you. He sees you out there every day. His own uncle."

"What did you go and bring him here for?"

"Finn would take him if he wasn't so busy."

"Finn," Nathaniel said. He was angry with his brother for not tending to his son when Finn had felt rejected by their father himself. Finn ought to know what that was like for a boy. He squatted down to meet Ezra's eyes, copper-green orbs suddenly looking right into him. He thought of Jacob, his skinny arms and legs.

"Row him around in the shallow part of the bay," Elizabeth said. She looked him in the eye in a way that made him turn away.

Nathaniel looked down at Ezra dragging his foot back and forth in the dirt, and he remembered his own longing to be out on the water when he was a young boy. Boys needed to learn about boats. Finn should be teaching Ezra how to row, how to cleat a line, and how to tie a square knot.

"Well?" Elizabeth asked.

"You wanna come, boy?"

Ezra nodded.

"Okay, then. I'll bring him home later," Nathaniel said, and Elizabeth waved as she watched them walk toward the skiff. The boy took Nathaniel's hand, and Nathaniel felt how small he was. He felt suddenly protective. Ezra reminded him of Jacob, and he didn't let go of the sweaty fingers until the boy let go himself. They walked in silence, Ezra running ahead with the dog, then coming back, then running ahead again on his spindly little-boy legs.

Nathaniel's mind drifted in the heat of the day. He thought over his conversation with Meredith and how easily the words had spilled out of him. One, two, three words and he was pouring himself out to her as if no time had passed. *You have to let him go.* He felt himself wishing for the pale candlelight against the wall and the quiet of the kitchen in the middle of the night. Only then did he feel like he could speak to her without some explanation for their ended relationship. He longed for her, he realized, as if some long-held hope had broken open inside him. When Ezra threw a rock into the water, Rascal took flight from the beach toward the splash. The boy squealed with excitement.

When the wet dog bumped into his legs, Nathaniel shoved him away. Rascal hadn't hung around this long before. The other two times he'd shown up nervous and skinny and took off before Nathaniel was done feeding him. No matter. He was here now. With Finn's boy.

"We need to get you into a life vest." Nathaniel dug under the bow seat for a cork life vest and fastened it onto the boy.

"It's too big," Ezra said.

"You won't think that if you fall overboard." Nathaniel wasn't going to take any chances with his nephew.

Ezra nodded and climbed into the stern seat where he sat with his knees tucked up, his whole body on the seat, while Rascal jumped aboard and sat in the bow of the boat, leaning forward over the prow like a ship's figurehead. Ezra waited while Nathaniel pushed the skiff into deeper water and climbed aboard. Nathaniel set the oars and rowed them out.

"Okay, you put your hands on mine and keep them there."

Ezra leaned forward to reach the oars. He held his hands over Nathaniel's and made each stroke of the oars, nice and slow, rowing from a backward position to get the hang of the motion.

"When you want to go left, you pull on the right oar. When you want to go right, you pull on the left oar. Backward, I know, but that's how it works. You get it?"

Ezra nodded. He looked nothing like Finn but more like Nathaniel and Finn's mother, Helen, with long limbs and an oval face and sandy-blond hair that he wore cropped close to his head.

All the way out of the harbor and along the jetty, the dog stood in the bow of the boat, feeling the breeze on his face and scanning the air for indications of what lay before them.

"Okay, you come sit in my lap now and try it for real," Nathaniel said.

The boy scrambled across the boat and sat on the seat with his back leaning into Nathaniel's chest, his hands wrapped around the oars. "They're heavy."

"I'll get you started."

Nathaniel wrapped his hands around Ezra's, and once they had some momentum, Nathaniel let the boy take over until he was rowing with the tide, his back leaning forward, then pulling on the oars with Nathaniel until he leaned against Nathaniel's front, back and forth until Nathaniel got used to him there in the curve of his body. This was how he'd taught Jacob to row, and the feeling of the boy's body, the heat and smell of him, brought a wave of grief that he tried to push away, but grief came on him like this, when he least expected it. He turned his attention to Ezra, then he slowly let go of the oars.

When Nathaniel waved his hands in the air in front of Ezra's face, the boy screamed with delight—he was rowing on his own.

They took turns rowing out into the bay until the water was dark and Nathaniel felt Jacob's presence in the very air around him. Like Jacob, Ezra had a lightness of spirit that came out when he was happy. Jacob got excited about everything, just the chance to sail and be with his brothers. After the accident, they had all been tossed by grief in different directions. But for Nathaniel, Jacob had remained at the center, as much a presence in death as he had been in life. Drifting in the tide with Ezra, Nathaniel felt close to Jacob, and he held on to the things he could remember, like that time Jacob woke up from a nightmare and climbed into Nathaniel's bed, his skinny elbows like branches poking Nathaniel's ribs, and the yeasty smell of him in the sheets. Or the way he hid his good shoes in a box beneath his bed because he hated how they pinched his feet and didn't want to wear them.

The dog yipped over the edge of the boat, and Nathaniel watched Ezra as he stared down into the water. Over Ezra's shoulder, he spotted Meredith on her lawn, spyglass aimed straight at them. He wanted to stand up and wave, say *Over here! Over here!* Then Rascal yipped again until Nathaniel set the oars to let Ezra to take over.

17

MEREDITH WATCHED RACHEL SLEEP, HER HEAD FALLEN BACK into the pillow as if thrust by a strong hand. She wasn't pretty at first glance, but upon knowing her, the collection of her features—squat nose and high forehead, small chin, freckled cheeks, and lush pink lips—gathered into a lovely portrait. When she fixed her eyes on you with her listening gaze, her interest enlivened her face, and that was when she became beautiful. Rachel's company had enriched Meredith's days, which were usually spent managing the maids, visiting her mother, or working with the church ladies on a volunteer project such as organizing a clothing drive for the less-fortunate families on the south side of town. With Rachel in her house, Meredith felt her maternal instincts and grief for the children she would never have. She wanted Rachel to stay. She imagined a life where the girl went to the schoolhouse each day and came home with books to read and math homework. She'd never thought to ask Rachel if she could read or if she'd gone to school.

When the girl woke up, she glanced around the room as if displaced, then getting her bearings, she said, "I never know where I am when I wake up. I'm so comfortable."

"I'm glad," Meredith said. "You've been sleeping for a while. It's good. You need the rest."

Rachel pulled herself up on the pillows and rubbed at her eyes. "I feel a little better today. I'll be leaving soon, I promise."

"I think you need to stay a while longer," Meredith said, slightly panicked at the thought of the empty house and an end to Nathaniel's visits.

As if reading Meredith's mind, Rachel asked, "How do you know Nathaniel?"

Meredith paused, as if assessing the question, then she spoke. "We knew each other from school when we were younger, but then we fell out of touch. Nathaniel moved out of his father's house to that island, which I'm sure you've heard about."

Meredith had seen him row out of the harbor with a dog in the boat. The rhythm of his stroke against the water and the way he held his head upright when he pulled back on the oars let her know it was him. In the low morning light, the dog appeared like a sentinel, searching the sky for birds, looking across the water for the shiny flecks of bass or the light water that meant a shoal, but the dog could not see these things; it was only what Meredith wished for Nathaniel: a devoted friend looking out for him.

The sound of an approaching horse in the driveway startled her from the window.

"What is it?" the girl asked, alarmed by the man's commanding voice easing the horse to a stop.

"It's my husband, Theo." Meredith didn't know how he would respond to Rachel. He liked to have Meredith's attention to himself.

Rachel sat up in her perch amid the pillows and blankets. She brushed her hair back from her forehead and ran her fingers through the tangles.

"I'll be back in a while. You rest," Meredith told her and pressed her palm gently to the girl's forehead.

In the foyer, Theo kissed his wife and dropped his coat on a chair by the door. "I'm so glad to see you, dear." He held Meredith by the arms and leaned back to take her in. Then he let her go, and he straightened the front of his frock coat and pulled his collar into place. He pressed his hair flat on either side of his part.

"You look concerned about something, Theo. What is it?"

Theo looked toward the bedroom, then distractedly, he said, "My poor father is not himself. He just can't work at the rate he's used to, and when I try to help him, he gets so angry. He wants to go to Boston to meet with a broker, but the trip is too much. When I talk to him about it and offer to go, he gets furious."

"You need to go with him." Meredith looked at her husband's graying hair, the paunch that pressed out against his shirt. She listened to his complaining and his stress, and she wondered what had happened to the man who'd taken her sailing when they first met. He'd had shining eyes that took her in as if he was happy with her in her entirety. This other man, the one who worked for his father and focused himself on ambition, had taken his place, and standing before him now, she wasn't sure how she felt. "Come in. You're late for dinner," she said.

They sat at the head of the long Shaker dining-room table that he ran his hands over as if he'd hewn the wood himself. He loved this piece of furniture because he'd gone with his father to buy it at auction when he was a boy. His father had let him carve his initials in the pedestal, since one day the table would be his. Meredith knew how proud Theo felt to have grown into the table and his role working with his father, his role as a businessman.

Theo stretched his long legs in front of him and waited for Dot and Rose to serve their meal. He wore his hair shorter now, and the firm line of his jaw was scattered with gray and sandy-blond beard. He was a man who needed to shave twice a day, and he enjoyed this as he believed it spoke to his virility.

"So who's this girl you've taken in? Is that her in the other room? I heard about it on my way through town, from Max Ballard. Nothing in this town is private."

"Her name is Rachel," Meredith said. "She sailed from Boston with the Boyds, then fell overboard and hit her head. She had twenty-six stitches, and she's quite banged up."

"How'd she come to be here?"

"I brought her," Meredith said. "She was badly injured, Theo." She didn't want to hide the truth, but she knew how Theo would react to the mention of Nathaniel's name, never mind the fact that Nathaniel had been in their home.

"It's kind of you, Meredith, but doesn't she have people of her own?"

"No, she doesn't. She's not from here. It doesn't hurt to do someone a good turn."

Once the food was on the table, Theo focused on eating as if there were nothing else in the house, no Meredith, no Rachel, nothing to aggravate or appease him beyond onion soup and stringy cheese he pulled off the top with his spoon.

"Dot, you'll bring a tray to Rachel, won't you?" Meredith asked.

"Yes, ma'am."

When they finished and Rose came to clear the table, the newspaper caught his eye, and he scanned the pages. "You haven't asked about my trip," he said.

"Well, how was it?" she asked.

"An utter failure. The men I met in Duxbury have signed on with a fleet from Gloucester. Father blames me for not pursuing other opportunities to expand our interests and has demanded that I get another contract by the end of next month. He's just frustrated that he can't manage these things himself. I don't take his anger personally, but still—"

"He's lucky to have you, Theo."

Theo folded his napkin and tucked it under his plate. He leaned back in his chair and stretched his arms out to the sides in a yawn.

"Come, meet the girl," Meredith said.

"Not tonight, dear. I'm tired out."

"It won't take a minute, Theo. She's our guest."

He pushed himself back from the table and groaned as he stood. "If you insist, but only for a minute. I've some papers to go through before bed."

"She's in the parlor."

"What if she's asleep?"

"She's not asleep, Theo. She's eating. Now, come on."

In the parlor, Rachel had finished her meal and left her tray at the end of the couch. She leaned back against the pillows and stared absently out the window when Meredith came in and announced the arrival of her husband.

"Rachel, I've someone for you to meet." She gestured to Theo, who leaned down to shake the girl's hand, which he held with the utmost delicacy.

"Theo Butler. Rachel, it's a pleasure to make your acquaintance. I only wish it was under better circumstances."

"Thank you, Mr. Butler, for your kindness."

"I'm afraid it's my wife's kindness you're relying on. I'm not home enough these days to offer much in the way of hospitality, but you are certainly welcome here, and I hope to see you up and about soon."

"Thank you, sir."

"I'll let you get some rest now. Meredith, I'm off to my study. Good night, ladies." With a bow of his head, he left Meredith and Rachel in the parlor while he disappeared to his room on the other side of the house.

He wouldn't sit with them like Nathaniel had, interested in their conversations, interested in what Meredith had to say. Meredith sighed and returned her attention to Rachel, glad to have someone who needed her.

"He doesn't want me here," Rachel said.

"No, he's just extremely busy with work right now."

"Do you miss him?"

"You need to rest." She patted Rachel on the hand and pulled the lightweight blanket up to her neck. "You just call me if you need anything," Meredith said, and she disappeared down the hallway where Nathaniel had first entered her house. She felt him there as surely as if he stood before her, but it was Theo in her house now, just beyond her reach, and she settled herself into the couch in the parlor with a patchy piece of needlework that bored her.

She worked the needle with her clumsy fingers while her mind drifted to a time when Nathaniel had stopped coming to school. She skipped out herself one day and followed him across the marsh. He didn't notice her until they were halfway out to the island, then he stopped and waited for her to join him.

"You're not in school," he said.

"Neither are you."

"Well, what are you doing out here?"

"I want to see what you get up to on the island," she said and took his hand. He carried a string of cod fillets in his other hand and smiled at her firm grip.

"It's not much."

"Well, it's something if it keeps you out here."

They crossed the big creek and walked across the seagrass to the island. Nathaniel led her through the bushes to the clearing where he'd placed stones for the fire. She saw the lean-to perched beneath one of the few trees, and a black chest. Full of supplies, she guessed.

"So this is it," she said.

"Not much, I know." He laid the cod on a bench and gathered some branches for kindling. With the fire going, he placed a metal grate along the stones, then the cod on the metal grate. He indicated the tree stump that Meredith could sit on like a stool.

"That smells so good," she said.

"Everything tastes better when it's cooked out here."

He led her to the lean-to where he unpacked a tarp and a blanket from the chest. He laid the tarp on the moist dirt, then the blanket on top of that. Meredith remembered making love and the way the sunlight fell through the branches of the lean-to, the smell of dried seaweed and dirt, and Nathaniel looking directly into her as if he could see the very core of her.

―⁓―

She looked into the needlework, a pale collection of flowers with the stitches all different shapes and going in the wrong direction. She laughed at her own lack of skill. *Who cares?* she thought, and she pushed Nathaniel from her mind and focused on making a perfect little stitch, then another right next to that, until the flowers began to look like flowers and she could put it down, knowing she had at least tried.

18

HERE HE WAS, LYING ON HIS COT, HIS MIND FILLED WITH THE rosewater smell of Meredith's perfume. He pictured her on her front lawn, spyglass aimed at him and Ezra as they rowed past the jetty. The way she'd pressed her hand to the girl's forehead, her forthright manner with the maids—all of it reminded him of the woman he'd loved before his life became one long circle of memory, going over and over the accident as if he could make things come out right.

Wind rattled the window and shook the shack in its frame.

Rascal stood by the bed, alert, vigilant. Nathaniel didn't know why the dog hadn't taken off. It was strange, the way Rascal looked at him as if for some kind of reassurance. Maybe he was afraid of going hungry, or maybe something had happened to him.

"It's only wind," Nathaniel said. The dog followed him outside past the edge of the clearing where he pissed in the woods. The wind was strong from the southeast, sending his stream off to the left of where he aimed. Wind rushed through the trees—*oak, cherry, birch,* Nathaniel thought. The cattails bent over in wavering arcs, but the sky was clear, no sign of a storm. He didn't have much that could be ruined by rain or wind or weather of any kind. He'd made sure of that when he started out. If he couldn't afford to lose it, it wasn't worth having. Still, he wandered around the clearing, looking for anything that should be brought inside.

While they ate, he gazed toward the bay and the distances beyond, where he could imagine himself as a speck that meant nothing. Nothingness eased him when he considered it—his pain a tiny dot in the world's worry of feelings.

He finished breakfast and walked with the dog along the path through the marsh. The Butler house showed its roof over the low tree-tops bending in the wind. *Meredith.* Her name rung through him like a lofty chord. He thought of the man he could be if he came off the marsh, a man who worked with his father and purchased land and owned a house, a man who Meredith could live with.

When he reached the harbor, there was Theo atop his horse, talking down to one of his fishing captains. When he saw Nathaniel, he tapped the horse into motion.

"Nathaniel," he said, coming alongside.

Nathaniel ignored him and kept walking. The dog's ears went up, and he walked on the other side of Nathaniel now, following his quick stride toward the water.

"I know you were in my house. The whole town knows," Theo said. "You go back there again, I'll have to do something about it. I mean it. I won't stand for it."

He kicked his boots into the sides of his horse and trotted out the harbor road.

As he watched Theo ride away, Nathaniel made up his mind. He was going to win Meredith back. He'd talk to his father about managing the land. He'd get a start building the life he and Meredith had dreamed of—a piece of land, a house built with his own hands. He threw a stick for Rascal, and the dog leapt across the creek and splashed the surface. He came up with the stick in his mouth and ran back with his tail wagging, his snout tilted up to meet Nathaniel's hand. Nathaniel wanted to know joy like the dog knew joy. He'd not thought such a thing in a long time. He threw the stick again and watched the dog. Over and again, he threw the stick until he made up his mind for sure. Now he knew what he had to do.

—⁓—

The smell of his father's cigar reached him before he saw the man smoking near the back door, turning the cigar between his fingers and puffing into the air.

"Nathaniel," Nathaniel Sr. said. He flicked ashes, then stubbed the cigar out on the bottom of his leather boot. "I wasn't expecting to see you after our last conversation."

Nathaniel followed his father into the study, the dog at his heels. He felt hemmed in by the shelves lined with leather-bound books his father hadn't read and a brass telescope he didn't use. When he was a boy, the room had been a simple one of whitewashed walls and portraits of his family, an old compass that the boys used when they went sailing, furniture their mother bought at auctions and refinished. Now the room reeked of formality; nothing of their simple early lives remained beyond the family portraits.

"Your dog is back," his father said. "I like him." He scratched Rascal under the chin, and the dog tilted his head high to receive Nathaniel Sr.'s hand.

Nathaniel lifted an antique theodolite from the desk and looked through the eyepiece to follow the edge of his father's yard toward the Butler house. He could work with his father if it meant he could win Meredith back. He had to show her the kind of man he could be.

The theodolite was used for surveying land, and his father collected them. Out the south-facing window, fields rolled like waves toward the far fence, skirting the acres of yard around the house with growth and other men's hard work, work that they paid his father for the privilege of doing. Farmers rented the land and provided a nice monthly income for his father, who sat back in his squeaking chair now to take in the length of his son standing before him in a faded-blue cotton shirt and worn leather boots.

"You've come to talk about working with me," his father said.

"I don't even know how to use one of these things," Nathaniel said, waving the theodolite in one hand.

His father suddenly looked toward the doorway, where Finn stood neither in nor out of the room. "What are you doing?" Finn asked.

"Son, I'm glad you've come to visit." Nathaniel Sr. smiled and gestured for Finn to come in, sit down. "Oh, you've come to discuss business. I can see it in your face," their father said with some disappointment. "I thought you were here just to see your old man."

Finn looked toward Nathaniel, who slid the theodolite back into place along the shelf. "I should go," he said.

"No, I want you to stay," their father said.

"I'd like to speak with you alone, Father."

"Speak," his father said.

Finn held onto his lapel, then eyed Nathaniel. "Does he really need to be here? Honestly, Father."

"Proceed," Nathaniel Sr. said.

Nathaniel heard the strain in his brother's voice as he began his proposal.

"My shop is flourishing, and I've enough profit to make payments on a boat. I'll bring in most of my own fish, and without having to pay for fish to sell, I can increase my profits. That's how I'll buy the second boat."

"I've heard all this before. There's nothing new here, Finn."

"What's new is that as an investor, you'll profit from the proceeds of my business. I'm not asking you to give me the money but rather invest in my enterprise."

As Nathaniel Sr. sat back in his chair to consider the proposal, Finn glanced over at Nathaniel, who looked away. Finn looked like a small boy standing before his father, asking for something he wanted, but this wasn't a small want—not a fishing rod or a new pair of waders— this was a valuable business proposition that he was, in fact, offering his father. Nathaniel worried about Finn facing up to their father; he worried about him being disappointed. Then he reminded himself that Finn wasn't a boy. He was a man with a man's ideas, and he could handle whatever their father had to say.

"Do you have figures for me to look at?" his father asked.

Finn pulled the folded papers from his inside pocket and opened them onto his father's desk.

His father put on his round spectacles and held each paper close to his face as he read through Finn's calculations. "This is good," he said.

Finn looked relieved, proud that his father liked his plan. "I've thought it through for some time," Finn said.

"Yes, but what about here?" His father placed one of the pages onto his desk and pointed to a row of numbers. "Do you really think it will cost this much for the schooner?"

Nathaniel felt his father's interest begin to turn, and he picked up the theodolite again and held it to his eye. He didn't know how to work the instrument, but it began to interest him. When he thought about Meredith, he thought about the man he'd wanted to be all those years ago. Maybe he could be that man now. *Maybe.*

He heard Finn's confident tone weakening.

"Yes, Father. I want to start with a good boat."

"I think you can do better on the price, go up Cape if you have to or to Maine. Do what it takes, Son."

"I talked to my friend Charles Daniels at a shipyard in Bath, Maine. These are the quotes he gave me. He's a fair and honest man, Father."

"Yes, I suppose he is." His father tapped his pencil on the pile of papers and seemed to be considering the plan, and more than that, he seemed to be considering Finn.

Finn leaned over his father's desk, his body vibrating with an anger he could barely control. He stood up, pulled the edges of his coat into place as if to steady himself. He looked toward Nathaniel, who held the theodolite at his side, then Finn shook his head as if to emphasize Nathaniel's disgrace. "I've got ambition, Father. You know I have."

"Yes, Son, I'm aware of your ambition. I just—"

"What?"

"You need to slow down. You're still a young man. You've got time to grow before you get into a larger business. For now, I want you to focus on the fish shop."

"I've taken the fish shop as far as it can go. What would you have me do?" There was that edge in his voice again. He turned from his father and focused on the rows of books along the bookshelf. "Nathaniel, say something."

"I think you should give him a chance, Father. He's been preparing for this since I can remember."

"Yes, and my business plan is solid. You need to review it again."

"Sit down." Their father's words to Finn were clipped and demanding. "Tell me what you think of my plan."

"The plan is solid, but I don't think you're ready," Nathaniel Sr. said.

"You'll never think I'm ready." Finn's voice was flat. He glared into his father's eyes as if he could do the man harm, then he turned to leave.

He knocked over the side table by his father's favorite chair, sending the lamp and newspaper and small crystal ashtray flying on his way out of the room.

The dog stood up, alert, vigilant, and Nathaniel wanted to break the mood. He picked up the lamp and the crystal ashtray, righted the table and arranged things as they'd been while his father watched him absently.

"He'll adjust himself," Nathaniel Sr. said. "If he hadn't delivered the schooner in a state of disrepair—"

"You need to give him a break about that," Nathaniel said. He fiddled with the lamp, centering it on the table, before turning to his father. "I've been doing some thinking." He sat across from Nathaniel Sr. in the chairs before the fire. His father still appeared agitated, but he brought his attention to Nathaniel.

"So you've been thinking," Nathaniel Sr. said, a swath of brown hair across his forehead. Hands on his knees, he leaned forward.

"Yes, about our last conversation."

His father waved his hands. "No, no, no. I'm sorry about that. I never meant to imply that I was ashamed of you. It's just—"

Nathaniel stood before the fireplace, his hands on the mantel.

"I didn't mean to insult you," Nathaniel Sr. said. "And I don't mean to insult your brother either."

"But you do."

They were both silent, looking away from each other now, at the air in the room, at the windows, at the sky. Nathaniel didn't want to talk about Finn, so he brought up what he'd come to discuss. "What would I do if I worked in your business?"

His father looked perplexed. He pushed his spectacles up on his head. "I told you, Son."

"Tell me again."

"First, you'd learn the surveying, from Michaels or myself, then I'd teach you how to parcel the timber lots. But I'd also like you to work with the tenants. Help them with their farming so that they are more profitable. We earn a percentage of what they take in, and I'd like to improve that aspect of the business."

"And you'll pay me?"

"Of course. But more than that, you'll be a part of my business."

"What about Finn?"

"Finn has his own business to consider. He has work to do before he can afford a fishing boat."

"I want you to help him start his fleet. He's hardworking and focused, and he deserves your support."

"I'll support him when he shows me—"

"Father, stop. You can't possibly believe that he won't succeed. He's been working on fishing boats since he was a kid, and he knows how to buy and sell fish. He's a very capable man, as you yourself are. Can't you see it hurts him, your lack of belief in him?"

"That's not your concern."

"But it is. If you want me to work with you, you need to help my brother, your son. It's not too much to ask."

"I'll consider it."

"No, you'll do it, or I won't work for you."

"That's blackmail."

"It runs in the family. Didn't you blackmail Finn to get me on that boat?"

"Fine," his father said, waving his hand as if he could shoo the conversation away.

Nathaniel looked toward the surveyor's tools on the shelf. He didn't feel ready to give up his life on the marsh, but he wanted to become a man worthy of Meredith. He wanted her, and he would prove to her that he could do more than fish for his dinner.

He'd never taken an interest in the tools of his father's work, but he picked up the theodolite and turned it in his hands again. His father told him to hold it up to his eyes. "You align the crosshairs on the main scope onto the point you want to measure. Then you record the horizontal and vertical angles and perform a few calculations to get the distances."

His father stood beside him then and adjusted Nathaniel's hands on the instrument. "Like this," he said, and they looked at each other then, and an understanding passed between them. Nathaniel agreed to learn how to survey the land and work with the tenants.

"You'll need training, Nathaniel, and proper clothing."

"Yes, Father."

"I'd like to train you myself, to get you started, then Michaels will take over. He's a good man, solid, skilled. You'll like him."

"I'll look upstairs for a suit. We can start soon."

"We'll start tomorrow."

19

R ACHEL PRETENDED THAT SHE WAS STILL ASLEEP WHILE SHE secretly watched Meredith puff cushions and straighten furniture. She wanted to see what Meredith was like when she thought she was alone. Meredith was a mystery to her. Even though she talked about her life, even though she spent her time tending to Rachel, she kept some essence of herself hidden. Rachel wondered what lingered behind her easy smile and efficient manner. When Meredith turned around, her eyes flashed, and she brushed the hair from her forehead.

"You're awake. If you're up to it today, Rachel, let's take a walk," Meredith said. "The air will do you good."

"Has Finn returned with my bag? I feel so strange without my things," she said.

"You needn't worry about Finn. He'll make sure that you get your things."

Rachel let Meredith help her up from the bed and wash in a basin. Meredith poured a pitcher of cool water into the bowl while Rachel wet a cloth and ran it over her face and under her arms. She didn't go near the cut on her head, nor did she try to fix her hair. Meredith gave her a cotton dress and covered her with a shawl. They walked slowly along the hallway out to the foyer where they stood for a moment before Meredith opened the front door. Daylight spilled onto the landing like water over a dam, all at once and rushing at them. Rachel squinted and pushed through, an arm at Meredith's crooked elbow. In spite of the throbbing in her head, her legs felt solid beneath her. Meredith walked on Rachel's right, where her sister, Katherine, used to be, and the daily ache eased with the warmth of Meredith's touch upon her arm. They walked around the house and took the short set of steps down to the beach, where the low tide left a wrack line of dried sea hay and shells covered in bright-green webs of seaweed. To the left was the jetty where a series of granite rocks tilted against one another. From across the marsh, the crack of a crate dropped onto the dock vibrated through Rachel's every bone.

"There, there," Meredith said, patting her on the hand. All that had been unpredictable in Rachel's early life—her mother's defection, her father's rage, and her sister's death—could be soothed by Meredith's hand tapping lightly on her skin. *There, there.*

Meredith led Rachel at a slow pace along a sandy trail to the salt marsh. Nathaniel's island sprouted as a thin line against the trees—she didn't know how many miles across the marsh.

"Does anyone ever go out there?" Rachel asked.

"Only Nathaniel."

"I want to see it," Rachel said. "Don't you?"

Meredith didn't answer, and Rachel didn't push. Rachel didn't know what she expected to see at the shack, maybe a sense of the man who'd saved her, or knowledge of him beyond his quiet reserve. Why would he choose to live out there? From where she stood, the structure appeared no larger than her thumb held up against the horizon, but she knew that it was large enough for him to live in, and she imagined that he'd made it homey. She imagined quilts made by some woman he held close to his heart, tintypes of his lost brother, and collections of rocks and shells from his travels along the shore.

She imagined a world that Nathaniel created for himself where he didn't need the noise of other people. Maybe he read books, she thought, shelves and shelves of books. She imagined *Arabian Nights*, *Huckleberry Finn*, and *The Count of Monte Cristo*. She imagined that she could visit him and sit before the fire, and he would read to her from his library. She wanted to know the world behind his sad eyes and how he filled his life after losing his brother. She filled her own life with work and with people. She couldn't know how someone else would live after such a loss as she'd experienced herself. She wanted to visit the shack, to see for herself the expanse of his grief.

"I'll get there one day," Rachel said.

"I expect you will."

20

THE GRASS WAS WARM ON NATHANIEL'S BARE FEET. THE SUN blurred his vision. When Meredith opened the door for him, the dog rushed around her, scratching the wooden floor of the kitchen and running his nose along the counter. Rascal didn't hesitate on his way into the parlor and toward the sound of human noise. When the dog saw Meredith and Rachel, he ran from one to the other while they lavished him with attention. Nathaniel sat in the chair across from Meredith and the girl. He crossed his legs one way, then another, until he finally stood up and poured a glass of water from the pitcher on the table.

"You look well, Rachel. I'm glad to see it."

The quiet of the first few days after her accident had passed over the last ten days into something he had not yet grasped.

"Where'd you get the dog?" Meredith asked.

"Oh, he shows up when he gets hungry." Nathaniel saw her happiness, but he didn't imagine that it could be for himself. They ate the lemon cake and cookies that Dot carried in on the silver tray. Sun fell through the windows in a bath of light. Rachel leaned back against the pillows and let the warmth onto the front of her body. Nathaniel watched Meredith's back arch slightly as she stretched herself out and sat in a chair by the couch.

"I saw you fishing the other day," Rachel said. "I could see you from that window there."

"Nathaniel has been fishing since he could walk," Meredith said. "The first time I saw him, he was a boy leaning over the water near the end of the jetty, peering into a minnow trap. I wanted to see what was in that trap. I wanted to catch minnows, but I had to get home and do my chores. Those boys ran wild as wolves, my mother said."

She'd never told him this, and it thrilled him to know she'd thought about him that long ago. He wanted her then, wanted to feel her more than physically. He reached for a piece of lemon cake, and she reached for a cookie at the same time. They looked into each other's eyes for a single moment that contained a decade of feeling—their love for each other and the rupture in their relationship, his defection to the island and her marriage, this room that they both found themselves in and the girl that brought them here, sadness and wistfulness—then they looked away. His longing for her made him want a home in a way he hadn't since the accident. Home had always been his parents' house, until he fell in love with Meredith, then home had become a place they dreamed together. When he looked around this house, he realized what a different home she'd chosen from the one he had once imagined for her, and it saddened him.

Meredith placed her glass of iced tea on the table, tilted her head to one side, and fiddled with her pearl earring, then she looked down as if she were studying the rug. Nathaniel watched her eyes running over the braided blue pattern that shimmered in the light like water. He didn't want his visits to her house to end. He panicked for a moment, imagining himself alone, then he told himself he liked his solitude and tried to fortify himself with this knowledge as he left.

Meredith followed him to the back door, and they lingered for a moment in the breeze from marsh. "Did you stay away because of our talk?" Meredith asked.

"It made me think," Nathaniel said.

"Me too."

"Let's go rowing."

"We can't go rowing. What will people say?" Meredith held her hands across her stomach and peered toward the water out the window.

"Do you remember that first time?"

"Of course I remember." She placed a hand on his arm, and she didn't remove her gaze from his face. It was as if no time had passed, and they were the same people they had been back then, only older and with layers of sadness that they hadn't known before. He looked into her eyes, at the startling green of them. When he touched her waist, her curves were like a memory. The utter beauty of her neck and shoulders, so close to his mouth that all he would have to do is lean down to kiss them. He was aware of her heat, the scent of skin and soap, and the firmness of her corset as she leaned against him.

"I'm going into business with my father," he said. "It's time for me to build a life, Meredith."

"You'll still come visit?"

"If you'd like?"

She nodded. He felt her there for a moment, then he turned to go.

—◊◊◊—

The sun burned down on Nathaniel's shoulders and scorched him through his shirt as he walked toward the shack. He felt full of love at the thought of Meredith. What emptiness had she filled that he hadn't known was there? He had an unexpected, deep feeling ringing through him, the sound of her voice, the vibration of her touch. He imagined the curve of her collarbone and the freckle on her right breast and how he wanted to kiss it right now. He walked faster through the muck of low tide. The dog followed him to the plank over the wide creek, and they made their way through the thickets that bordered the island. The shack stood straight as any house he'd ever seen, made to withstand any weather.

He wanted to build a house for him and Meredith, but there was no way that could happen, he realized.

He drank water from the pump and wiped his mouth with the back of his hand. Glancing around the clearing at the single chair, the empty clothesline, the small circle of stones where he cooked his meals, he saw the paucity of his life and felt ashamed. What did he have to offer Meredith? Not even a plot of land to build a house upon. He kicked at the circle of stones, then sat on the chair, frustrated. Meredith would never leave her marriage. What was he thinking? Still, he couldn't let go of the thought that if he could provide a home for her, she would come to him. She loved him still. He was sure of it.

As soon as he had that thought, though, he lost its surety. Why would she love him after all that he put her through? If he returned to her house, Theo would be furious. Nathaniel didn't know what violence the man was capable of. He took the broom from where it rested against the side of the shack and swept in wide arcs around the clearing, swiping away leaves and rocks and clods of dirt. He took apart the campfire stones and stacked them again, one by one, into an orderly circle. Inside, he brushed the floor and took his sheets outside to hang on the clothesline, opened the windows to let the breeze through the shack. He lay back on his mattress, but he couldn't relax. He prepared a large meal of salt beef, turnips, and onion that he shared with Rascal. He drank a cup of water to wash it all down, and only then could he sleep.

21

TWO DAYS AFTER DR. HOWE REMOVED THE STITCHES, RACHEL convinced Meredith to return to her normal activities. Rachel was fine on her own, and she wanted to be alone for a while. She didn't tell Meredith that now that her headaches had stopped, she was bored with lying on the couch, bored by the same old routine. She wanted to find a place of her own, a job. She wanted to start building her new life. Nathaniel had mentioned that he could help her, but she wanted to take responsibility for herself. She didn't want them to think she was a helpless child.

When the carriage that carried Meredith across town toward her mother's house disappeared down the driveway, Rachel rose from the couch where Meredith had covered her in a summer blanket. She peeked out the windows to make sure that Meredith was out of sight, then she took her dress from where Meredith had folded it onto a chair for safekeeping. The dress smelled clean, like fresh air and lavender, as she pulled it on over her head. She found her jacket, clean as well, hanging on a hook in the back hallway. She had to find her bag before Finn stole her money.

Once she was dressed, she opened the side door as quietly as she could. She didn't know why. Nobody was home, but she felt as if she was sneaking away. She wanted to come back and show Meredith that she could take care of herself. There was something in the woman that was beginning to oppress Rachel. Maybe because she'd never been cared for in that way, or maybe because she wanted to get moving again, she didn't know. What had been a caring attitude had seemed to become a need within Meredith to keep Rachel close. It only made Rachel want to get away.

As she walked toward the harbor, she could see the shingled buildings with plumes of smoke curling from brick chimneys, low-lying brambles and gangly scrub pines, the pure lack of growth that to her signified potential. Even the noise welcomed her with its ease. The men she passed by were friendly, and the few women she saw carrying baskets of vegetables and fish greeted her as she walked without direction. For a minute, she stood motionless.

"You look lost, miss." The boy pulled his shoulders back and held his chest forward as if this could make him look older, but he was not more than fifteen years old, blond and skinny. "My name's Davey Sampson. I work at the fish shop over there."

Rachel followed the line of his finger toward Finn's fish shop. That was where he was hiding her bag. She was sure of it, but she didn't know how to get to him. She needed a room first, then a job, then she could get her bag back. She hoped.

She turned to Davey, whose eyes warmed her, eager and trusting, wanting to please her. Her! A girl from nowhere Maine, dressed in a cotton dress and faded skirts, a thin wool coat that dragged along the ground, frayed with travel. As she lifted her skirt to step over mud in the road, she was reminded of how small she was compared to her mother and sister.

"I'm not lost," she said. "I need a room to let."

"Mrs. O'Shea there on the end," he said. She didn't respond, and after a moment, he led her toward the building farthest from the bay.

"You're that girl staying over at the Butlers'. What, did they kick you out finally or what? Must've been nice living in luxury for a while, huh?"

Rachel watched him speak, but she didn't know what to say to him. The greasy smell of fried eggs and buttered toast from a small restaurant mixed with the odors of the sea, and for the first time in weeks, Rachel was hungry.

"She's short a waitress," Davey said. "I'll bet she can help you out, you know? Give you some work maybe?"

Rachel looked through the front window of the restaurant, then back at Davey with something like a question on the tip of her tongue.

"You want me to come in with you?"

"No, but thank you."

"Okay. I'll see you around," he said and waved on his way to the fish shop.

Inside the restaurant, the sound of voices assailed her, and she placed her hand to her head. The only woman in the place stood behind the counter, wiping the wood in circles. She hadn't taken her eyes off Rachel since she walked in the door.

"Excuse me," Rachel said.

The woman stopped, folded her cloth, and hung it on a rod. "You must be that girl," she said.

"I guess so," Rachel said.

"Well, what can I do for you?"

"Davey said you might have a place to rent?"

"You come back this afternoon, and I'll take you up to see it."

"You wouldn't know anyone who needs help around here, would you? I'm a good worker. I've waited tables." Rachel couldn't get herself to ask the woman for a job, not after she'd just asked her for a place to live.

"I guess I can help you out with that, too. I'm Mrs. O'Shea. I'm willing to give you a chance, but if you mess it up, I can't help you. Grab an apron from the back of the door, and wipe down the counters over there. That'll get you started, and we'll see how you do."

22

F INN WATCHED AS RACHEL POURED COFFEE AND JUGGLED JARS OF maple syrup. She maneuvered amid a barrage of breakfast orders, the comings and goings of men, and the scuff of their boots along the wooden floor. He'd heard from his brother that Rachel had started work here a week ago, and he had to see for himself.

He sat with the newspaper spread across the table and the carpetbag at his feet. When she came to take his order, he looked up from the paper into the curiosity on her face.

"Finn," she said, then she looked around the restaurant as if checking on other customers. "Did you come with my bag?"

"It's at the shop," he said, hoping she'd come over after work, and he could see her again.

"I'll be sure to stop by then." There was a warmth in her voice, as if she was fond of him. The scar on her head looked roughly sewn together, a nubbly line of red tissue that receded into her hairline. He only wanted to win her over. He wanted her to know that he'd saved her as much as Nathaniel had. If he hadn't sailed the boat, they would've been wrecked by the squall.

She took his order and smiled. Out of all these men, he wanted to be the only one that she was here to take care of. The other men ordering their breakfasts were a mere distraction. He was the one who mattered, and she was the relief he needed from the cold reception he received at home. He ate slowly and watched her swipe tips from the tables into her apron pocket. He deserved a woman who paid attention to him, and Rachel had paid attention to him on the boat.

As the restaurant emptied, Rachel washed down the tables. She appeared to be waiting for him to leave. The way her backside filled out her dress as she leaned over a table to close a window, the threadbare fabric pulled so that the seams of her underthings showed. He imagined her body beneath the dress, the soft pale skin over each curve of hip and thigh, her legs strong, pliant beneath her stockings, and her arms around him. With her face turned up to him, he would receive her like a gift.

"How about keeping me company for a minute?" Finn called to her.

"Work doesn't stop when everyone leaves," she said. She ran the rag across the table, then wiped her hands on her apron.

"Everyone needs a rest during such a busy day," Finn said.

He pushed the chair across the table out with his foot, then watched her consider him from across the room. She was still tired from the accident and not used to being on her feet all day, he could see that. Mrs. O'Shea wouldn't mind if she joined him.

"It looks like you've healed well," he said, tapping his forehead. "I'm glad."

"Mrs. Butler took very good care of me."

"I went to visit you, but Meredith sent me away. I don't like her," he said.

"She took very good care of me."

"It was rude. I only wanted to see how you were doing," he said. "I wanted to tell you how sorry I was that you were injured. I sailed the boat over to you and Nathaniel and helped pull you onboard, but you were unconscious. We were so worried—"

"It was a storm. There was nothing you could do about it. I was hors-ing around. I should have gone below like I was told. It was my own fault."

Finn wanted to change the subject. "We had fun before that."

"When you were flirting with me?"

"You flirted back."

When Rachel didn't respond, he said, "You work hard." He pressed his fingers down on the tines of a fork to rock it up and down like a seesaw. "I'm surprised there isn't a young man come along to take care of you."

"Maybe that's not what I'm looking for." She turned from him to face the window, bounced her leg up and down as if she were about to run from him.

"That's what every young woman is looking for."

"I'm not every woman."

Rachel watched the harbor where the fishermen on the mackerel smacks unloaded crates of fish. Finn followed the line of her gaze to the wagon from Butler Fishing Company that stood by while fish were packed with ice, the crates nailed shut, then stacked on the wagon like tiny coffins. When she turned away from him, he leaned closer with his elbows on the table. His loneliness opened like a ditch. He was over-taken with the impulse to hold her hand, so he put his hands back in his lap and continued.

"You're the nicest thing I've seen around here in ages."

Rachel turned to watch the gulls near the jetty, then she pushed herself back from the table. "You'll have to excuse me," she said. "I need to get back to work, but I'll see you this afternoon." She turned to go.

"Yes, of course," he said. He waited until she disappeared into the kitchen before he took his leave, thinking maybe, after all, he could get something he wanted.

III

23

F INN GAZED ACROSS THE ROLLING LAND TOWARD THE BAY, WHERE
sometimes a break in the woods allowed a glimpse of the water
and the world of his dreams. On the road, a man rocked by on his
wagon seat, reins held limply in his hands as the horses skulked along
the road. A flock of boys ran alongside a wagonload of chickens and
squawked as if this were the funniest thing in the world.

Parcels of land were marked with stone walls that rambled over the
bumpy ground like a child's drawing. The town looked neat and trim
with small shingled houses set back from the road on generous pieces of
land. More and more people came each year from places like Boston and
Worcester. Farming, fishing, building—there was money to be made
and an optimism in the air they breathed. There was a feeling of signifi-
cance that accompanied everyday activities. The townsfolk knew they
were building something that would stand over time—a life for their
children, a town and a way of life that would go on after they were gone.

Past the old Garvey place, there was a piece of land that Captain
Sears had stripped of timber to sell to the shipbuilding yard. More and
more of the land was stripped, and this was what his father wanted, to
wait for the demand for wood to increase so that he could get a higher
price for the timber on his land. The longer he waited, the more the
shipbuilders and house builders and railroad lines would pay for each
tree.

As Finn approached one of his father's pieces of timberland near the bank, he was surprised to see his brother and father walking the perimeter, his father pointing out the land boundaries. He ducked behind an elm tree that bordered the road and watched while his father showed Nathaniel how to hold a measuring rod on the ground and count off in increments.

Finn stepped out from behind the elm and walked across the tamped-down dirt of the road, then over the bumpy earth and along the edge of woods that marked his father's property. His brother stood with one foot pressed against the rod on the ground. When he saw Finn, Nathaniel brushed the hair from his face, turned the back of his wrist to wipe the sweat from his forehead. Their father fidgeted with the theodolite he used to triangulate distances and measure his land along with the older method of using metal rods. They both looked down at their tools, then up at Finn.

"What are you doing?" Finn asked.

"We're measuring this parcel of timber," his father said. "It might be time to sell it off. The market price is good, and we were thinking—"

"You were thinking what?" Finn's voice came out like a demand.

Nathaniel and his father stood with their backs firm, tools held at their sides, expressions of guilt upon their faces. His father put the theodolite on the ground and stepped toward Finn. The earthy smell of him, the dirt and sweat and leafy odor, his face flushed with heat, all of it too close. Finn stepped back. "What are you doing, Father?"

"Son, Nathaniel and I—"

"I can see exactly what's going on here," Finn said. He turned away from them, placed the balls of his hands to his cheekbones as if to push back his rage. When he turned to his father again, he was nearly shaking with the effort of controlling himself. "You'll take Nathaniel into your business, but you don't think I'm ready. After all the hard work I've done, the dedication I've shown." Finn stared at his father then, as if he could make out something in the man's face that would explain this treachery. "To hell with you!" He nearly spat his words in his father's face.

"Son," Nathaniel Sr. said. "I will help you, when you're ready. I've told you."

"When will I be ready, Father? When?" Finn demanded an answer, but their father stood mute, confused as to what to say. He seemed to weigh his options for calming Finn down, but Finn would not be stopped. He spat on the ground at his father's feet. "You don't care for me. You never have."

"That's not true, Finn. Now calm down."

"Father," Nathaniel said, holding his hand up to stop Nathaniel Sr. from saying any more. "It's true. You haven't supported him. He's ready now. His plan is smart and ambitious, or you wouldn't have bothered to read it beyond the first page."

"That's not true," Nathaniel Sr. said, turning from his sons to stare across the fields as if the expanse of land would provide some relief from his two boys.

"It is true, Father," Nathaniel said. "He deserves a chance, like you've given me."

"After what happened on Edwin George's boat...I can barely look the man in the face." Their father looked at them again. He was determined, stern. "I'll not have the two of you talk to me like this. It's disrespectful." Nathaniel Sr. stood with his hands on his hips, not budging. His stiff arms, the set of his face, everything about him said *no!*

"I've seen everything I need to see. I'm done trying to please you," Finn said. He shook his head, disgusted, and took off down the street. He left his father and Nathaniel standing with their tools held at their sides.

"Finn," Nathaniel called after him, but Finn waved him off.

He continued up the road toward the bank, kicking a rock that nearly turned his ankle, then picking it up and hurling it into the woods with the force of his anger. What difference did it make if Nathaniel worked with their father? It wasn't going to influence the old man either way regarding his business plan. The old man would never invest in anything Finn worked out, whether it was the fish store or a fishing fleet.

He tried to think about something else—the thin streaks of clouds stretched across the sky over the trees, the stone wall built by Davey's father that followed the road—then he pictured Rachel sitting across from him in the restaurant, her strawberry hair and her pretty lips forming words, the tiny freckles beneath her eyes. If he could focus on the details of the girl's face, he could push everything else from his mind. She'd flirted with him on the boat and stirred some longing in him that he wasn't able to satisfy with his wife. He needed something of his own, and the girl gave him a sense of hope that he could move beyond this frustration with his father, his business, and his marriage.

He inhaled with every two steps, then exhaled, then inhaled with the next two steps, then exhaled, until his heart slowed down to a steady thump.

He walked back toward the familiarity of his fish shop, toward Rachel and her bag of money.

Finn was truly on his own, he realized. His father was never going to help him, and when he realized this, he went to the side of the road and stared off into the woods. What had he done to wind up so alone? Couldn't his father see that all he did, he did for the family legacy, to continue their name in town as the Boyds of the harbor, the landowning Boyds, the fishing Boyds? They could be an even more successful lot if Finn wasn't always punished for his drive. He held back tears until a cutting anger took him over. He quivered from the force of it until his anger drove him back up the road, walking fast, almost jogging, as if he could create his own oblivion in the scrape of his breath against his throat, the thrum of his heart in his chest, and that mind-numbing ringing in his ears. He jogged until he ran, his arms swinging, his boots slapping the road. At least he would get to see the girl.

He didn't care how much his legs hurt or how his breath tore at him. *Let it tear*, he thought. *Let it rip me apart.*

24

N ATHANIEL FOLLOWED THE WOODS ALONG THE EDGE OF THE marsh and perched himself against a stone wall so that he was hidden from the Butler house by a fall of grapevines. The syrupy-sweet smell, the light and shadows playing with his senses, and his loneliness made him lazy as he sat in the shade. He didn't know where Rascal had gone off to. He wasn't surprised the dog had taken off, but he missed him in a way he hadn't missed him before. He'd guarded himself against loneliness for so long, but visiting Rachel and Meredith over the few weeks had broken him open. He'd found comfort, even pleasure sitting in the parlor amid their voices. It disturbed him, his desire for Meredith. She'd saved him with a tender touch. She gave him hope. Hope could be dangerous, but here he was, filled to the brim. He felt his body hum with pleasure, the relaxed feel of his back leaning against a strand of vines, his long legs stretched before him.

The moist air on his face, the breeze ruffling his hair, even the calluses on his palms felt good and strong to him, but then the image of Finn walking away from him and his father overtook him. He felt pity for his brother, then a sense of annoyance. Why couldn't he be happy with the fish shop? Why did he have to always push, push, push for more? But he knew Finn, and he knew that nothing could stop him from going after what he wanted. Nathaniel wanted to find a way to placate Finn, to ease his own feelings of culpability. Wasn't he supposed to look after his younger brother? Frustrated, he picked at his teeth with a piece of sea hay and looked toward the bay where the wind traveled in ripples across flat water.

His gaze turned back to Meredith's yard, where she stood looking toward his shack with a spyglass. She leaned toward his cabin as if to bring the shack into closer view, and he saw that she longed for him. He felt the warm rush of his love. Meredith made him think of clean sheets and a house filled with the smell of a fish stew simmering on the stove. He watched as Meredith closed the spyglass and walked toward her house. She took one last look over her shoulder as if she might catch sight of him. What was this pleasure in watching? Feeling himself at a remove? He felt hope like a rope held down to him, and all he had to do was grab hold.

He drifted back to the night they first kissed. It was after skating on Dennis Pond with a group of children from school. They'd held hands making loops around the pond. When they sat on the sandy beach to unlace their skates, he leaned in to her. They were almost adults, he told her, and he lifted her hand to his lips. Then he tilted his face down to kiss her, and she took in his kiss as if she'd been waiting. Their romance was solidified with that kiss, and from there, they began to imagine a future together, as if their love was a truth that they both had to accommodate now that it was in the open.

He remembered the house he'd wanted to build, a real Cape house with the south side all windows to let in the sun and provide heat during the colder months. He would build a four-poster bed from pine he gathered from his own land while Meredith sewed curtains and planted her vegetable garden. It had been a dream that felt real, an inevitable reality. Now here he was, a pauper, which was right where he'd wanted to be until he landed in Meredith's sitting room. He leaned back into the sea hay and stared at the sky where stars appeared like tiny promises, and he felt a quiet solace take hold of him as he lay back into a sleep that came over him as if he'd taken a tincture of laudanum.

—⁓—

Nathaniel woke at dawn to the creeping tide, his feet wet and puckered. For a moment, he couldn't remember what he was doing on this far edge of marsh, but the thick smell of grapes let him know where he was, and there through the vines, he saw Meredith's house. That was what brought him here. He'd fallen asleep with dreams of her hair in his face, the smell of her neck beneath her ear, and her voice speaking into him. *It's as if nothing has changed.* He wrestled himself up from the weeds and brushed the bottom of his pants, wiped the dirt and moisture onto his thighs to clean his hands. Meredith's house was white against a background of green and blue, grass and sky.

At the shack, Nathaniel sat on a wooden bench and bent over at the waist in an attitude of defeat. He wanted to recall the ease he'd found in the quiet on his island, the simplicity of his life looking at the red-winged blackbirds perched on a branch or listening to a woodpecker digging for insects in the nearby trees. He wanted to look up and remember the feeling of building his shack and the satisfaction he felt each night lying down to sleep under a roof he'd constructed with his own hard work, but these small consolations eluded him now that he knew the comfort of Meredith's anchoring gaze.

"Nathaniel." The raspy voice, thick and slurred, belonged to his brother, who stood in the doorway, leaning out of the shack, his linen shirt hanging loose from his trousers, shoes untied. Unshaven and with hair tousled around his heavy brow, he looked like a castaway. He swayed in the doorway. He was clearly drunk. His head swung to one side, then the other, as if he was trying to make sense of where he was.

Nathaniel could see the skin on Finn's neck flushed red and sweating, could smell the alcohol and musky, fishy odor of him. His brother stood there, disheveled, angry, and out of place.

"I'm as surprised to see me here as you are," Finn said, words slurred.

"I don't think so."

"So you finally got tired of living in a shack, Nathaniel. Is that why you're working with Father? I guess it would have to happen sooner or later." His drunkenness overwhelmed his anger, and he stumbled back into the chair that leaned up against the shack. "It's that Meredith Butler, isn't it?" His voice was a venom in the quiet air.

Nathaniel didn't speak.

"I knew it," Finn said. "She's married. You know that, don't you?"

"Finn."

"Well, at least Father will be happy to get you off the marsh. You think you're ready to face up to your life now and live like the rest of us? You think it's going to be easy?" Finn spat on the ground and stood up from the chair. "Huh? You think it's going to be easy?" He hovered near Nathaniel. If Finn was angry, the worst thing to do was try to fight him. It would only entice him.

"What do you want, Finn?"

Finn scratched his day's growth of beard and wiped his hand across his mouth. "I want you to talk Father into loaning me money. I want that girl at O'Shea's. You know who I mean."

"You're out of line."

"Father listens to you."

"I mean about the girl. She's too young, and she's here on her own." Nathaniel got up from the bench to stand in front of his brother, as if his words would have more force when spoken into Finn's face. "You stay away from her."

"You think you know anything about her?"

"More than you do."

"You know all about that girl… You have no idea."

Finn spat into the dirt and turned away from his brother. He stuck his hands in the bucket by the pump and splashed cold water on his face, wiped at his face with his shirttails. "What about Father? You'll talk to him?"

"You need to come up with a business plan that will get his attention. You need to take his advice," Nathaniel said, but even he didn't believe the words as they came out of his mouth.

Finn stared at him as if he were trying to find a way into Nathaniel's mind. "Goddamn you. You're a selfish bastard," Finn said. "How do you think it feels? Father doesn't trust me. He never has. Why? I want to know why?" Finn demanded an answer, but Nathaniel didn't know how to help him, and he wasn't sure he wanted to.

"You need to go home," Nathaniel said.

Finn hitched up his pants and gazed around the clearing as if to make sure he didn't forget anything. Nathaniel felt as if something between them had shifted, and it would not go back to the way it was when Nathaniel sold Finn his fish and Finn was in charge. Nathaniel had the upper hand now, and he wasn't sure he wanted it.

25

MEREDITH HADN'T SEEN RACHEL. SHE'D COME HOME TO FIND A pile of blankets where the girl should be. She'd gone from room to room searching, talked to the maids, and scanned the yard, filled with a kind of dread that was worry for the girl's safety and worry for herself. If the girl left, Meredith would be on her own with no one to care for and no visits from Nathaniel. It wasn't until she found the note that her fears came true. Rachel wanted to establish herself in town and prove to herself that she could make it on her own. At first, Meredith was hurt, then angry, then she realized that it wasn't fair to keep Rachel here when she wanted to move on. Still, without her, Meredith was confronted with the loneliness of her house.

Without Nathaniel's visits, she found herself looking across the marsh for a glimpse of him. She tried to distract herself with ordering Dot and Rose around the kitchen, busying herself with needlework, and writing letters. But nothing took her mind from the length of his body standing in her doorway, the deep look in his eyes when he sought her out, or the concern he showed for the girl. Upstairs, she stood before the mirror and applied face cream and powder, changed into an ironed cotton dress with blue posies along the hem and capped sleeves that showed off her arms. She liked the look of her arms, their pale skin and fine movements. Her physical grace came naturally. She unfastened the bun on the back of her neck and brushed her hair down over her shoulders, then refastened the bun in a loose twirl. She knew from the first day Nathaniel had appeared on her lawn that she still loved him. A familiar current had run through her and ran through her still.

She wanted to hold off her feelings, brush them aside, but the walls she'd erected around herself since Nathaniel moved out to the island cracked open, and the thinnest sliver of hope shone through. She remembered how miserable she'd been when he left her, how hopeless and strange her life became. Her mother had fed her broth, held the spoon to her lips. She'd held Meredith while she sobbed. Then Theo had offered her an alternative to loneliness, and she'd taken it at her mother's urging, because he was a good man, solid and caring. But happy memories of her past with Nathaniel, yearning for the dreams they'd shared, and physical craving overtook her senses now so that she couldn't remember her misery and the cruelty of Nathaniel's abandonment. She couldn't bring to mind her mother's words. *Be done with him once and for all, Meredith.*

She went downstairs to find something to do and found herself looking out the window toward Nathaniel's skiff. When she didn't see him, she took the spyglass and went on the lawn to search for him, then there he was, walking from around her house to greet her with the dog running ahead like a scout. His wide smile and the mischievous glint in his eyes reminded her of the old Nathaniel.

They stood before each other and almost laughed with delight, then he said, "Come out in the boat with me."

Meredith considered his offer, glanced toward the harbor where boats traveled to and from the docks. "People will see us." Meredith twirled her earring where it was fastened to her right earlobe as she considered his request.

"We can row into the creeks away from the harbor where it's hidden."

"I'm married, Nathaniel." She spoke to remind herself of this one fact that felt like an impediment now to her happiness. She thought of her husband with a feeling like foreboding, and she didn't want to acknowledge him at all.

"Your husband is never here." Nathaniel looked over her shoulder and past her as if searching for something to say that would persuade her.

"Come inside," she said.

In the parlor, they sat on the settee together, one on either end while the dog lay at their feet.

"I want to go rowing with you. I'm just frightened."

"Of getting caught?"

"Yes, of getting caught, but more than that. The more time we spend together, the more confused I am. I'm a married woman."

"Then you still love me?"

Meredith fiddled with her earring, twirling it with her fingers. "You have to ask me that?"

"I want you to say it."

"It's as if nothing has changed, as if we were still those young people hiding in the boatyard. I wait for you every day. No matter how much I try not to think of you—" She clasped her hands together in her lap and straightened her back. "Does that make you happy?"

"Yes," he said. "And I wanted to tell you that I've taken a job with my father. It's time I made my way in this town. I'm going to leave the marsh, Meredith. I'm going to make a life." Nathaniel stood to go before she could ask him any questions. She wanted to hold him back, make him sit for another few minutes on the couch. She wanted to ask if he was doing it for her, but she stopped herself.

"I'll be back," he said. "You can count on it."

Meredith sat in the kitchen and ignored her toast. Bands of yellow daylight striped the floor, and she stood in the midst of them. With the sun on her back, she looked toward Nathaniel's shack, then cursed herself for her disloyalty, then sank into sadness. He hadn't been by in days. She didn't know what to do with herself. With the girl gone and Nathaniel working for his father and visiting less, she was lonely in a way she hadn't known before they'd arrived in her house.

She found herself thinking of Nathaniel's long body moving over the marsh like he owned it, how he had unfurled a stream of memories she'd left behind when she met Theo Butler. Letting Theo love her had been admitting that Nathaniel was gone. He would never come in from that island. Never talk about what happened to his brother. Never let her close to him again. When he sat on her couch last week, she'd felt as if she could reach through the years and place her hand on his cheek, and say *Here, let's start here.* The intimacy between them had lingered, untended and ignored, and all the while, she'd imagined that Nathaniel as she'd known him was gone, as if leaving the land of those he loved made him no more. But he was still himself, a sadder version of himself, but he moved his long limbs with the same humble grace and spoke with the same gentle tone.

When she looked toward his shack, she wondered what he gained by removing himself from everyday life. Young Jacob was gone, and no amount of suffering on Nathaniel's part would bring him back, nor could it ease the pain of that loss. Nathaniel denied himself the simple pleasures of companionship and home and family. He denied himself his love for her. Didn't he understand that when he'd left the world, he'd left her, too? The language of his body moved through her house, and she couldn't say, *I know you. I've loved you. And you left.*

—⁓—

When Theo came home, Meredith shook herself loose from the weight of her longing. Her husband was all bristling energy and wanted only to be left alone, but Meredith needed the distraction of his attention. She brought him a drink in his study, asked him what he would like for dinner.

"Meredith, I don't care what we have for dinner," he said, looking up from a pile of papers.

"Will you take a walk with me?"

"I'd love to, dear, but I've got to attend to work. Can't you see?"

"Yes." Meredith groaned, frustrated with her own anxious energy. She sat in the armchair across from her husband and bounced one leg.

"Stop it," Theo said. "You're acting like a child."

"I'm sorry."

"What is it? What's the matter?"

"Nothing. I just want to spend time with you, but I understand. You're busy." She wanted him to convince her to love him again, but she only saw him sitting there with his pale, pale skin, the bags under his eyes. She stood from the chair and took a sip of Theo's whiskey before leaving the room. A warm glow permeated her chest, then spread out through her limbs. She decided to take a walk without him. She wasn't surprised to find herself on the east side of the house with the spyglass on Nathaniel's shack. When she didn't see him, she thought of scanning the bay for his boat, but then she scolded herself. *You're a married woman, Meredith Butler. Mind yourself.*

Back in the house, she reached for her shawl. She should go visit her mother. She would ride Daisy there herself. The air would do her good. As she called to Theo, her voice sounded lonely in the stillness of their rooms.

"Send my regards," Theo said.

26

TWO DAYS LATER, FINN WENT INTO O'SHEA'S AFTER THE breakfast rush and stayed until the last few customers swiped toast across their empty plates. He sat in the corner where he could watch Rachel. Why did she appear so confident stacking a row of dishes up her arm? When he looked at her, he didn't think about his wife ignoring him or his father turning him down for a loan. He felt the excitement of a young man. He asked Rachel for more coffee and invited her to sit with him a minute.

"I went by your shop," she said, wiping a cloth across his table and waiting for him to respond.

"I'm sorry. Trouble at home," he lied.

"I hope it's nothing serious."

"Not at all," he said, lying easily.

"I need my bag," she said, looking into his eyes now. "It's everything I own."

"I'll be there today," he said. "I promise."

She took his plate and cleared another table before disappearing into the kitchen. He had no problem chasing her if that was what she wanted. She was young and beautiful, and she deserved to be flattered. When she reappeared from the kitchen, he could hardly stand the slightest sway of her hip, the smile in her eyes, and that distant look that could be a place she went to have space for her own thoughts. All of it made him want to know her. When she took time to talk with another customer, he longed to have her all to himself. Even the smallest amount of attention she paid him, a smile when she poured his coffee, a hello, gave him hope that he could know her.

When she returned from the kitchen and saw that he was the only one left in the restaurant, she came over to his table.

"I know I don't deserve your attention, but maybe you'd indulge me for a few minutes."

"What do you want?" She pushed her hair to the side and glanced around at the empty tables. The restaurant was quiet except for the sounds from the kitchen of the grill hissing as the cook cleaned it and the dishwasher clanking plates.

"I just want to talk." Finn indicated the seat across from him, but she didn't sit. "Since I first saw you…you have a way about you."

"What's that supposed to mean?"

"You're kind and warm. You give off this glow that makes me want to be around you." He spoke in the most unfiltered way he could muster and thought himself a fool, but it was the only way he knew to get her attention. If he could reel her in with words, he'd hold himself wide open for her.

"You have the wrong person," she said, but he could tell she was flattered, and he reached across the table for her hand, but she pulled away from him. "What is it you want?"

"I want you to take a walk with me."

"A walk?"

"I know you like to go out and get some air after work. We can go someplace away from here, just the two of us. We can talk and get to know each other."

Rachel stood with her arms crossed over her chest. She considered him for a moment, and a series of thoughts flickered in her eyes, and he felt an anticipation he could hardly stand as she stared out the window toward the fishing fleet.

"I don't have much time to myself," she said, looking fearful when there was nothing to be afraid of.

"We'll keep it short." He looked at her with eyes full of longing. "A walk never hurt anyone."

"Monday's my day off," she said.

He didn't know what had changed her mind, but he put down a generous tip and left the restaurant, thinking, *Monday, that isn't so far off.*

27

TWO ROOMS ON THE SECOND FLOOR SERVED AS STORAGE, ONE FOR the restaurant, and one for items Mrs. O'Shea had packed away when she moved from the house she'd shared with her husband. As the only boarder on the second floor, Rachel enjoyed her privacy, but today the hallway felt lonesome. Two days since she'd left Meredith's house, and already, she missed the warm press of Meredith's hand against her forehead and Nathaniel's quiet presence. The cast-iron latch on her flimsy door rattled. Two south-facing windows let in late-day sun that fell in a slant across the floor and dropped soft light onto the crimson quilt Mrs. O'Shea had provided.

Out the windows, the harbor at Yarmouth Port didn't seem so much a well-laid plan as a sprawling row of buildings and intermittent docks built to accommodate the growing town. More fishermen, more settlers, more everything—and the town flourished. In spite of the quick growth, there was a permanence to the place, a solid construction of small buildings made to withstand the tests of weather and sea. It was a place where people longed to stay, to put down roots and thrive. And Rachel wanted to thrive here, too. The maple night table, the braided rug, and the small fireplace were her home now. As she sat on the edge of her bed and unlaced her boots, she felt relieved to be home.

She folded down one corner of the quilt and swiped her hand across the sheets as if to clear them of some other night's memories. When she thought of Nathaniel, she wanted to be near him the way shed been near him at Meredith's house. Maybe she would go out to the island when she knew he was there. They could sit together instead of alone in their quiet rooms, then she could get close to the sadness he carried that felt so much like her own. She wanted to wade into his grief and reside there with him if only for a while. To say, *I know.* Have him say, *Me too.*

But as she blew out the wick in the lamp, she knew that Meredith was more likely to welcome a visit, to serve a pot of tea and talk into the night about everything or nothing and it wouldn't matter. Meredith would enjoy the sound of their voices and the feeling of Rachel in the room, as Rachel would soak in the warmth of Meredith's attentions.

Rachel flattened her pillow by thwacking it with the palm of her hand, then she lay on her side with it bunched under her head. She felt soothed thinking about her friends, soothed by the sound of ropes snapping against wooden masts outside her window and the last of the voices on the docks, soothed by the easy flow of a day in the harbor village.

She didn't know what to think of Finn Boyd coming into the restaurant to see her. His attention was a game, their flirtations like a ball they bounced between them. She believed he kept her bag as an excuse to see her again, but she was frightened now about the money. She had to find the bag, and she was certain that he kept it in the shop, since that was where he appeared to spend most of his time. She had to get it.

In the morning, she walked behind the shops toward O'Shea's. When she saw Davey behind the fish shop, she watched him dump a bucket of detritus into a trash barrel. So focused was he on his work, running the bucket under the pump to clean it and covering the trash barrel before he went back into the shop, that he didn't notice her. She admired the way he worked, and she was grateful to him for sending her to Mrs.

O'Shea. He didn't have to help her like that, but he did. Maybe he'd help her now.

She kept walking past the backs of the shops into Mrs. O'Shea's kitchen and bought a fresh-baked loaf of bread with her tips.

"Aren't you the one, spoiling yourself," Mrs. O'Shea said, beads of sweat gathered along her hairline, her hair loose from her bun at the back of her neck. Her kind, brownish-green eyes shone like the seaweed that washed onto the beach, a little cloudy but with a beauty all their own.

"Thank you, Mrs. O'Shea," Rachel said with a wave, and off she went along the trail behind the shops. The cooking smells from O'Shea's, the smell of fish, and the salty odor of the jetty and marsh were becoming home to her. For hours at a time, she forgot entirely the place she'd fled.

When she reached the back door at the fish shop, she stopped to watch Davey work. His face was a meditation. His eyebrows were bleached from the sun, his fair skin freckled along his cheeks.

"Davey," she said.

He looked up as if startled.

"I've brought you some bread. I thought you might like it."

He went to the sink to clean his hands, and he took off his apron. She could see the heat on his face, blushing as he walked outside, beyond the smell of the shop.

"Why, no need to thank me." He accepted the bread as if she were handing him her heart in a paper bag. Not knowing what to do with the package and nearly quivering with emotion, he shifted it from one hand to the other. His youth, his shyness, and his awkwardness with the gift were endearing.

Rachel wasn't sure how to put Davey at ease, so she said, "I was wondering if you could help me with something?"

"Anything," he said, all eagerness.

"I left my carpetbag on the schooner after the accident. Finn said that I could come by and get it."

"I haven't seen any bag around, but you can come inside for a look. I have to warn you, the stench will knock you over."

"I can handle it," she said, and she followed him into the back of the shop. "Where's Finn?"

"He leaves me in charge sometimes when it's slow. We can look in his office if we don't touch anything."

Rachel watched from the doorway as Davey searched. "I don't see it," he said, standing up from where he'd bent beneath the desk for a look. "You're going to have to come back. Sorry, Rachel."

"Don't you worry about it," she said. "You better get to work now. You don't want to get in trouble with Finn."

Davey turned from her, and she watched him roll his sleeves for work as she stepped outside into the fresh air, panicked about her money.

28

W HEN NATHANIEL SAW HIS BROTHER TALKING WITH RACHEL inside O'Shea's, he'd had such a rush of feeling he didn't dare go inside to say hello. Rachel was his responsibility. He'd saved her. The thought wasn't right, and he knew it. *You don't own her; you barely know her.* But still, Nathaniel felt protective, then outraged. Finn was a married man, and there he was flirting with a young girl. Rachel was naive, and he could imagine her easily taken in by a man who showed her kindness. Then again, it was none of Nathaniel's business: his brother's attempts at attracting the girl or the girl's willingness.

Nathaniel continued past the docks and storefronts until he reached his skiff. He sat in the boat where it bobbed in the tide, firmly anchored to the beach. The sun burned his back, and he squinted into the bay, then looked into the bilge where water splashed along the seams. He didn't know what to do about Finn. He ran the bailer along the bilge and dumped water over the side until there was no water left in the boat.

He sat back on the stern seat to rest his arm, then he wondered how many days it had been since he'd been to see Meredith. He'd been working with his father, and he couldn't keep track. Today was hot. The heat permeated his body until every cell of his skin down through his muscles felt on fire. When had heat been so unrelenting? He crossed the marsh to the Butler house, knocked on the door, and listened for her footsteps. The doorknob turned, and he stepped back so as not to appear too eager.

"You're here," she said. "I've been watching you for days." Her face was aflame with the heat or surprise; he didn't know which. He only felt relieved to see her, to step inside out of the heat into the shadowed coolness of the hallway where they stood close together for a moment, just to feel each other there.

"I was hoping you'd come back," she said, and her words released some spring held down in him. "Come in. We can sit in the parlor."

She led him through the hallway. "I haven't been able to stop thinking about you," she said as she walked, as if it were the most natural thing in the world to speak this freely. "No matter what I do, there you are, occupying my mind as if no time has passed."

He sat on the settee. She sat beside him and poured water from the pitcher into two crystal glasses.

"Rose will bring iced tea and cake," she said as if she hadn't just revealed her innermost thoughts.

"I've wanted to come since the other day," he said. "But, you know, Theo."

"Yes," she said.

"There's something I've come to tell you." He took her hand, and when he let it go, she took his hand and held it firmly. "I've started working with my father. I'm going to live with him in the house until I figure out what to do. I want you, Meredith, as much as you want me."

"Don't do this for me," she said.

"It's time. I'm ready."

"I'm married."

"I know, but things can change. They have to change."

Meredith smiled into Nathaniel's face and leaned across the settee to kiss him. He kissed her back, receiving her body as she leaned into him. "There's something else," he said.

"Well, what is it?"

He wanted to say something about Finn, but he didn't know how to put it, so he said the first thing that came to mind. "My brother has been talking to Rachel, taking too much of an interest."

"How do you know?"

"I've seen them."

"Are you sure? How can you be sure?" She stood from the settee and paced the room.

"You could talk to her, Meredith. She needs a woman's point of view. She has no family here to guide her."

Meredith dropped her weight onto the settee next to him and appeared to be turning the facts over in her mind. "She's young, and the attention of a handsome older man can be flattering. Girls that age can have very poor judgment. Have you talked to your brother? What is he thinking?"

When Rose came in with tea, Meredith shooed her away and told her they needed the room to themselves.

"Not yet. I'm waiting until I can speak to him rationally."

"Don't wait too long," Meredith said. "I feel like she's my daughter. She was only here a couple of weeks, but I feel protective of her."

He leaned against her, felt her arm against his. Meredith turned to him then and leaned her face toward him, brushed her cheek against his. Nathaniel wrapped his arms around her, and she let herself fall against him. They sat like that for some time, breathing in rhythm like they had so many years ago. He ran his hands along her back, which was small but strong and tapered at the waist. When she picked her head up again, they locked eyes, and he felt years of knowing in her steady gaze. The truth existed between them from that early connection, and he knew then that she'd never stopped loving him. When he kissed her, something in him came home. He was brought back to the schooner in the boatyard where they'd first made love, and that early innocence felt palpable to him.

Meredith ran her hands along his face, feeling the tears along his cheeks, the worry in his forehead, the creases at the corners of his eyes from squinting into distances he couldn't fathom.

When Meredith led him upstairs, he didn't resist. Theo was in Boston for the week.

She sent the maids home.

29

FINN PLACED A BUNDLE OF FISH ON THE KITCHEN COUNTER AND looked into the parlor where the girls played on the floor. He poured a short glass of whiskey and sat at the kitchen table. The girls' tender voices could erupt into shrieks over the smallest infringement, and often it was something he didn't understand. He recognized Elizabeth's heavy tread on the wooden floor. "Come on, girls. Wash up for dinner." She clapped her hands to stun them from their game, and they groaned and dragged themselves up from the floor.

She took up the broom from the corner and started to sweep the kitchen. "Where were you last night?"

"I went to see Nathaniel on the island. I slept on the floor of his shack. Did you know he's working for my father? Can you believe it? My father who won't even help me with a loan." Finn shook his head and looked at his wife for some sympathy.

"You didn't think to let me know? Do you think I slept at all for worrying?"

"Elizabeth, do you hear what I'm telling you?"

He stepped toward her and placed a hand on her hip, seeking the comfort of her body, but she didn't move to receive him. He pulled her toward him then and felt her heat and the worried length of her. He wanted to calm her, but he didn't know what to do. The nonsensical sounds of the children playing, the drip from the pump, and the tick of the old kitchen clock captured him in a moment that contained the life they'd built together and the love they shared. He wanted to capture that love and carry it with him always, but it felt thin and fragile.

"Elizabeth," he said.

"I don't know what to do, Finn." She pushed herself back from him so that she could look into his eyes. "It's one thing that you're hardly here, but the least you can do is sleep in our bed."

And when I'm here, it's as if I don't exist. He stopped himself from saying the words, but he began to pace, working to keep his anger down. Where was that wisp of love? That good feeling was gone in the turn of a phrase.

"We need you, Finn."

"I'm at the shop before dawn so I can take care of our family. I have plans, Elizabeth, plans for us."

"It would be better if you were here." Elizabeth's voice grew shrill, and Finn hated that. He tipped his glass to drink down the end of his whiskey and slammed it on the counter on his way out the door.

30

I T STARTED WITH A RESTLESS CLEANING-OUT OF KITCHEN DRAWERS, tossing out dented measuring spoons and tarnished serving forks. Dot and Rose kept the kitchen clean, but they didn't make commonsense decisions about replacing things. Meredith took down the curtains with their ruffled bottoms that overfluffed the room, which in itself was lovely, with south-facing windows and space for the large cook's stove as well as a kitchen table where the maids could eat or Meredith could take her breakfast. She often woke in the night and sat in the kitchen to watch the stars shift over the harbor. She enjoyed her time to herself then. It was during the day when the world rushed on about her that she felt most alone.

The kitchen was only hers in the middle of the night, as it was mainly the domain of Dot and Rose, but Meredith was determined to make it her own. In spite of the shine of the stove, she scrubbed it down with water-soaked rags. Her hands felt their way around the contours of iron and the flat surfaces. She removed the burners and cleaned in and around the grooves that held them. When she finished her work, she felt like the stove was hers. The floors were next, and then beneath the sink where the maids kept the root vegetables. She touched every square inch of the kitchen until the room took shape within her and became a space she could inhabit.

After tea, she focused on the parlor where she'd tended Rachel.

This room offended her the most, with its shelves of crystal bowls and small statues of dogs that cluttered the shelves with memories of Theo's family. One at a time, she packed them away into boxes that she carried up to the attic. As she emptied the shelves, space opened up, space to fill with anything she liked, anything at all, and there was no one to stop her. With the last candlesticks packed away, she sat on the easy chair and gazed around the room. The dreary art would have to go, but not just now. One thing at a time. The patterned wallpaper darkened the room, which was a shame. Perhaps a light shade of paint instead, something to brighten the room even in the winter months.

She went upstairs to her room to draw herself a bath. Her hair was full of dust and dirt, and she needed a good soak. Meredith lay in the tub and gazed out the windows at the water. This wasn't a bad house. How many people could see the bay from their bathing tub? She'd never taken the time to make it her own. Over the years, she'd accepted the house as part of her life with Theo, but that wasn't enough for her anymore. She needed something that was hers.

She climbed out of the tub and considered herself in front of the mirror. What did Nathaniel think of her after all these years? Her breasts didn't sag or droop, her stomach was lean, and her were arms strong. By all standards, she was an attractive woman. She wanted more than the comfort and familiarity of her husband's body in bed. She wanted the passion she had with Nathaniel.

"You're a disgrace," she imagined her mother saying, but she didn't feel like a disgrace. She felt like she'd been waiting for Nathaniel and only realized it when he'd walked across the lawn carrying Rachel in his arms after the storm had wrecked their boat. She worried about Dot and Rose telling Theo about Nathaniel coming to their house, but any good help knew to keep their employer's secrets, didn't they?

She dressed in a white cotton dress with lace across the chest, then she took the stairs down past the old portraits of Theo's family. *I'll get rid of you soon*, she thought. She'd decided to have a late lunch at O'Shea's where she could see Rachel and maybe catch up with her after work.

When Meredith reached the restaurant, the place was nearly empty. She stood inside the front door and glanced about in search of the most appealing table. By the window, she thought and sat with her back toward the wall with the open room on one side of her and the harbor view on the other. Men's voices warmed the room, and she watched for Rachel. The open window let heat onto her wrists, and she rolled her palms facing up and felt the heat on the insides of her arms. She closed her eyes and waited for Rachel to come with food.

Next thing she knew, the girl was shaking her by the shoulder.

"Meredith, you fell asleep. I'm so glad to see you. I ordered for you, a lobster salad with some potatoes. You like that, don't you? I'll clear a few tables, and then we'll talk. Now, drink your coffee."

The girl's eyes offered such kindness. Meredith took her hand. She wanted to thank her in some small way for noticing her, but Rachel was off again, her apron strings hanging down her backside as she breezed from table to table. She lined her forearms with plates and silverware and carried them into the kitchen. As she moved from one table to the next, her eyes scanned the room. She pushed in chairs and adjusted tables as she worked her way back to the kitchen.

Meredith drank her coffee black, and the heat of it cooled her down for a moment. She was tired. Her arms ached.

"I hope you're hungry," Rachel called across the empty room.

"I'm half-starved," Meredith said.

Once Rachel sat down, Meredith didn't know what to say. She missed the girl, but now that Rachel looked across the table at her with an unwavering gaze, Meredith realized that that was all she wanted—Rachel's uninterrupted attention.

Meredith ate as if she'd never eaten before and smiled at Rachel between bites. When she finished, she said, "It seems you've found a good place for yourself. I'm glad."

"I'm grateful for everything you've done for me," Rachel said. "Truly."

Meredith nodded and pushed her plate into the center of the table. Rachel reached for it, but Meredith placed her hand on top of the girl's. "You'll come to visit, won't you?"

Rachel promised that she would, and that was all that Meredith could ask for. She nodded to the girl and watched her sweep the plate up in her hand and carry it off. She left before Rachel returned.

31

THE NEXT DAY, WHEN FINN APPEARED AT THE RESTAURANT, Rachel wasn't surprised. He ordered lunch without referring to her bag. She was angry, but she made sure to be extra nice to him. He finished his lunch and ordered coffee, and she knew then that he was going to wait until she finished work. She began to lose track of orders. She forgot to bring Max Ballard his home fries, and one of the visiting fisherman got his eggs scrambled when he'd ordered them sunny-side up.

"Is Finn Boyd pestering you again?" Mrs. O'Shea asked. "You want me to get rid of him?"

"No, no, it'll be fine. I'm sorry."

When the last of the customers was gone and Rachel had cleared the tables, Finn folded up his newspaper.

"I thought you were going to come by the shop. I was really looking forward to it."

Rachel kept wiping tables. "I did come by the shop. You weren't there. I told you how much I need my things."

Finn leaned forward onto his elbows. "What about our walk?"

"You're taking advantage of me, and I don't like it. I need my bag."

"Where did you get the money, Rachel?"

"That's not your business."

"You made it my business when you brought it aboard the schooner."

"Please," she said.

"Our walk?"

"I can't see you like that, Mr. Boyd."

"Why not?"

"It's not right and proper, and you shouldn't be asking me."

"You're a lovely girl. I'd do nothing but spoil you and treat you right. In spite of everything, I'd only make your life better. You can count on me to do that."

Rachel shifted from foot to foot and looked around for Mrs. O'Shea. "No, it's not right. You're keeping my bag to trick me into seeing you. Please, go get the bag for me."

"You flirted with me on the boat. Obviously, there's something between us."

"No, I can't."

"Has Mrs. O'Shea or my brother been talking to you?"

"I make my own decisions, thank you very much, and I need you to respect them."

Mrs. O'Shea came from the kitchen and found something to do behind the counter. Her authoritative personality, the respect she received from members of the village, and the sheer fact of her presence drove Finn up from the table.

"If that's your decision," he said curtly and made his way to the door. Rachel could forget about her money. He'd find out where it came from, that was for sure. Then he'd see what she had to say for herself.

Rachel joined Mrs. O'Shea behind the counter and stood close to the woman. "Bye, bye now," Mrs. O'Shea said, waving her dishrag and smiling.

32

FINN RUSHED UP THE DRIVEWAY TO HIS FATHER'S HOUSE STILL angry and embarrassed at how Rachel had sent him away. He'd had enough of people turning him down, and he was going to change his father's mind. It was time, he was ready, and his father needed to see the facts. Finn had a successful business in the fishing industry. He was an experienced fisherman. Didn't it follow that purchasing a fishing boat was the next logical step for him? Hadn't he proven himself over and over again? He pushed through the door and let it slam behind him, then he called from the kitchen, "Father, I've come to talk."

"I'm in my study." Nathaniel Sr.'s voice was harsh, and Finn wondered what was wrong with him. He wasn't going to let his father's bad mood deter him. He needed to stay focused and strong and show his father a firm resolve.

Finn went to the study where Nathaniel Sr. leaned over his desk, account books spread across the expanse of polished mahogany. He worked with a pencil up and down columns of numbers, his spectacles fogged from the sweat on his face.

"I want to talk with you about my business plan," Finn said.

"Not now," Nathaniel Sr. nearly barked at his son. "It seems I've been robbed."

"What are you talking about?"

"There are discrepancies in the reporting from two land holdings in Barnstable managed by the same man, a Mr. Reynolds, who recently moved with his family to Boston. Since he moved three weeks ago, no one's seen him, nor has he corresponded to follow up on outstanding business." Nathaniel Sr. shuffled papers, then slammed his pencil onto the desk and pushed his spectacles back on his head.

Finn was shocked that his father could make a mistake. He was frightened to see his father in a vulnerable position. Believing in his father was what made Finn believe in himself.

"That's preposterous," Finn said, searching his mind for how there could be some mistake, but he couldn't think of anything. He only felt this vague sense of loss. "Don't you check the books every month?"

"Yes, but Reynolds hid it quite well."

"But the bookkeeper, isn't he to blame in this as well?"

"Yes, but it's not his money."

Finn was not only outraged but worried about his father. "How can I help, Father?"

"There's nothing you can do, nothing anyone can do. The money is gone."

"I'm sorry, Father." Finn poured two glasses of whiskey. Nathaniel Sr. sat in his chair in front of the fireplace, and they drank in silence. Outside, Finn inhaled a deep breath of brine and salty air. He resented the intrusion on his thoughts. All this time, he'd been thinking about himself and his own problems and ambitions while his father suffered this terrible blow. His father must be as frightened as Finn was about this moment of vulnerability. How could this happen? Finn wondered over and over again.

Nathaniel Sr. ran his hands over the top of his head, then looked at Finn. "Well, I've given it some thought. I'll look at your business plan again." In his voice, there was both a resignation and a wish to set things right. Finn didn't like his father's ambivalence.

"This isn't the right time."

"You can leave it on my desk."

Nathaniel Sr. finished the whiskey in the bottom of his glass. He said goodbye and went to his bedroom. Finn had another glass of whiskey while sitting in his father's chair. What must it be like to have failed in this way that his father had failed? He wouldn't wish his father's loss on anyone, and he wanted to learn this lesson well. Never trust anyone with your money. Not family, not loyal employees—no one.

Finn finished his drink and carried the empty glasses to the kitchen. He wanted to feel relieved that his father would look at his plan, but he didn't want it to happen like this. He wanted to earn it, not have his father do it because he'd made a mistake and felt more forgiving toward his son for any mistakes he might make. He let the door slam behind him, then reached back to pull it shut as if he could close this day out of his mind. Between Rachel and his father, he felt in a state of disorder. He would go home on the dirt road, where the walk home would be his and his alone.

33

R ACHEL WALKED ALONG THE JETTY, DAVEY KEEPING UP WITH HER brisk step. Beyond the backs of the shops, Rachel could see a single mast sticking up, swaying to the left, then to the right with the rhythm of the waves, but it was Nathaniel she searched for along the horizon. She needed his help and the sooner, the better, or Finn would continue to taunt her, promising her bag and never delivering it.

Past the jetty, the channel was quiet, not a single boat coming in or going out. The only place to look for Nathaniel now was the island, and she walked toward the marsh, Davey still on her heels. He wouldn't care where they were going as long as he had her attention. To distract him from the fact that they were going to the island, she said, "You've never told me much about yourself, Davey."

"Like what do you want to know?"

"What do you think about when you're cutting all those fish?"

"I don't know."

"You must think of something."

"If you want to know the truth, I think about moving off Cape. I want to open a general store or some other type of business that can grow. I can make my own success and not rely on someone like Finn. I've been working since I was twelve years old. I've got money saved, a good amount of it, too. Finn's let me take on more responsibility. He's even given me a raise, but I can't fillet fish for the rest of my life. I'm learning about business, though, how to turn a profit and keep track of money, how to treat customers so they keep coming back."

"That's wonderful," Rachel said, surprised at his ambition. "Isn't your family here in town?"

"My mother is, but she understands. My father ran off," Davey said. "But I remember him. He let me work with him sometimes. He chose me instead of hiring a man to work, said I was strong and a good worker. Maybe he was too cheap to pay for someone, but it made me work hard and feel like a man, even as a small boy. He'd bring me lunch, and we ate with our backs leaning on the stone wall we were building, drinking water from the same bottle. When he left, I found the job with Finn. He'd seen me work with my father and took me on. He's been good to me for the most part. He's just moody, and lately something's gotten into him."

Davey carried a strand of sea hay and peeled away the layers of leaves around the stem. "I want to be my own man," he said.

"Then you will be."

He stopped to look at Rachel as if to assess the verity of her response, and finding it ample, he said, "That means a lot coming from you, Rachel. It truly does."

"Let's walk through the marsh," Rachel said. She liked his sincerity, but sometimes the intensity of his gaze overwhelmed her, and she had to turn away. "I've never been out that way."

They walked behind the Butlers' house and picked up a narrow path tamped down in the grass. Toward the creek, the soil turned to wet clay, and their feet sank slightly into the surface of the earth. Cattails leaned over the path, and they pushed them out of the way to step into the open marsh. There was no wind now, only stillness and the sound of their breathing. In the distance, Nathaniel's shack leaned out of the trees on the island, but neither of them mentioned that as they walked toward it. Davey took her hand and she let him, and they walked in the heat and the sun as if the air kissed their bodies and life didn't exist beyond this day on the marsh with nothing to think about except what to do next.

"Don't get any ideas," Rachel said. She pulled down the edge of her bonnet as the sun drifted directly overhead. "We're friends."

"But—"

"Friends," she said.

He let go of her hand and fell behind her along the trail, sulking. She let him mope for a while, then she cajoled him into walking with her again. His spirits lifted easily, like a young pup, and he stammered on about his plans to build a house above his store.

"I envy your certainty. I've no idea what I'll do," Rachel said.

"You'll marry, won't you?"

Rachel thought for a moment about her father, marriage. She didn't know if she would marry. "I suppose," she answered.

They reached a creek with a weathered board stretched across. Rachel held her skirt up and stepped onto the board, testing its strength before she put her full weight on it. She took another step, then another until she was over the creek. When it was Davey's turn, he scurried over the board like any marsh rat.

They caught their breath and stared at Nathaniel's shack.

"What are we doing?" Davey asked.

"I need to talk to Nathaniel."

"He doesn't like people out here. Let's go back." He reached for Rachel's hand, but she pulled it away. He followed her across another creek, and the shack took on shape and dimension. The wood structure had a west-facing window they could see through the trees, and there was a clearing evident from where the trees thinned out and revealed open, airy light.

They walked side by side, then one behind the other as they followed the bushes, looking for an opening to the clearing. "Here it is," Rachel said, and she stopped in the middle of the path.

"Stop," Davey whispered, but he followed as Rachel pushed brambles out of the way, taking care not to let one go and hit Davey. The rustling sound of the woods—squirrels foraging, branches scratching, sparrows rushing through the trees—filled the stillness of the afternoon. It was the music of the woods, she told herself as she stepped into the clearing. "Nathaniel," she called, not wanting to startle him if he was in the shack.

"He's not here," Davey said. "Let's go."

Rachel was taken with the raw beauty of the shack, the simplicity of a single chair leaning against the building, the circle of stones with the grate where he must cook the fish he caught.

She squatted by the fire and imagined cooking over the grate.

"What if he finds out we were here? There's no telling what he'll do. If he's anything like Finn, we're in big trouble." Davey looked into the distance as if Nathaniel would appear walking across the marsh at any moment.

Rachel placed her hand on the shack's door latch. "He's nothing like Finn. Come on. I'm curious." The rusty iron was warm beneath her thumb, but she opened the door and stepped inside the shack. It was dark, but as her eyes adjusted, she saw the bed, the impression of his head on the pillow. A wooden counter had been built along one wall, and there was flour in a jar and salt. A basket with potatoes, turnips, and onions. Wrapped in cheesecloth, salt cod, and left on the counter, a loaf of bread. Not much to live on, but enough. The few items he had, he kept in order: the bed was made, the food lined neatly on the counter.

A fork, spoon, and knife stood in a jar next to a tin cup, and a small ceramic bowl sat atop a tin plate.

On a shelf on one wall was a scattering of tintypes, one of the three brothers around the time of the accident, she thought, based on their ages. She held the picture in the light from the door. Nathaniel always had that serious, brooding look, only it was deeper now. Finn, dark and handsome, looked worried and cocky at the same time, while the young boy who must have been Jacob smiled at his brothers in the most carefree manner. He must have eased them in some way, Rachel thought, with his handsome smile and apparent lightness of heart.

"Hurry up," Davey said. "What are you doing in there?"

Rachel left the shack and pulled the door shut behind her. She went to the pump and raised the handle until a thin stream of cold water ran over her hand, then she poked a stick in the ashes of the fire pit. Rachel felt an intimacy with Nathaniel, knowing the inside of his shack, the spare quality of the small room. None of the books she'd imagined. None of the comforts of soft quilts for rugs or paint to brighten things up. Only a rustic wooden space with the bare essentials he needed to live, and that made sense when she thought about it. That was Nathaniel, nothing more than the bare essentials—the way he talked to people, the way his body had nothing extra, the way he only fished for what he ate. A life stripped to the bone.

"Isn't this place just like him?"

"I don't know what you're talking about."

"You don't know him like I do."

"Just because he came to visit you a few times doesn't mean you know him."

"But he rescued me. He risked his life." Nathaniel made her feel safe in a way that no one ever had, and that was worth something.

Davey grimaced and chucked a rock through the trees. "Can we go now?"

After she circled the shack, she let Davey lead her back across the marsh. She didn't look back but let her gaze drift beyond the bay to the line of haze that hovered at the horizon. She looked at the sun glittering off the vibrant green seagrass as it drifted listlessly in the summer air. At the way the water in the creeks eddied and swirled and the bits of seaweed and algae drifted along in the incoming tide. The world was always in motion, and Rachel was in motion along with it, with that marvelous world of hope: hope that she could move beyond her fate as the daughter of a derelict, a girl who poisoned her father.

She didn't complain when Davey nearly ran. She didn't complain when she was out of breath and struggling to keep up. When they reached the marsh near the Butlers', they slowed to a walk, but still, she struggled to keep up with him all the way to the fish shop.

"Do you know where he's hiding my bag?"

"What bag?"

Finn appeared in the doorway then, rubbing his bloody hands together. "I gotta do everything around here? Get your skinny ass in here and work."

Davey started toward the door, and Finn disappeared back into the shop. Before Davey crossed the threshold, he looked back at Rachel. "We'll walk together again?"

"Yes," she said. "Soon."

34

MEREDITH NARROWED HER EYES INTO THE DISTANCE WHERE strings of pale clouds punctuated a sky as blue as the water winding through the marsh. She stared at Nathaniel's shack barely visible through the trees, looking for the source of her joy, but there was no sign of him. She felt a sense of possibility, as if somehow she'd forgotten her life, and it had all come rushing back the minute Nathaniel put his arms around her. This agitation made her want change like she wouldn't have imagined possible a few weeks ago.

Now that Nathaniel was going to come in off the marsh, what was she going to do about Theo? She turned from the window and went to her needlepoint in the sitting room. She worked the stitches quickly until she stabbed her finger with the needle and bled drops of red onto jagged blue stitches. With her thumb pressed against the pinprick, she tried to stop the blood, but she felt a larger wound, one that wouldn't heal until she left this house.

What would she say to Theo? How would she begin? *I don't love you, Theo. I no longer want to be your wife.* They could get an annulment from the church or simply decide to live apart. She hesitated when she thought of the impropriety. She imagined the conversations with her mother. "Meredith, how could you even think of such a thing. I will not allow it!"

"It's my decision, Mother."

"And it's a very poor one indeed." Her mother would cross her arms over her chest and wait for Meredith to respond, but Meredith knew that nothing would change her mother's mind and that she would have to live with the consequences of her decision alone. She knew that her mother would die of shame, her own daughter an adulteress. Would Meredith be ashamed, too, to have the world know of her affair? Adultery was completely against everything she'd been raised to believe. While she loved and cared for Theo, she had always loved Nathaniel in a passionate way that couldn't be held back, and this final fact drove her up from her chair to look toward his shack. *He was there. He was right there.*

Meredith shook herself loose from the view and returned to her needlepoint in the parlor. Her thumb began to feel like a pincushion with each nervous stick. When the front door clattered open, her husband entered the hall. He didn't bother to remove his coat and boots on his way into the parlor. His smile brightened his eyes. He leaned forward to kiss her, and she tilted her head to accept his lips on her cheek.

"I've had a winning week," he said. "I've gotten a contract with a large outfit out of Boston, and Father has put me in charge of the account."

Theo poured them each a bit of bourbon, and they toasted his success.

That night when Theo took her to bed, she watched the white shape of him emerge from his clothes, and she knew how he would fold the sheets back into a triangle before he slid beneath them, how he would raise himself on one elbow to look down at her before he kissed her, even the rhythm of his hips upon her. She felt the weight of her duty to be his wife because she knew him in this most intimate way, but when she stared into his eyes, she saw a man she no longer loved, and she turned away from him to hide her tears.

In the morning, Theo began to examine the changes Meredith had made around the house.

"You've moved things around," he said. "I'm not sure I like it."

"Well, why not?"

"It's different. Where's my mother's crystal?"

"We never use it, Theo. Aren't you tired of those old things? Can't we find the things we like together and put those out?"

"Those were the things I liked," he said, hurt in his voice. "I thought you liked them, too."

"I do. It's just—"

"You don't, or you wouldn't have changed everything."

He picked up a tintype of her mother and sister that she'd placed on the bookshelf next to a tintype of his parents. Never had she brought her own pictures into his family collection. Then he examined a daguerreotype of his own mother and father, himself with his brother when he was a boy. There seemed no end to his interest in himself. She sat in the easy chair and watched her husband rapt with his own memories. She removed her earrings, two round pearls that she rolled in her palm with her thumb. The curtains were drawn against the August sun, the light dim but enough to see by, and what caught her eye were the portraits of Theo's distant relatives, people neither of them had ever met.

"Theo," she said.

"I want you to put everything back." He didn't look up from the pictures in his hands.

"I won't."

"You must. This is our family home."

"It's your family home." Meredith rose from the chair and faced him. He was taller than her, and in his coat, he looked oddly official. "There's nothing of me here, Theo. You must see—"

"You're everywhere. You're my home."

"I don't feel that way. You have an entire life going on at your business, and I'm here all day, in this house that is drenched with your family. I need to make it more livable for me. Frankly, I'm surprised it's taken me as long as it has."

"I don't know who you are anymore, taking in that girl and letting Nathaniel Boyd into our house. If ever there was a stray dog."

Meredith was stunned. She didn't think he knew that Nathaniel visited her.

"You think I didn't know?" Theo shouted. "Everyone in town knows. You know how people talk. How could you humiliate me like that?"

"Don't raise your voice. You've no idea what it's like to be in this house day after day with your ancestors starting down at me, as if blaming me for simply being here."

He stared at her, infuriated. "I'm talking about Nathaniel!"

Meredith was silent now. The dimensions of the room felt close and airless, and she stood near the window.

"Ever since that girl came into our house," Theo said.

He launched himself out of the room and up the stairs to their bedroom. She heard the door to his wardrobe swing open and bang against the wall. He'd always meant to pull the piece out from the wall so that the door wouldn't hit, but it was one of the things he never found the time to do.

When he appeared in fresh clothes, he looked in on Meredith, but he didn't say *goodbye* or *I'm leaving*. He left in a clatter of boots on the floor, and the door slammed in an angry burst that was his final word.

Meredith was relieved when she heard the clomp of horse hooves down the drive. She drank her tea and ate a biscuit to sooth her nerves. She knew then that she would leave him.

When she went out the front door to the edge of the yard, she looked with the spyglass to see if Nathaniel was at his shack. When she didn't see him, she swung the spyglass around to look toward his boat, but he wasn't there. She went back into the house to wait for him, and when he finally entered through the kitchen door, she ran her fingers through the sweaty path on the back of his neck. She kissed him hard, his lips, his neck. Then she stopped.

"I didn't touch him," she said.

35

FINN SAT BY THE FIRE IN NATHANIEL SR.'S LIVING ROOM. HE didn't know how some things could go so right and some so wrong. Since the day he'd helped his father review the accounts, Nathaniel Sr. had spoken to him not as a son who had to prove himself but as a man with insight and an opinion. This was a swing in the tide of events that he never could've predicted, and all because his father had been swindled. It amazed him how life could change in a matter of days. He waited while Nathaniel Sr. poured drinks in the mahogany-paneled room, rich with the smell of oiled wood. Finn loved the house he'd grown up in, even though any trace of that former life had been replaced with the face of his father's wealth. The combination of memories and money held him in the promise of his own potential.

"Here you go, Son." His father passed a glass of whiskey. "So what brings you up here?"

"Elizabeth—"

His father nodded and sipped his whiskey. He didn't pursue whatever was wrong with Finn's marriage. He looked pale in the firelight, not his usual ruddy, suntanned self. In his eyes, something soft shone, a kind of love, Finn thought, or wanted to believe.

"You been getting out, Father?"

"I must admit, I haven't been feeling in top form."

"You seem tired out."

"I haven't been sleeping."

Finn was concerned to see his father looking so weak. He could be strong for his father, yet he felt this strange current of vulnerability when faced with his father's fragility. His father had always been stronger than all of them in spirit and physicality. To see him diminished was to feel that they could all be diminished, and this frightened Finn. Was it his father's health, or was it the errors he'd made that had led to the embezzlement, or was it both? If it was his health, why hadn't Finn seen it before this?

"Let's have our dinner. Bea's left a pot roast and potatoes."

"I thought I smelled something delicious," Finn said, glad to have the conversation turn to something ordinary.

—⌇⌇⌇—

Finn didn't know what inspired him to walk up the hill toward his father's house the day after having dinner with him. It was unfamiliar, this feeling of concern, but Nathaniel Sr. hadn't looked well last night.

"Hello, Father," Finn called into the quiet. In the kitchen, he saw the glass on the table, then his father, pale and sprawled in the most unnatural position on the floor. Finn dropped to his knees, lowered his ear to his father's mouth to listen for his breathing. The sounds of the kitchen—the slow tick of the clock, the pump dripping into the sink, the icebox creaking—were exaggerated by his father's faint, shallow breaths.

"Father," Finn said, pulling his father's right arm out from beneath him. "Father."

His father groaned. Finn soaked a dish towel in cold water from the pump, then pressed it to his father's forehead.

"Father, I'm here. Wake up," but his father didn't wake up, and Finn began to panic.

"I'm going for the doctor. Don't move. Please, don't move."

But it was Finn who couldn't move. He held his father's wide hand. The lack of color in his father's face and the slack look of his jaw frightened him.

"I'll be back," he said, and he lay his father's hand on the floor as if it were a bird with a broken wing.

IV

36

THE READING OF THE WILL TOOK PLACE IN FRANCIS MILLER'S office. Nathaniel sat in a heavy wooden chair next to his brother, his elbows on the armrests as if the chair could hold him to this place and the inevitability of his father's final words. Bookshelves lined the walls with leather-bound books, the gold lettering like doorways to cold, hard facts. Finn sat in his chair with one leg jittering until he stood up and gazed around the room, at the gavel on a wooden pedestal, the diplomas from Harvard in curly maple frames.

"Sit down," Nathaniel said. "You're getting on my nerves." Finn complied. He straightened his tie, then loosened it, then tightened it again. He undid the top button on his frock coat and stretched the fabric loose from around his throat. Nathaniel knew now that Finn would have more than enough money to start a fishing fleet. He would go to Boston to purchase boats, and he'd need a crew to sail them back for him. Nets, hauling winches, navigational equipment—there would be a lot to do. He believed that Finn was ready for it. Every ounce of effort in his body would be spent on managing the fleet, managing his wealth. Maybe Finn would move his family into their father's house. Nathaniel certainly didn't want it.

A dark band of clouds blew in from the east, and the office grew full of shadows. They waited for Francis in silence. Nathaniel sat still as a board, thinking of their father laid out in the living room of the family home. There had been a prosaic beauty to his father in repose, as if all of his busyness had stopped and had left in its place only the quietude of his being. Finn hadn't been able to look at their father. Death up close frightened him, and he stayed in the kitchen and drank whiskey.

Nathaniel wore a new brown frock coat, cut loose on his thin figure, and a beige shirt with a brown-plaid tie that had little gold and white stripes running through it. When he'd put the suit on at his father's house, he'd stood before the mirror. In spite of the new clothes, he still looked rough. He needed a haircut, a shave, but he'd only had time to comb his hair back and flatten it with his father's pomade.

Francis Miller came into the room, and in a huff of rustling papers, he slammed the door shut behind him. He wore a white shirt with balloon sleeves rolled to the elbow and linen pants that rode high on his waist.

"Now, let's see, boys. We've got some business to attend to. I'm very sorry to hear about your father. He was a fine man. He will be remembered well."

Their father's funeral had been well attended, with people waiting in line to view his body, then gathering in crowds at the cemetery. The boys had escorted the casket, solemn, eyes downcast. They'd stood at the graveside and followed the minister's prayers by rote, so stunned were they that their father was gone. When people gave their condolences, they nodded and said thank you with a numb sense of duty.

Francis shuffled through papers on his desk, moved books from one pile to another, then having placed his hand on the document he sought, he leaned back in his chair.

"Your father had an appointment to revise his will, but we never got to it. I don't know what his intentions were, but I think you two might have some idea."

"Well, what does it say?" Finn asked.

"I'm not sure how to say this, but to get right to the point..." Francis looked down into the will and took in a suck of breath before he said, "He's left the entire estate to Nathaniel."

"What? That's not possible!" Finn leapt from his chair and leaned over Francis's desk. "You need to explain this to me."

"He wanted Nathaniel to take over his interests. Your father left it at Nathaniel's discretion to distribute the money."

"That's utter rubbish. He wouldn't do that." Then he pointed at Nathaniel. "You! You'd really stoop this low to win Meredith over? How could you?"

Nathaniel touched his brother's arm, but Finn yanked away. "I had nothing to do with this," Nathaniel said.

"Shut up!" Finn paced across the small room, sweat forming on his hairline, then he returned to stand in front of Francis's desk. He went from fighting anger to a look of despair.

"As I said, he had an appointment to revise his will," Francis said. "You have time to sort things out between yourselves. I suggest that you let it sit for a while and think about what your father would've wanted. I'm sorry it's such a mess, boys, but I have every confidence you can sort it out." He straightened the pile of papers on his desk and slid them into a folder. Nathaniel knew that this was their signal to go. He didn't want to inherit everything. He didn't want the responsibility, nor did he know what to do with his father's assets. Finn should've been the one to take over the estate.

After taking their leave, they walked to the harbor in silence, the drizzle a mist on their skin. Finn held his head facing directly into the mist, his gait determined, as if he had somewhere to go that was more important than walking right here with his brother.

"I'm sure he was going to change the will," Nathaniel said.

"You can't know that." Finn kicked a rock along the road. "He never trusted me. It's obvious now." Nathaniel knew that their father's disappointment in Finn had started when they were boys. Every fear Finn'd ever had about his father's love had come true in a simple swipe of the pen signing the will.

"There's plenty of money, Finn. You can get a schooner, start your fleet. We'll manage the estate together." Nathaniel wanted to ease his brother, as if sharing the estate could make up for the fact that their father had denied Finn this final time. "We have to get his land interests sorted out, meet with the bookkeeper and business lawyer about that. He had a lot of projects going on."

Nathaniel stopped in the middle of the road. He wanted to be on the marsh or working on his father's timberland, not worrying about the responsibilities of an estate. These thoughts passed over his mind like wafting streaks of clouds that then were gone, and he focused on the situation in front of him. "We'll be partners, Finn. That's what Father would've wanted. You'll have to deal with the business accounts. That's your strength, not mine."

"Yes," Finn said. "I'll take care of that." He walked in silence for a while, looking at the willow trees that hung over the swamp, watching the cardinal that swooped onto a branch that hung over the road. Then he said, "He hated me, it's clear now."

"That's not true."

"He hated me because I was just like him, hard-working, ambitious." Nathaniel stood by and watched his brother pull a branch from the side of the road. Finn went into the woods and swung the branch at a tree as if he could beat all feeling out of himself. "There's nothing left for me, Nathaniel. Don't you understand?"

"But I said—"

"It doesn't matter. He died hating me."

"He didn't hate you, Finn." Nathaniel's words fell into the under-growth as if they hadn't existed.

Finn dropped the branch and bent over to catch his breath, then he left the woods, and they walked up the road toward the harbor. "Do you think you can handle the land, the tenants, the wealth of his estate?"

"We'll do it together," Nathaniel said.

"Once you get your hands on the money, there's no telling what you'll do."

"How can you say that?"

"I'd learn Father's business. He should've trained me before he died. He should've trusted me."

"Yes," Nathaniel said. "He should've."

———

The next morning, Nathaniel woke from a sporadic sleep and saw the white plaster ceiling above him and the heavy wooden beam painted white to match. He'd been staying in his father's house since the funeral. Sun poured in the tall windows, bathing the room in a soft glare. He noticed that the candle had burned down and scolded himself for falling asleep with it lit. Memories of the past week clamored through his mind—his father's death, the will, Finn's rage. All of it made him tired, too tired to sleep. He'd woken every hour, frustrated that it wasn't morning yet, frustrated that sleep wouldn't carry him away. He rustled through his closet for a pair of trousers and a linen shirt, casual but nice clothes. He didn't know what to expect of the day in his father's absence or how he was supposed to make sense of the estate. The smell of ham cooking on the griddle reached him from the kitchen, and he pulled on a pair of shoes with no socks and went downstairs.

Bea, with her hefty backside to him, didn't turn around. She pushed the ham back and forth, flipped it over, and waited for Nathaniel to say something, but he had nothing to say. "Coffee's right there," she said, pointing with the spatula.

—⁓—

After breakfast, Nathaniel walked toward the fish shop, but when he neared the harbor, he turned across the marsh toward Meredith's house. The sun was a white blare, the air a salty tinge in his nostrils.

When she opened the door, he said, "He left me everything, Meredith."

She led him through the hallway, walking with her hand on his hip, guiding him forward. He stood before the settee in the parlor as if on his feet, he could face his uncertainty. Meredith sat and looked up at him, waiting for what he would say.

"Now I'm responsible for his life's work—the land business, his investments, all of it. If I give half the estate to Finn, am I shirking my responsibilities?" He let his weight drop onto the cushion beside Meredith and turned to face her. "Did he just not make it back to the lawyer in time to change his will, or did he really want to leave me the money?"

"Your father trusted you. That's why he left the money to you."

"He did it to get me off the island."

Meredith turned her silver bracelets around on her wrist as if straightening them out. They jangled as she fiddled with them, then she shook her wrist as if she could shake the bracelets into place and herself along with them. She reached a hand out to him, and he clasped her fingers as if they were a lifeline.

"I don't know what to do," he said. "About this estate, about us, about anything."

"I want to leave Theo," Meredith said. "I need to tell him."

"Are you sure?"

"I'll go to my mother's for a while. I don't want to stay here."

"You'll be with me, Meredith?"

She ran her hand through Nathaniel's hair and brushed her fingers down his cheek. "I can't stand living here any longer and waiting for you to visit me. I want to wake up with you and fall asleep in the same bed. I want our old dream."

"I want that, too," he said. He took her jaw lightly in his hand and leaned his face toward her. They kissed deeply, and she leaned her body into him. "When will you tell him?"

Theo's horse clomped in the drive, and Meredith let Nathaniel's hand go. "You have to go," she whispered. She led him to the side door and kissed him quickly on the mouth. He turned from her and hurried down to the beach, where he walked along the water to the harbor. He didn't turn around or look over his shoulder to catch sight of Theo. He knew well enough what the man would do if he saw Nathaniel leaving his house. He hastened his step, then took the road to the foot of his father's driveway. It was his driveway now, and he wanted to walk up the hill like he owned it, but he felt like a visitor.

At his father's house, the air was cool as it whisked in from the bay. The strain of the windmill, the steady chirp of crickets, the creak of the barn door—all of it was familiar, and Nathaniel tried to relax into his father's chair in the living room. He thought of how his father's body had looked empty without him in it. The way his hair had been combed to the left over his forehead didn't look right. His father wore his hair combed back. Nathaniel had stood in the downstairs bedroom where they'd lifted his father onto the bed. Heat had pressed against the windows. Heat hung in the room like an unwelcome mourner. Nathaniel hadn't made it in time to say good-bye and felt the loss of those last words. Loss had become part of the air he breathed, and he imagined that his father's death would settle in among the rest.

He recalled the look on his father's face when he and Finn turned up after the wreck without Jacob, the look of terror as he counted only two sons, then the relief of having two sons back, and then the terrible grief. He was a man, after all, with losses of his own. What difference did it make if he hadn't been able to accept Nathaniel's life? All that mattered now was that his father had wanted only to do what he thought was best for him. In realizing this, Nathaniel softened toward the man. He felt sadness that his father was gone and their shared sadness for losing Jacob, and then the sobs came all at once.

He went outside where he could see Meredith's house, the windows aglow with lantern light. He waited for some sign of her—a curtain pulled back or a candle lit in an upstairs window—but there was no sign, only the certain knowledge that she was there. This eased him enough that he felt sleepy and went back into the house where the press of the settee against his body held him in his dreams.

37

THE STAIRS TO RACHEL'S ROOM RAN UP THE BACK OF THE restaurant and faced out over the marsh. Beneath the stairs, amid trash barrels, discarded flour sacks, and an old bicycle tire, Finn waited. He didn't know what to say to her. He scratched his foot back and forth in the dirt, then he sat on the ground and leaned against the building, waiting.

He heard Rachel coming before he saw her, her feet sweeping along the marsh grass. He grabbed the bottom of a stair and pulled himself up from the ground, but he kept himself hidden. He waited in the cave of his anticipation, his mind racing with images of her pressed against him, her face turned up in expectation. She walked with purpose, one hand holding the edge of her skirt, her other arm swinging with her forward motion. As she approached, her hair became visible, the way it came loose at her brow and stuck to her forehead with the heat of her body, her eyes bright. The soft curve of her nose made a shadow against her cheek as she tilted her head, and her lips appeared painted as dark outlines.

"Rachel," he wanted to say, but he couldn't utter the words.

She hesitated before she stepped toward the bottom of the stairs. He heard the even sound of her breathing, smelled the lavender soap on her skin, the sweet, young smell of her sweat. She looked up the alley between buildings toward the harbor, then up the stairs.

When her hand was on the bannister, Finn stepped out.

"Rachel," he said.

She stepped back away from him, startled. "What are you doing here?"

"I've come to see you. My father—"

"I'm sorry about your father, Mr. Boyd."

"Please, call me Finn."

"I'm sorry, but you can't be here."

He stepped toward her. "Rachel, what can I do? I'll do anything."

"Please go," she said, her voice cross now.

He wanted to have a simple conversation. He wanted the chance to know her and be the kind of man he felt beneath his anger, a softer man, a hurt man. Didn't she know that he had feelings, too? Wouldn't she ever forgive him?

When she backed away from him, he panicked. "I only want to know you," he said. She turned away, and he saw every loss he'd ever known— his father denying him, his wife forgetting him, Jacob. He had to stop thinking about it. Before he knew what he was doing, he grabbed her by the upper arms and shook her as if he could make her understand that he only wanted to love her. "Tell me, what do I have to do?"

"Let me go!"

He pushed her against the building and pinned her shoulders to the wall. He searched her face for some sign of love, and finding none, he pressed his lips against hers as if he could breathe love into her. She turned her face away as he tried to meet her lips, but he took her jaw with a firm grip and held her still, pressed his lips to hers.

"See what you make me do?"

"Stop it," she yelled. "I don't love you. You have to stop this!"

He leaned in to her, his face close enough that he could whisper in her ear. "I know who you are," he said. "You're a liar and a thief. You want your money back, but you're not willing to give anything in return."

She pushed against his shoulders to shove him away, but he leaned his weight in to her, holding her back against the wall. "You're a criminal," he said. "You think if I told Nathaniel, he wouldn't send you back where you came from?"

"Go ahead," she yelled. "Tell him! Do whatever you want. Just get off of me!"

When he eased his weight back from her, she broke away. He didn't chase her—this wasn't how he wanted her. He wanted her to yield to him as he would yield to her. He watched her run along the back of the shops to the road. He spat into the dirt and let her go.

38

THERE WAS BARELY ENOUGH MOONLIGHT TO SEE BY, BUT HER FEET followed a rut in the gravel and sand. She kept running toward the Boyd house. If anyone could keep Finn away from her, it was Nathaniel. Her skirt swung at her legs until she nearly tripped. She ran until she couldn't run anymore, then she could do nothing but walk at a quickened pace, arms swinging at her sides to pull her body along. Her breath scraped her lungs and tore through her nostrils. She had to stop, rest, but fear was fully upon her. She never should've flirted with him that first day on the boat or sat with him in the restaurant. She never should've told him that she would take a walk. How was she to know that he would react like this? As she ran up the hill, she felt the threat of him behind her. The sweat along her back and under her arms wet her dress. She didn't want to cry, not now, not before she got up the hill. She started walking again, nearly staggering, toward the house.

Her heart lifted at the sight of a dim light in the first-floor window, and she slowed now that she knew Nathaniel was there. The light grew brighter, and she cut through the hedge and went around to the kitchen door.

"Nathaniel!" She called out to him. "It's Rachel."

He appeared shirtless, startled, his hair pressed up on one side where he'd been sleeping on it. He led her to the chair by the kitchen table and directed her to sit. "Tell me," he said.

"Your brother," she said.

"What's happened?"

Rachel began trembling. "You can't tell him I told you."

"You can tell me," Nathaniel said.

"He waited for me in the dark, beneath the stairs to my room. He forced himself on me, kissed me on the mouth, threatened me."

Nathaniel stood up. He turned from the girl and looked out the window toward the harbor and his brother's shop.

"He'll do it again," Rachel said. "I'm afraid."

"I'll stop him."

"If he knows I told you—"

"It will not happen again, Rachel. I promise you." Nathaniel leaned toward her and let her rest against the curve of his body.

A ragged intake of breath, and she began sobbing. She wanted to tell him about the money, but she was afraid of what he would do. She wanted to go home, but she didn't know where to go. Home was suddenly just an idea in her head, a misty feeling that she couldn't associate with any place she knew.

39

THE NEXT DAY, NATHANIEL SENT FOR HIS BROTHER UNDER THE guise of discussing business. When Finn arrived, Nathaniel poured him a drink, but Finn pushed Nathaniel's hand away from the bottle and poured it himself. A silence hung below the sound of the men, a silence that contained the absence of their father, the absence of their mother and Jacob and the life they had lived together. The silence contained the inevitability of death and the fact of their father's will.

In the living room, Nathaniel prepared himself to speak. He watched Finn sip his drink and look around the room as if there was something he wanted and couldn't find.

"I know what you did to Rachel," Nathaniel said.

"I don't know what you're talking about."

"This will stop, and it will stop right now." Nathaniel stood over his brother where Finn sat in their father's chair. "You've no right to go after her like that."

"I've as much of a right as the next man." Finn looked up at Nathaniel over the edge of his glass.

"You don't have any right to force yourself on her."

"You don't know anything about that girl."

"I can't rely on you to be responsible for our father's money if you lose control like that. How can I trust you?"

"I have every right to be angry." Finn stood now and paced before the empty fireplace. "Father left everything to you. You've no idea what that feels like."

"You can't take it out on Rachel."

"I wasn't taking it out on her. You must know that I regret it." Finn finished the whiskey in two swift gulps, and his expression turned smug as he lit a cigar. "What are you going to do with Father's cigars?"

His sudden lack of interest in the situation infuriated Nathaniel. "Until you prove that you can leave her alone, I'll not give you a dime, Finn."

Finn stared at him as if trying to find a foothold, and finding none, he shoved his brother back against the fireplace. Nathaniel shook his head, knowing that Finn had just proved that he couldn't control his rage.

"It's not your money, Nathaniel! He was going to change the will."

"But he didn't. It's your anger, Finn. You're not trustworthy."

Nathaniel wanted to feel confident in having made a decision, but he only felt a sense of regret for having been put in charge of his father's estate. He didn't want to use his position against his brother, but he could think of no other way to keep Finn away from Rachel.

Finn poured another shot of whiskey, then took a drink from the bottle. "You think you can control me," he said.

"Go home," Nathaniel said.

"I'm taking this with me," Finn told him, swinging the bottle as if it was all the power he had in the world.

40

FINN STOOD IN THE FRONT WINDOW OF HIS SHOP, LOOKING OVER the few fishing boats that had remained in the harbor for the day, their masts gently rocking with the rhythm of the waves. If he wanted a boat, he needed to appease his brother, which meant he needed to apologize to the girl. He removed his apron and rolled it into a ball that he placed on the stool by the cash register. He finally knew the right thing to do. Once Rachel understood his remorse, she'd forgive him. He'd promise that it would never happen again. He'd promise to leave her alone. Then it occurred to him, the bag. That was the only way he could win her over.

The bells rang over the restaurant door, and he stood near the entrance, waiting for her to emerge from the kitchen. There she was with a series of plates up one arm, her strawberry-blond hair pulled up in a neat little bun, her face radiant. She served a table of fishermen, sliding each plate across the table and chatting affably with the men until she wiped her hands on her apron and turned to check the next table. That was when she saw him.

"You've no right," she said in front of everyone, then her eyes settled on her bag.

Mrs. O'Shea came out from behind the counter and confronted Finn with the heft of her presence. "You're not welcome here," she said.

"I've come to apologize," he said, stepping toward Rachel, holding the bag out in front of him.

"Go," Mrs. O'Shea told him.

Faces looked up from plates of food. Eyes watched to see what he would do.

"Rachel, I'm sorry. I never meant to—"

"Get out, now." Mrs. O'Shea shoved him toward the door.

Rachel ran into the kitchen and away from him.

"Rachel," he called.

But she couldn't hear him.

Mrs. O'Shea pushed him outside, grabbed the bag for Rachel, and closed the door against him.

He went back to his shop, and there was Davey standing at the counter like he owned the place. "What are you doing standing around? Isn't there fish needs filleting?"

"I'm working the counter. You asked me to—"

"I'm telling you now," Finn said as he slammed his fist on the counter. "Get to work out back."

Davey took his bloody work apron from the nail over the gutting table and shook it out before putting it on over his clean clothes. He stepped into the front of the shop where Finn leaned over the cash register, staring into the rows of iced fish.

"I know what you did," Davey said. "You can't get away with that. It's not right."

"You don't know anything, you runt." Finn pushed Davey out of his way and went to the gutting table. "Get out of here. I'll do it myself." When Davey handed Finn the apron, Finn threw it on the floor. He opened a crate of haddock and took a fish in each hand, then slapped them down on the table. "You think you know your way around a fish," he said.

He took a knife from the block and held the first fish down with the palm of his left hand while he cut with his right. He made clean, even strokes with the knife to free the guts from the fish, and then he folded the fillets back from skeleton. His precision energized him until he recalled the sight of Rachel's back as she ran away from him into the kitchen, and he felt Mrs. O'Shea's hands on him, pushing him out of the restaurant. His cuts into the second fish became jagged, and the fillet was a ragged mess. "Goddammit!"

He stabbed the knife into the counter so that the blade twanged and swung from where it stuck in the wood.

"What are you standing there staring at me for? Get to work!"

Davey shook his head and went to the front of the shop where the work was cleaner and he could deal with customers like a grown man. When Finn appeared from the back of the store, wiping the blood from his hands on a rag and dabbing the rag at the blood on his shirt, he stared at Davey where he was wiping down the counter. "You think every kid has the opportunity I give you?"

Davey stopped his work, startled.

"My own father didn't give me the chances I give you." The boy looked scared, and this made Finn feel better. He said, "Get back to work."

41

THE STEELY-GRAY SKY HUNG LOW OVER RACHEL AND DAVEY AS they walked along the jetty. The sky was like a bad mood, a foreboding, and a rush of cool air sweeping up from between the rocks shook her. "He's out of control," Rachel said. Davey would know she was talking about Finn. He always knew what she was talking about.

"He's not going to leave you alone," Davey said, stopping on the rocks and turning Rachel toward him. "You know I have plans. I'll leave with you. I'll take you anywhere you want to go."

"There's no need for anyone to go anywhere." Now that she had her bag back, she wanted to feel a sense of ease, but the money only frightened her. Why hadn't Finn stolen any of it? What if he came after her again?

"You don't know what he's capable of," Davey said. He told her about Finn with the knife, about his unpredictable moods and his bad temper.

Rachel stared blankly across the water, into distances Davey couldn't know about. She'd already run away from home. She wasn't going to run away again.

"I'm going either way, with or without you. I've got steady work with Finn, but I'm never going to get anywhere cutting up fish for a living. I want more." He looked past her then, toward the road that led off the Cape. "I'm going to take my savings and find some place where I can make a good start. If it's not with you, so be it, Rachel, but I think it's a mistake for you to stay here. You could come with me."

She didn't know if he said that only to force her to make a decision or if he really meant it. Would he really leave? She thought of Finn coming into the restaurant and how Mrs. O'Shea had protected her. It made her feel safe, and she knew that Nathaniel would protect her, too.

"I want you to come with me. It's the perfect time to make a fresh start. We can do it together. We can make something of ourselves, Rachel."

She wanted to please him, but her place was here.

"Please stay," she said.

"I'm leaving at the end of the week when I get paid. You can come with me or not."

"Please," she said.

—◁◦▷—

The sound of the tenant downstairs, the turn of another roomer's keys in a door, even the familiar harbor sounds drove Rachel to slide the dresser in front of her door. The tenant below her banged a broom against the ceiling and yelled something that Rachel couldn't hear. She looked under her bed to make sure her bag was still there, then frightened anew, she sat in the only chair and looked at the tintypes of her mother and sister. What would they want her to do? They would want her to be happy, and she was happy right here in Yarmouth Port. Her life had felt filled with promise until Finn Boyd stepped into it.

She undressed quickly, as if her very nakedness was a threat. In her nightdress, she slid beneath the covers. The candlelight flickered and left corners of the room in darkness. She kept her eyes from those places and tried to focus on the globe of light in her proximity. She didn't want Davey to go. Even though he was barely a man, she felt his devotion to her. She had leaned on that more than she wanted to admit. She didn't want to blow out the candle. She'd let it burn down and go out once she was asleep. With her pillow firmly tucked beneath her head and another pillow tucked by her belly as if she were spooning her sister, Katherine—for this was how she'd slept for most of her life, and she could fall asleep no other way—she closed her eyes. Every creak in the floorboards, moth against the window, brush of wind upon her face forced her eyes open, and she squeezed the pillow closer and shut her eyes once more.

She made her mind play a story that she had practiced with Katherine to help them fall asleep. She imagined bubbles pouring into her toes until her toes were tingling. Then the bubbles moved into her foot until her foot was tingling, then up into her calves. Whenever she heard a sound, she forced her mind to the tingling in her knees until finally she fell asleep, clutching her sister in her dreams.

42

FINN SAT ON THE SWING OUTSIDE HIS OWN HOUSE LIKE AN INTER-loper. He wanted to go in, but he didn't want to go in. He swung the bottle of whiskey at his side, then took a hard swig. He watched his family sitting at the kitchen table, looking down while Elizabeth said grace. She was wearing an apple-green dress with a modest neckline, and she'd rolled the sleeves up her forearms so that they wouldn't dip into the potatoes as she spooned them onto each plate. The children were tired, hair mussed and eyes fading.

When he entered through the kitchen door and into the midst of their meal, Elizabeth dropped the spoon onto the table and stood upright.

Then she picked up the spoon and continued to serve each child. She didn't look up at Finn, only at the children, whose manners she corrected and whose mouths she wiped.

Finn ignored her, too, and went to his study, a small room off the living room that had formerly been the borning room. He'd converted it by adding bookshelves and a desk, and he often brought his ledger from the fish shop to work on in there. He listened absently while Elizabeth put the children to bed. It soothed him, the sounds of his family getting ready for sleep, their voices overhead, their footsteps padding the floor.

He listened to the house until it grew quiet and Elizabeth's footsteps came softly down the stairs. He met her in the living room and waited for her to speak. She turned to adjust the lantern flame and wipe a smudge from the glass. Her head was turned to one side, her throat long and pale, vulnerable in a way he didn't often think of her. She seemed remote, and he felt helpless.

"I don't know what you want," she said, turning from the lantern. The light cast her face in shadows he didn't understand. "That girl, you think I don't know?"

"If I had you, I wouldn't need her. A man needs to feel welcomed in his own home."

"Why would I welcome you? You're never here! You're busy chasing a young girl, a runaway, around town like you've a right to." Her voice grew shrill, and Finn wanted her to shut up.

She threw her head back as if to toss him off, and she went to the kitchen to wash the dishes.

"I'll have money now," he said. "I can get you the help you need to take care of the children." He stood behind her and placed his hand on her shoulder. He hadn't expected to feel this longing.

He felt her shoulder move as she washed the dishes. Her silence annoyed him. He was overcome with desire and loneliness.

"It's not the money," she said without turning around. But he felt her resistance, and he knew she'd closed her heart to him. Now he wanted only to possess her, because she, his wife, belonged to him. Even if she didn't want him, he would lay claim to what was rightfully his and restore the confidence on which his life depended. He pushed her forward over the sink and hitched her dress up. Her arms splayed out to either side as she tried to push back and writhe away from him, but he shoved her down until she froze.

He unbuckled his belt and felt his own strength as he held her down with one hand, pressing her forward over the sink. She tried to pull away, but his weight pinned her. When he entered her, she groaned, not with pleasure but with something like disdain, and he pounded himself against her, feeling the soft curve of her buttocks against his thighs, and there was no sound then but for the roaring in his ears like the sound of the ocean. All his energy was focused on holding his wife at the counter with the force of his thrusts against her until he finished. That was when she freed herself and pushed him off.

"You pig. You're disgusting. Get out! Just get out!"

There was that shrill tone again. He buttoned his pants and fastened himself up.

"Now," she screamed.

"Shut up," he said.

"Get out!" That high-pitched tone.

He slapped the back of his hand across her face. He had nothing now. Nothing. When she looked up at him, stunned, he stepped around her and left by the kitchen door.

43

THEO SAT IN THE PARLOR IN A CHAIR BY THE WINDOW WITH HIS legs crossed, a drink in one hand, the paper folded neatly and held up in the other hand. Meredith stood in the doorway and watched him, knowing what she was about to tell him and wanting to let him bask in the peacefulness of the moment before his world changed. She felt powerful then, with a power she didn't want to have, and she resisted telling him as she stood with a manufactured stillness. She'd readied a small bag, and the horse was packed and waiting by the side of the house.

"Meredith," he said, looking up from his paper. "How long have you been standing there?"

He dropped the paper onto the side table and stood from his chair, holding his arms wide to welcome her.

She crossed the room, unsteady until she thought of Nathaniel, and only then was she able to gather herself.

She sat in the chair across from Theo and smoothed her skirt across her legs. She didn't look at him but at the shelves emptied of the crystal statues, at the pictures of her family and the brighter shade of wallpaper where she'd removed one of Theo's family portraits.

"What is it?" he asked.

Meredith pulled at her pearl earring and looked out the window, then she turned to Theo.

"I have something to tell you." She pushed the words out with the force of her will. "I don't love you, Theo. I don't want to be your wife."

The words fell like stones onto the floor, and Theo stared at her as if she'd spoken a foreign language. He looked confused, then stunned.

"Meredith—"

He stood from his chair and kneeled before her, clasping her hands. His hair fell over his brow as he bowed his head before her.

Then he looked up, his eyes pleading. "What do you mean?"

Meredith patted his hand where it gripped her own. There was a delicacy about him now, a thinness about the wrists and hands from working indoors. She wanted to give him something, a silver pocket watch to slide into his vest pocket, a nice one with his initials inscribed on the back. She didn't want to say any more or make him feel more pain than he already did, but she had to tell him the truth.

"Theo, I'm not in love with you."

He stood up then and glared down at her.

"It's Nathaniel. That scoundrel, right under my own roof. I should've known better than to trust that man. I should've known—"

"Theo, I fell out of love with you before he came here."

He looked deflated, a new confusion on his face. "Why, Meredith?" When she didn't answer, he let his arms fall down at his sides. "I don't want to lose you. I'll do anything. Just ask me."

"You don't love me, Theo."

"Of course I love you. How can you say such a thing? I've always wanted to be with you."

She saw his vulnerability and what could've been called love, but she didn't feel that he saw her the way Nathaniel saw her.

"I'll leave," Meredith said.

"You'll not leave this house." Theo's voice took on a surprising authority. He stared at Meredith as he spoke words that went right into her. "You're my wife. I love you, and we can work this out. You'll stop seeing Nathaniel. You'll come to your senses this minute."

She turned her back to him and stared into a daguerreotype of her with her mother in front of the house she'd grown up in, a small cottage with only two windows on the front to spare the money it would've cost to buy the glass.

"I do love you, Meredith. I do. I've loved you since that first day we went sailing and you took such joy in the boat, in saying 'ready about' and 'hard alee.' I've never stopped loving you."

Since they hadn't been able to have children, Meredith's passion had been replaced by a dull interest in her husband that waned as time went by. She was physically distant with him, and he didn't complain. "We don't go out in the boat anymore or do anything together. But it's more than that," Meredith stammered, not wanting to break open the hard kernel of truth that was the failure between them.

Theo sat in the chair and put his head between his legs as if to get the blood back to his brain. He ran his fingers through his graying hair and sat upright again. "So what are we to do?" She saw in his confusion a genuine curiosity that was something like an opening between them. If he could be curious, maybe she could be curious, too. In that moment, she felt their shared history, the years of lying together in the same bed, trying to have children and maintain a life together.

"I don't know what we're to do," Meredith said, and in that moment, she didn't. She'd grieved Nathaniel for years, even after she married Theo. Nathaniel had left her without warning, and now she was going to trust him with her heart and her life? She felt a moment of panic, then she thought of the length of him stretched across her sheets, his white buttocks a contrast to his suntanned back, the thin hair on his legs bleached nearly white from the sun. An erotic feeling overcame her, and she pulled her mind back to this moment.

"I'll work less. I'll tell my father right away. We can spend time together like we used to. We can think about adopting a child. Would you like that?"

She wanted him to stop, but he kept on.

"I don't want to lose you, Meredith."

"There's nothing between us anymore. There hasn't been for some time, or this other thing, it never would've happened."

"There are ten years of marriage between us. And love. Don't say there isn't. I love you, and I know you love me." He took her hand then, and she let him. "Please reconsider. I'll always take care of you. Even if it means spending less time in the business. Even if it means selling this house and leading a different kind of life. There's nothing we can't do."

"I'm surprised that you'd be willing to do that."

"You've shaken me awake." He stood and paced by the windows, trying to think of what to say next that could convince her not to leave. She could see the fear on his face, the worried lines on his forehead. His desperation frightened her, and she wasn't sure what to do. "I'm going to my mother's," she said finally.

"You're leaving?"

"I need to think, Theo. Please give me some room to think." She left him standing in the living room with his arms crossed over his chest as if to hold in his grief. The part of her that was his friend wanted to soothe him, but she couldn't soothe him now.

She rode the horse sidesaddle with her bag strapped on one side. She hadn't anticipated Theo's openness. His vulnerability touched her, and she felt the love she'd once felt for him. It was a different love than the love she shared with Nathaniel, a more quiet, settled kind of love. But when she thought of Nathaniel, she felt relief and a sense of her life as a different kind of woman, not a woman who gave up her desires, not a woman who lived in a home that wasn't her own. Rather, a woman who could be moved by the mere sight of a man with his hair blown in the wind as he walked toward her. The aliveness she felt vibrating within her was part fear, part sadness, and a large part of love for the man she'd unknowingly longed for these past ten years.

A feeling of freedom overtook her, and she guided the horse toward Nathaniel in what was now his house on the hill. Less than an hour and already she was making decisions for herself. She didn't care about what people would think of her, but when she pictured the hurt on Theo's face, her reservations tumbled down on her. She was giving up a life of honor and loyalty with Theo, who had never left her like Nathaniel had. Could she trust Nathaniel not to run away again if something awful happened? Could she trust their passion to carry them through life, or would it fade with time?

All these thoughts, but when the Boyd house came into view, the white clapboards glowing in the sun, the widow's walk rising high on the hill, she rode faster without stopping.

At the top of the hill, she walked the horse into the barn. There was a vegetable garden behind the kitchen that she remembered from when she was a girl. At the kitchen door, she called Nathaniel's name, and there he was at the sink, pumping water into a pitcher. He pulled a chair out for her, but she didn't sit down. She glanced around the kitchen as if taking stock of everything that had changed in the ten years since she'd last stood in this room.

"You told him?" Nathaniel asked.

"I did. And he insisted on me staying."

"But you didn't."

"He was so broken by it. I feel awful, but when I see you, my sadness and fear evaporate."

Nathaniel took her by the hand and led her through the living room, where she glanced at the fireplace, the surveying tools, the floor-to-ceiling bookshelves. She walked up to get a closer look at the tintype of Nathaniel with Finn and Jacob. "That was right before the trip," she said. She followed Nathaniel to the downstairs bedroom where he was staying. She straightened the sheets, then pulled the blanket up and fluffed the pillows.

"I wasn't expecting company," Nathaniel said.

Meredith went to him then. She ran her fingers along the line of his jaw. When he dipped his head to kiss her, they fell onto the bed. They made love lying side by side, Nathaniel reaching under layers of skirts, Meredith opening to him. When they finished, they lay together on their backs, looking up into the beams on the plaster ceiling. The room had a quiet, contained feeling that Meredith wanted to wrap around her and carry everywhere. She felt free, and she felt in love, and she felt that she had made contact with some previously unreachable part of Nathaniel. It was the part of him that went to live on the marsh.

"Do you remember what we dreamed together as children?" Meredith asked.

"Yes, the house that I would build, a house that we would design together."

"Why couldn't we still do that?"

"How did you leave things with Theo?"

"I don't know. Unresolved."

"What do you mean, unresolved? You told him, didn't you?"

"Yes, but he was so…so hurt." If Theo had gotten angry with her or sent her away, she wouldn't have any reservation about leaving him, but his sincerity had cracked the hard shell she'd created around herself. Leaving him would be harder now.

Nathaniel didn't speak. He sat on the edge of the bed, looking away from her, as if distracted by something more important on the far wall.

"We've been married for ten years, ever since you left. That's not nothing, Nathaniel."

"I know it," he said, getting up from the bed. "Are you going to leave him?"

Meredith pulled the sheet up to cover her body. She watched Nathaniel pour a glass of water from the tin pitcher. His torso was tanned, but he was white from the waist down from wearing no shirt with his pants. His body was lithe and sinewy, without any body fat to cushion the jut of his hip or the ripple of his ribs. She wanted to run her fingers over those ribs, to feel his breath moving in and out of his lungs.

"You have to leave him," Nathaniel said.

"I will."

"Forever?"

"He'll die of humiliation."

"That's not an answer. You have to choose, Meredith."

Meredith looked into his eyes, the same eyes she'd looked into as a girl. She remembered their time in the boatyard and rowing on the bay, their engagement at the end of the jetty. She still had the ring. She'd kept it all these years.

She cupped Nathaniel's face in her hands and kissed him on the mouth. Then she said, "I choose you." She leaned back from him. "I have to be honest with him. I have to let him go." A great wave of sadness shook her body, and she didn't want to cry, but her tears came.

Nathaniel wiped them away with the tip of his finger. "You can cry," he said.

—⁓—

Later, they sat at the kitchen table, eating scrambled eggs from a cast-iron pan, when Elizabeth knocked on the back door. Nathaniel wore a sheet wrapped around his waist, and Meredith pulled her bathrobe, his bathrobe, closer around her body.

"Nathaniel, may I come in?" Elizabeth said. She pushed herself through the doorway before he had the chance to invite her in. Strands of hair hung in her face, plastered by sweat from her brow. "Oh no," she said. She covered her eyes as she turned her head away. "I had no idea. I'm sorry. I can come back later."

"It's okay, Elizabeth. We're all adults."

"No, it isn't okay," Elizabeth said. Meredith left the room, and Nathaniel excused himself to get dressed. When he returned, he was tucking his shirt in as he entered the kitchen.

"What's the matter?" he asked. "Can I get you a glass of water?"

"Yes, please." She drank half the glass before she said, "You have to do something about Finn." Her eyes pled, and Nathaniel felt pity for her, but he didn't know what had caused her distress.

"Did he hurt you?"

"It's been building over the past months, his anger, his rage. He was coming home later and later, then he didn't come home at all. When I didn't give him the attention he wanted, he went into a rage."

"Did he hit you?"

"He was a brute." She took a cloth from the table and dabbed at her tears.

Whatever Finn had done to frighten her, she was keeping it to herself. "I can talk to him," Nathaniel said.

"That's not good enough. You have to stop him. Keep him away from our house. Get him to stay here."

"I can try," Nathaniel said, "but he's angry with me, too."

"I don't want him to get violent with the children around or, God forbid, with the children themselves."

"Of course not," Meredith said. She reached over and covered Elizabeth's hand with her own.

"He was absolutely terrifying. I've never seen him like that. What's happened to him?"

"He's angry about the will, about his business..." Nathaniel said.

"The children have been noticing the difference in their father. Ezra has grown shy with other children. He's not himself, not confident. A boy needs his father. The girls are lonely for him at bedtime. He used to tell them stories to ward off the demons. Now he's never home, and they feel unprotected without him in the house."

"You go home and get some rest. I'll find him first thing in the morning and have a talk. We'll put an end to this right away. You can bring the children here for the night if you're worried about Finn coming home."

"No, he's not coming home tonight. He left in a rage." Elizabeth stood from the table. "You'll talk to him?"

"First thing in the morning. He can stay here in the house with me. I'll keep an eye on him."

"Thank you," she said.

"I'll walk you home," Nathaniel told her.

"No, no, no," Elizabeth told him. "There's no need. I'll let you get back to your meal. I'm sorry to have intruded, but you understand?"

"Of course."

Nathaniel watched her pass across the lawn to the driveway as she nearly ran for home.

44

Rachel waited behind O'Shea's for Davey to pass by on his way home. She wanted to stop him from leaving. It was all he talked about now: riding to New Bedford and heading northwest from there, starting fresh. She would do anything to get him to stay, she thought. She'd tell him how she loved him, and that friends should stay together. That he was too young—they were both too young—to leave a place where they had work and people who cared about them. She imagined his eyes on her, assessing her love and finding it not enough. He wanted to court her; she knew this. But did she love him that way? She loved him dearly as a friend. She didn't want to give him false hope, but part of her didn't mind holding out hope if that meant he would stay.

When he didn't pass by, she walked out to glance along the backs of the buildings toward the fish shop. Barrels leaned against the wall, and empty crates were stacked to burn. The back door was open. What if Finn was there? She tucked herself beneath the stairway and waited in the shadows. Seagulls called out from the harbor. Wind rattled the shutters on the front of O'Shea's. She leaned against the wall and waited, counting *one, two...fifty-seven, fifty-eight*. Then she peered out from the stairwell and saw the fish shop was dark, the back door closed. Surely, Davey would walk past on his way home. She waited beneath the stairs for the sound of his footsteps along the marsh, then she stepped out from beneath the stairs into Finn Boyd's shadow.

His broad shoulders and brooding expression, the way he wore his hair slicked back, his beard thick with a day's growth—everything that had made him attractive in the beginning terrified her now, and she turned to run up the stairs.

"Wait," he said, his voice gentle.

When she didn't stop, he caught her by the arm, holding her harder than he meant to.

"Let go of me." She flung her arm back and forth, but his fingers dug into her.

"I just want to talk. Will you stay still?" He pushed her back against the railing to get her to stop moving. She was pinned, but she couldn't stop struggling.

The coffee and onion smell of him, the weight of him against her, repulsed her, and she kneed Finn in the groin. He doubled over for a minute, then shoved her harder.

"Listen to me," he yelled. "I'm sorry for what I did to you. You don't understand how much I want you. Don't you care for me at all?"

"No," she said. "I don't know why you think I do."

"The way we flirted on the boat, that day you sat in the restaurant with me... I gave you your bag."

"You're married!"

"But I could give you everything. Elizabeth is nothing to me now." He nearly spat these last words out as he glared at her.

When she saw the desperation in his eyes, she turned away. "I don't love you," she said.

At these words, Finn's top lip pulled back in a sneer, and his rage unfurled and drove him to shake her by the arms so hard that her head tossed back and forth. She tried to push him away, but he grabbed her by the elbow and dragged her along the backs of the buildings. He kicked open the door to his shop and pushed her inside. She tried not to resist him then, thinking that he would relax if she softened toward him.

"See what you made me do? You're a stupid girl." He pushed her back against the gut table. He pressed his weight into her.

When he lifted her onto the table, she reached back, flailing for something to grab, anything to hit him with. She writhed until her fingers touched the whetstone, then she tipped it toward her and took it in her hand. She cocked her elbow and swung the whetstone as hard as she could at Finn's head.

"You bitch," he said.

Davey called through the door, "I forgot my—"

"Davey!"

Davey looked at Rachel with the whetstone in her hand, her hair pulled loose, and a pleading look in her eyes. The knife block on the gut table had been knocked to the floor, and the room stank of fish.

"Get off me!" Rachel yelled at Finn and tried to wriggle herself from beneath him. Davey ran to her, then dove at Finn to get him off her. The assault seemed to enrage Finn further, because he shoved himself against Rachel and took her by the throat.

Davey reached for a mallet and swung it at Finn's knees. When Finn bent over, Davey swung the mallet up against Finn's face, but Finn blocked the shot with one arm, never taking his hand from Rachel's neck. She knew not to move. *Just breathe.* She felt Katherine on her right. Was this what it felt like, Katherine, this slow suffocation? She thought of their father hovering over Katherine, her stifled crying as he slapped her across the face for no reason other than his drunkenness and no dinner on the table. Katherine, long and lean, who looked like their mother. Rachel longed for the safety of Meredith's house with its sweeping curtains and puffed cushions. She longed for the silent presence of Nathaniel sitting in the corner. She held her fear at arm's length and tried to find a way through the chaos around her.

When Finn stared into her face, she tried to hold his gaze, thinking maybe he wouldn't hurt her if Davey was there. Maybe if she stared into his eyes, he would remember what he loved and spare her any more pain. But she felt his power over her as he tightened his grip. Davey's yelling sounded faint and faraway. There was a noise like wind spinning through her ears. She grasped at Finn's fingers and tried to pry them loose. She kicked hysterically, as if her legs were windmills run without her own will. She'd come so far to find this place. She'd felt safe and known people who cared about her. Was that enough for a lifetime, to know peace? No, she didn't think so. He shook her neck and banged her head back against the table until she grew tired and the wind in her ears rushed through her body. She couldn't breathe. She was hungry for air. *Give me some air!*

"Rachel!" Davey screamed, pulling on Finn's arm, kicking him in the legs until he remembered the large gutting knife. Davey went for the knife and swung it through the air to get Finn's attention, but Finn didn't take his hands from the girl's neck. Davey stepped up behind him and pressed the tip of the knife to Finn's kidney.

"Let her go," Davey said.

Finn clenched the girl tighter for a moment, tighter still, then the pain struck as Davey guided the knife no more than an inch into his skin, same as he'd slide the blade into a fish. Finn lurched back. He held his hands out to his sides in an attitude of surrender long enough for the girl to slide from the table. She scrambled to her feet, looked at Davey blankly, then staggered out the back door.

Rachel walked as fast as she could toward Nathaniel's house until she got her breath back, and then she ran. Her feet twisted in the gravel along the road. From the Boyd house, a single window issued a pale light like a beacon. She didn't listen for Finn behind her. She ran harder until she only heard her own breath pounding the night air, her feet slapping the dirt with a violence that could save her. She remembered getting on the boat in Bath, Maine, afraid of getting caught with all that money, wanting only to escape her past, and now here she was, running for her life, a pain around her throat that she tried to ignore as she ran harder toward the Boyds' hill.

She didn't want Davey to leave. Not ever. If he hadn't been there, Finn would've killed her. She ran up the hill and thought of the last time she'd escaped Finn's rage. Nathaniel had tried to save her, but there was no stopping Finn. Maybe Davey was right. Maybe they had to leave. She tried to put these thoughts from her mind and catch her breath. *Run,* she told herself. *Run and don't stop.*

45

W HERE DID THE GIRL GO? WHEN FINN STEPPED OUTSIDE THE FISH
shop, he couldn't see into the night, and he heard no trace
of her. He slammed the door and hurried to the back of her building
where the staircase climbed into the dark. She'd run to Meredith's, he
thought. Where else would she go?

He knew that Davey and the girl were going to tell Nathaniel what
had happened, and now he would never give Finn his rightful inheri-
tance. Nathaniel was in the way. Nathaniel was always going to be in the
way. Finn walked deliberately across the marsh toward Meredith's house.

When he finally reached the house, he peered in the parlor windows,
but the room was empty. The kitchen was dark, but the door was
unlatched, and he stepped inside. The silence was disarming as he felt
his way along the walls into the darkened parlor. Not a light aglow in
the whole house. Not a voice to be heard. He glanced out the window
toward his father's house where a dim light shone on top of the hill. He
kneeled down and fixed his gaze upon that light. That was when he saw
a shadow moving across the thin glow, then another unlikely shape, and
he knew Rachel had gone to his brother. He fled the house and ran back
across the marsh toward the harbor road. He could keep her from telling Nathaniel. He'd shut her up once and for all with all he knew about
her. Once he reached the hill up to the house, the light from the window
was clear, and Finn made his way toward it.

He snuck around the bushes to the back of the house where he heard his brother talking to Rachel. They were in the kitchen, and Finn crouched down and listened through an open window. Davey's voice rose above the rest. How did that kid get here before him? Finn pushed his anger down and tried to make out the words, but he only heard the urgent tone in that swell of voices. He crept closer to the open window and tilted his head toward the voices, but still he couldn't make out what they were saying. He crept toward the shadow of the barn. The darkness was complete, and he sat on his haunches. When the kitchen door slammed, he leaned around the edge of the barn.

Finn looked down into the dirt by his feet, then into the dark at the vegetable garden and the apple trees that Nathaniel had tended as a boy. How he hated Nathaniel, for his years of indolence and his control over their father's estate. He'd never hated a person more than he hated his brother right now. He leaned around the barn again and saw Nathaniel standing in the kitchen window at the pump by the sink. Then the kitchen door slammed, and he saw the long skirts and the hourglass figure, the bun perched high on her head—it was Meredith walking in a circle by the door.

She sighed, then appeared to be taking deep breaths of the night air. Finn watched as she crossed the yard toward the front of the house, where the view of the harbor beneath the night sky might capture her mind and bring her a certain amount of peace, he thought. He followed her past the hedge, keeping his distance, crouching down, stopping when she slowed. He stepped gently in the grass, staying in the shadows of the old elm tree, then edged along the front of the house behind her.

He watched her, trying to see what his brother saw in her, and then he realized that Nathaniel saw everything in her.

"Meredith," he said.

She gasped and turned toward the front door, but he dove at her. He put his hand over her mouth to stifle her. He was fast, and she didn't have time to resist him. He held her from behind, one hand over her mouth, until she flailed in his arms. He pulled her in close, feeling the life in her. The fight she put up tired him out, but he held on. She wasn't as strong as Rachel. She was thinner, and her body had a lightness to it that he could control. His rage had become like love to him, the way it moved in warm currents through his body, the calamity of reactions it inspired.

He felt her skirts brush against his legs. The firm bones of her bodice pressed up against him. He remembered her standing in the doorway of her house and sending him away. She'd wanted to keep him from Rachel all along, but she couldn't control him. Nobody could. With his hand over Meredith's mouth, he pinched her nose to keep her from breathing. This restored a feeling of justice upon which his life depended. What better way to ruin Nathaniel?

Her hair in his mouth smelled of lavender, her skin of fresh rose water. Would every woman fight him until the end?

Nathaniel came around the front of the house, squinting his eyes into the dark, and then he ran toward them. Finn would give up everything to ruin his brother. He didn't care anymore. Finn knew that he would always be working at the fish shop with an unhappy wife and a house full of children who didn't know him.

"What in—?" Nathaniel grabbed Finn by the arm. He swung him around and pushed him to the ground. "Let go of her." Nathaniel yelled, but Meredith fell limp in Finn's arms.

"I just wanted to scare her." Finn dropped her on the ground, and Nathaniel fell on top of her, shaking her. "He pounded her on the back, and finally shook her, until she groaned and rolled her head against the ground. "You nearly killed her! You've gone 'round the bend, Finn."

When Finn tried to leave, Nathaniel scrambled to his feet and shoved him to the ground. Finn leaned back from his position in the dirt and stared up at Nathaniel, his dark hair a tangle over his forehead. Nathaniel kicked him in the stomach, and Finn doubled over. Nathaniel kicked again, and when Finn tried to get up, Nathaniel kicked him in the face.

"You can't kill me, Nathaniel. You're a coward." Finn spat dirt and blood from his mouth. He wiped his filthy shirtsleeve across his brow.

"Shut up," Nathaniel shouted in his face.

"What are you going to do?" Finn asked, struggling to stand up.

Nathaniel let him stand, then came at him with fists raised. He flung himself at Finn. Finn fought him off even as his arms lashed out. Nathaniel punched him in the face, punched at his chest and his stomach, but Finn easily pushed him to the ground and went into the house. He couldn't stay in town. There was nothing left for him here. He felt an emptiness that frightened him. He needed money, a gun, a horse. His body was exhausted, but a strange energy carried him forward.

He went to his father's safe, an old black box with a silver wheel; the series of numbers were the days of the boys' birthdays, 27, 25, 26, and as he turned the wheel in each direction, Finn heard the clank of pins falling into place until the final bolt sounded and he pulled the door open. The safe was empty. "Goddammit!" He looted through his father's desk drawers, looking for cash, then ran up to his father's bedroom and ransacked his dresser, beneath his mattress, and his dressing room. There was no money, and Finn couldn't waste any more time.

Nathaniel appeared in the doorway. "You're not leaving. You can fight me all you want, but you're not going to get away with this, Finn."

"Try to stop me." Finn tried to get around Nathaniel where he stood in the doorway, but Nathaniel stood strong. Finn had to pry his brother's hands from the doorframe, and then he punched Nathaniel in the stomach so that he bent over and gasped. "Stay out of my way."

Nathaniel spun around and followed Finn around the house. "Davey went for the sheriff. You don't believe me? You wait, Finn. You're not going to get away."

"I'm already gone, Brother."

In his father's barn, the horse, Martha, didn't want the saddle, but Finn tightened the bridle until the horse stayed still. He tossed the saddle over her and fastened it quickly so that she'd get used to the idea and simmer down. Nathaniel struggled to stand up and found his brother in the barn. He picked up a hoe and held it over his shoulder, ready to swing. Finn could see that his brother was tired, more tired than he'd probably ever been. He lunged at Nathaniel and pulled the hoe from him, knocked Nathaniel to the ground, and held the wooden handle to his neck. "I could kill you right here."

"But you won't. You're a coward."

Finn pushed the handle harder against his brother's neck until Nathaniel flailed beneath him, reaching both arms for Finn's neck, but Finn was stronger. He held his brother down. "Now leave me alone," Finn commanded. He tied a large sack of oats over the back of the horse and trotted down his father's drive, but there was one more thing he had to do before he left. He steered Martha toward the marsh and along a narrow trail where the ground was packed hard. They followed the path along the back of the woods. The sweep of marsh between them and the shack was barely lit by the moon, the ground too soft for a horse, but Finn could make it on his own. He slid down from the saddle and led the animal to a low-hanging branch where he fastened the reins.

"You stay here." He patted her on the nose, scratched the grassy-smelling hairs there, and stepped off into the night.

46

THERE WAS NO WIND AND THE TREES HUSHED THEIR BRANCHES, and the world seemed to hover and wait. Nathaniel wanted to run after his brother, but he couldn't leave Meredith. She sat on the ground, tears on her face and her eyes blinking. "Meredith," he whispered as he kneeled before her. He wiped the hair from her face where it was plastered in sweat across her forehead. "I'm so sorry," he said, and he pulled her toward him, but she pushed him away.

"Don't touch me." She swept her skirt beneath her and struggled to stand, swatted Nathaniel's hand away as if he'd been the one who attacked her, who'd placed those bruises along the pale skin of her neck. "I want to go home, to my mother's house. I want to go there now."

"I'll take you." Nathaniel's voice was a plea, but Rachel placed her hand on his shoulder and gently led him one step away from Meredith.

"I'll take myself." Meredith stood next to them, frightened and angry. She looked around as if to get her bearings, then she stopped and pointed toward the island.

Nathaniel followed the line of her arm, the length of her finger toward the marsh. Plumes of fire rolled up from the island where the shack used to be. Black clouds wafted across the moonlit sky. "Finn," Nathaniel said.

They stood transfixed, watching the crackle and snap of wood as it burned. Nathaniel wanted to feel sad or angry or some urgency to stop the fire, but he only felt worried about Meredith.

"Where's Davey with the sheriff?" he asked, and he felt better for thinking of something, as if a simple thought could save them when it was too late to make any difference at all. He'd lost both of his brothers, and he tried not to feel that it was his fault, but some part of him believed that if he'd been able to protect them, even protect Finn from himself, they would all still be here, and he wouldn't be alone. He reached for Meredith again, but she stepped away from him.

"Meredith," he said. "Please." But she stood on the lawn looking toward the Butler house where she'd made her life with Theo. Nathaniel thought he saw regret on her face, regret for leaving the safety of that life. He wanted to reassure her that she was safe, but she was gone from him. He could tell by the way she stood with her arms crossed over her chest, her eyes looking anywhere but at him.

"Take me home," she said finally, looking into the night toward the driveway. "I want to go home."

47

THREE WEEKS GONE AND THE SEARCH FOR PHINNEAS BOYD HAD been reduced to posters scattered from Yarmouth Port to New Bedford and Boston. Most guessed he was on his way to the Caribbean to try his luck on a whaler or a merchant vessel, anything to get away from Yarmouth Port and the fact of his crimes. How he could live with himself was a matter of some speculation.

Meredith moved to her mother's house and refused to see anyone. Nathaniel took comfort in knowing that he'd saved her from Finn's rage. When her eyes had finally opened and set themselves on him, knowing she was out of danger released some of the guilt and sense of failure he'd carried with him for years. Now her stony silence, her remove, left him with a loneliness he hadn't known before he walked across her lawn with Rachel in his arms. He felt desolate, like he did after losing Jacob, when he'd moved out to the marsh. It frightened him, and he knew he didn't want to go back to that place in himself. He wanted Meredith's love, her kindness.

There was a moment each morning when he opened his eyes and didn't know where he was. His memories of the shack permeated his dreams—the smells of salty air, clay, and wet wood. The feeling of clean sheets disoriented him. There was no shack to go back to. The thought troubled him, then settled into the facts of his life: Meredith across town and out of reach, his father's house around him, and an estate to manage without Finn. *Finn*, he thought. *What will become of him?*

He rose to splash cold water from the basin onto his face. His old bedroom was filled with mementoes of his childhood—a small fishing pole, a daguerreotype of him standing by *Lulu* when he was about nine years old, a wooden model of a schooner painted with a green hull. Nathaniel went to the window ledge and swung the schooner's boom to and fro with the tip of his finger. He touched the mast and ran the back of his hand along the cotton sail. Once he started emptying the room, he couldn't stop. He dumped everything into Finn's room—the box of board games from under his bed, the bag of marbles, the rough fishing lures he'd made as a boy. He maneuvered the mattress through the doorway and tipped it into Finn's room, then dragged the bedstead.

When his room was empty, other than the chart of Cape Cod framed over the spot where his bed used to be, he stood in the dusty light. There was a shiny spot of wood like an island where the bed had protected the floor from the sun. The rest of the floor was faded and worn smooth. He ran his bare feet over the like-new floor and wondered what to put there. The double bed from the guest room. The quilt from his father's bed, the one his mother had made with the compass rose in the center of a navy-blue and white field. He would turn this into a man's bedroom, and he would live here like he'd never lived on the island.

In the kitchen, Nathaniel poured coffee into a mug. He sat at the table and leaned back in a chair, the shape of it so familiar to his body that part of him relaxed into it while another part of him remained clenched against the worry that Meredith was lost to him. This was not how he wanted to spend his day, but with every day that passed, Nathaniel found himself deeper into a life without her. Why hadn't his father given Finn the money? Why did his father try to control them? Meredith would've been spared the terror of Finn's rage. She might be sitting at the table with him now and not suffering her fear.

Out by the side of the barn, Bea and the gardener kept a vegetable garden, and Nathaniel set himself to weeding. Squatting in the dirt, he worked until his back burned. He tried not to think about the fact that he and Meredith may never share a simple domestic life. The pleasure of bringing her a basket of vegetables may never be his, or waking to each other's faces first thing in the morning and getting dressed together in the same room, or washing from the same basin. They may never sit around the table and talk over breakfast or decide whether to have children. He snipped rotted lettuce leaves between his thumbnail and middle finger, picked cherry tomatoes and tossed them into the bucket kept in the corner for just that purpose, ran his hands through kale and onion shoots and turnip leaves, and finally watered row after row of green growth.

That afternoon, his longing for Meredith made him tired, and no amount of coffee could help him with his grief.

Bea stepped into the room to announce the presence of his father's lawyer. "He insists on a meeting with you, Nathaniel. He says it's quite urgent."

Nathaniel looked at her with her black hair curled back behind her ears, her loose skin and the age that she wore like a survivor.

"I want to take care of the garden, Bea. Do you mind if I do that?"

"No, certainly not. But the lawyer—"

"I can't talk right now," Nathaniel said. "Send him away."

When the lawyer showed up again looking for Nathaniel, Bea didn't even bother him before turning the man away.

The thought of lawyers and the papers stacked on his father's desk drove Nathaniel outside. The walk down the hill and across the marsh was easy. He hadn't been to the island since the fire, and he wanted to see for himself the place he'd called home. The sounds of the harbor drifted over him, but he was in a fog, and he didn't hear a thing. As he approached the island, the smell of burnt wood drove him faster. The bushes that surrounded the island were gone. In their place was a charred expanse of clay and bits of grass. The damage was complete. The shack reduced to cinders. Only the ashy outlines of his bed and his chair stood out against the dust. He kicked at the embers, and there by the door, he saw what remained of Jacob's hat. When he squatted down and poked at it, he felt a loss so deep a shiver ran through him. He held back his tears and inhaled the deep aftermath of fire. He held his hand to his mouth and let out a heavy breath of air. *My God.*

He felt a well of loss around him, and he didn't want to fall down into it. He'd lost his father and two brothers—he wasn't going to lose Meredith. The wish to live alone had left him. Even after Finn's attack and disappearance, Nathaniel didn't want to move to the island or row all day on the harbor by himself. He wanted a life with Meredith.

Back at the house, he changed his clothes—a linen suit and brown leather shoes—and he saddled the horse Evie. He lifted himself into the saddle and settled in for the ride. On his way south through Yarmouth Port, he kept his head down and tried to think of what to say. *I'm sorry.* Or, *Please.* Anything to get Meredith to talk with him. He wanted her more than he ever had. He rode high in the saddle, firm in his conviction that he could bring Meredith back with him.

Across the middle of Cape Cod, as he rode from the north shore to the south, the old-growth forests were nearly gone. Home building, firewood collection, shipbuilding, and the construction of the Old Colony Railroad had depleted the land of wood so that the parcels Nathaniel Sr.

had collected over time held a high value for their timber. What use was his father's money if Nathaniel couldn't do something good with it? He imagined building a small house for him and Meredith, somewhere by the water, where he could manage his father's estate without being knee-deep in the past.

He arrived at Oakum Road, a thin strip of dirt wide enough for a horse and wagon. Meredith's family home looked just as it had when they were children—the window boxes overflowing with blossoms, the white shutters brilliant in the sun, the footpath groomed and scattered with broken clamshells. It was a two-room cottage with a kitchen and living area on one side and sleeping quarters on the other. He'd only been inside once, invited by Meredith's mother over tea, when they'd told her of their engagement. He tied Evie to a birch tree by the fence. Standing there with his hands on the bridle, he slipped the horse an apple and waited. For what? Did he expect Meredith to hear his horse and open the door to greet him? He shook his head. "Foolish," he muttered.

On the front stoop, he knocked gently.

Footsteps on the other side of the door, then the crack of an opening.

"It's Nathaniel."

Jane, Meredith's mother—she'd always insisted that he call her Jane—answered the door. With her hair in a neat bun perched on the back of her neck and her white cotton dress smelling of bleach, she presented herself as the tidy person that Nathaniel remembered her to be.

"You're not welcome here, Nathaniel. You oughta know that without me having to tell you."

"I love her, Jane. I couldn't know Finn would—"

"She won't see you. You need to go."

"But—"

"The girl is shocked and confused. You need to let her be."

Nathaniel stood for a moment, disbelieving, then he walked toward the road. He was so close to Meredith that he couldn't stand it. He turned back to look at the house where she lived without him, and there she was, dropping the curtain from the window, her shadowed figure moving behind the muslin like the thin wisp of a promise.

He stood with the horse and waited for Meredith to return to the window, waited for the muslin curtain to reveal her face, but the window remained empty, and he rode home along the narrow road north. He wouldn't give up. He would aim himself toward getting Meredith back. He kicked the sides of the horse into a gallop and rose in the stirrups, felt the wind on his face and the road rushing toward him as he moved forward along it.

48

MEREDITH LAY ON HER BED, ANGRY THAT NATHANIEL HAD come to see her and bereft not to be with him. She knew he'd only go back to the marsh now that Finn had vanished. He'd never be able to stand losing another brother, running his father's business, or settling down with her. She should've known this all along. She felt as if she had a rock in her belly that weighed her down. No matter which way she sat or lay or stood, she got no relief from the pain that kept her from eating.

When there was a knock at the bedroom door, Meredith sat up and pushed her hair back from her face. Another knock. "Who is it?"

"It's me, dear."

"Come in," Meredith said. She loved her mother, but she didn't want advice right now.

"I know you love him," her mother said. "So why won't you see him?"

"He's just going to disappear, and I can't bear that a second time. And what if Finn comes back? What then?"

"Where's he going to disappear to?"

"He could just remove himself, like last time, emotionally, physically. I can't stop thinking about that."

Her mother sat on the bed beside her daughter. "You didn't leave your husband for no reason. It might take time, Meredith, but you'll come around."

"Are you terribly ashamed?"

"Why would I be ashamed? Theo was never right for you. I pushed you into that marriage."

"I had to do something to move on after Nathaniel left. That was the only thing I could think to do. And I loved Theo, in a quiet kind of familial way. God, what have I done?" Meredith burst into sobs while her mother held her close against her chest. She ran her hand over Meredith's head in a soothing gesture until she stopped crying altogether.

"You'll be fine," her mother said. "Just you wait and see." She stood up and looked down at her daughter. "What are you going to do with yourself, Meredith? You can't sit here all day."

"Mother, please."

"I mean it. If you can't find anything to do, I'll put you to work. God knows, there's plenty to do."

Her mother reached for Meredith's hand, and she took it to let her mother pull her up from the bed. She feigned reluctance, but she was interested to see what her mother would come up for her to do. It had to be better than lying around all day.

"You want to start with the windows?"

"Sure." Meredith liked washing windows because she saw the impact of her work as she stared out the clean glass.

"Get started then. You know what to do."

"I know just what to do. Thank you, Mother." Maybe cleaning the glass, moving her body, and standing in the fresh air would remove this dread from her belly.

49

NATHANIEL WOKE ON THE SETTEE IN THE LIVING ROOM TO THE sound of Bea calling his name. His head swam as if with fog, and he struggled to pull himself upright.

"Nathaniel," Elizabeth said. She'd woven her dark braid with a navy-blue ribbon.

"What are you doing here?"

"Ezra wanted to come, but he was too shy. He made you this." She held out a sailor's-knot rope bracelet in a Turk's head design. "He made one for himself, too. I helped him a little, but it was his idea."

Nathaniel looked at the bracelet, feeling the twine in his fingers, the tight knot, then he pulled it on over his calloused hand.

Elizabeth spun the bracelet on his wrist to see the different colors. "It looks good," she said, then she gathered her skirts and stood to go. Still, she hesitated, watching Nathaniel for a moment for some sign—of what? "I'll bring Ezra next time," she said as if that would solve something, but when Nathaniel didn't get up from the couch to see her out, she said, "You know, Nathaniel, I was married to your brother. I lost him, even before he disappeared, even before his despicable acts. What he did makes me feel dirty, as if I'm somehow complicit by association. Everyone in town looks at me with pity or disgust, and I can't go to the harbor for the shame of it. Can you imagine what it's like for me?"

She had Nathaniel's attention now.

"He was a monster, but he was a man, too, and the father of my children. They don't understand. I'm afraid to send Ezra to school, because I'm afraid of what the other children will say. I'm considering keeping him at home longer."

Nathaniel sat up and brushed his hair from his face with his long fingers. "I hadn't thought of that."

"He could use a friend right now."

She left through the kitchen, and Nathaniel tuned out the sound of Bea and Elizabeth talking.

As he sat on the couch, Rascal came running through the door to the kitchen, his tail wagging as if he was the happiest thing in the world. He ran over to Nathaniel and stuck his nose under Nathaniel's hand to get him to scratch his head. Nathaniel leaned over and rubbed the dog's head, then along his back to feel his thick body. Someone had been feeding him; that much was clear. He grabbed Rascal around his body and hugged him.

With the dog hovering around him, he dragged himself up from the couch, stretched his arms out to the sides, and took a few deep breaths. He knew that he needed to take responsibility for his affairs, but he wondered about his ability to do this. Standing over his father's desk, he decided that first he would address the papers spread and stacked in seemingly no order whatsoever. He scanned each page to see whether it pertained to land or fishing interests or other businesses, and he filed each paper accordingly. Slowly, he got a sense of the expanse of his father's enterprise. He worked his way through layers of papers, filling file folders and desk drawers.

When he found what looked like a letter in a folder marked *Boyd Estate*, he sat back in his father's chair and opened the envelope. The letter was dated only a week before his father died. He must've known his heart was failing.

> I, Nathaniel Boyd, Sr., a resident of Barnstable County in the Commonwealth of Massachusetts, being of sound mind and body, hereby declare this amendment to my last will and testament.
>
> To my son Nathaniel Boyd, I leave forty percent of my land holdings and forty percent of my cash holdings.
>
> To my son Phinneas Boyd, I leave sixty percent of my land holdings, sixty percent of my cash holdings, and one hundred percent of my business interests.

Nathaniel didn't know what to make of the letter. His father meant to leave the larger share of his estate to Finn. Finn would've gotten what he wanted: his father's approval as well as the means to build his fleet. Nathaniel began to realize that Meredith might have been spared. She might still be his if they had discovered the codicil to the will sooner. Finn's rage might've been eased. Nathaniel tried to back up and review the facts as if knowing the facts could provide him with answers to questions. *How did this happen? Why didn't Father discuss this with me? Why did we not find this?*

His mind raced. He thought of Rachel pressed beneath Finn's weight, of Meredith on the ground with no breath. He began to shake violently with the piece of paper in his hands, and then he slammed it onto the desk. He swiped everything on the desktop to the floor, then turned around and shoved the chair out of his way. How could this be true? He leaned against the wall and slid down into a crouching position. He couldn't catch his breath. The sobs took hold of him and shook him hard.

Rascal thought that Nathaniel was on the floor to play, and he leaned into Nathaniel's legs, wiggling his body and tossing his head. "Not now, Rascal. Not now." But he patted the dog and pulled himself up from the floor as if he could shake himself loose from grief. At the desk, he stared into the pile of his father's papers, but he couldn't bring himself to read any more. Finn had left him alone with this mess, alone without Meredith. He'd wanted to ruin Nathaniel, but Nathaniel would not be ruined. He wouldn't let Finn win.

50

R ACHEL KNOCKED ON THE BACK DOOR, BUT NATHANIEL DIDN'T answer. She'd seen the candlelight from the front windows, but the door was locked. She knocked again, louder and more determined. Davey stood beside her, facing away from the door. Rachel knew he didn't want to be here, that he still considered the Boyds above him somehow, but she needed him beside her. He provided a comfort to her with his sheer presence. He was kind and solid in a way that surprised her. He ran the shop in Finn's absence and didn't ask for anything from Nathaniel. He was more than a boy, she realized, and she liked having him there with her.

"Nathaniel, it's Rachel. Will you come to the door?" She pressed her ear to the glass, but there was no sound from inside the house.

"He's not going to answer," Davey said. "Just leave it for him."

She placed the basket she'd prepared by the door, folded the red-and-white-checked napkin over the loaf of bread and package of fresh fish that she wanted to cook for him. She left and walked down the hill, the dark swelling around her.

"We'll come back," she said.

They walked down the driveway toward Rachel's room with the sun setting behind them. The gulls swarmed around the fishing smacks, and the cacophony of their cries and the men's voices and the sound of crates sliding onto the wagons created an evening song. Rachel let her head drop onto Davey's shoulder. She listened to that music as if it had been composed from the wellspring of her own spirit.

"Remember when you brought me the loaf of bread?" Davey said. "I thought you loved me then."

"I love you now. We are the best of friends."

Davey shook his head and looked down into the sand. He scraped the ground with the toe of his boot, uncovered a scallop shell half-covered in seaweed. "I have to tell you something." He spoke without looking up, as if the scallop shell held all meaning for him now. "I'm leaving for Worcester."

"No!" After everything she'd shared with him, how could he leave? Wasn't their friendship enough to make him stay?

"I need work, and I don't want to live here without you. It hurts, Rachel. I know that you're older than me, and you don't see me as someone who could court you. It's okay. Maybe one day, you will come to me."

"You can't just leave, not after everything."

"I've made up my mind." He was resolute, and she felt him already on the road off the Cape, his mind planning the route toward Worcester.

"What can I do to convince you to stay?"

"I'm leaving the day after tomorrow."

—*ᨠᨠ*—

She went to see him in the early morning before the town shook itself awake. He said goodbye to his mother as she stood in the doorway with a frightened look on her face. Rachel waited for him at the bottom of the steps, then took his hand.

"I'll write to you," he said, and he let her hand go. He stood before the horse, his leather hat cocked to one side. He didn't need to take the stagecoach because Nathaniel had given him a sturdy mare. "I don't like long goodbyes, Rachel."

She shoved a small package of money into his hands before he stepped up into the saddle. "For the road," she said.

He nodded. His body looked bigger perched atop the horse, not only with the height of the animal but with a new confidence. He looked down at her, and she felt him gone in her heart. She burst into tears, then, embarrassed, she wiped her face with the back of her hand.

"Sorry," she said. She fortified herself against him leaving, then looked up at him until their eyes met. "You go along now. You have a long journey."

He nodded and clucked the horse into motion. She gazed after him, and as he disappeared around the corner of the road, he held one hand up to wave goodbye. He didn't turn around.

The next evening, a pinkish light hovered over the lawn and lit the trees as Rachel walked toward the Boyd house with a fresh basket of scallops. She felt a lightness in her chest now that she'd given Davey the money, as if she'd been released from the fact of her own guilt. She imagined him shoving the package into his satchel and forgetting about it until he reached his destination. She didn't need the money, and she had other things to think about now. She was not going to give up on Nathaniel, even though her spirit sagged with Davey gone. She knocked loudly on the door, then waited. The basket of food she'd left for him sat right where she'd left it. The stench of day-old fish hit her nostrils, and she tried not to feel hurt.

"Nathaniel, it's Rachel. Please open up." When he didn't answer the door, she spoke to him as if he were on the other side of the glass. "Davey's left town. There's nobody watching the fish shop. He's closed it up for now." She wiggled the doorknob, and it was open. She stepped into the kitchen, slid her basket onto the counter. In the sink, an empty glass, a dirty bowl, a spoon. She walked through the pantry into the dining room, then into the library where Nathaniel sat with the last rays of sun in his eyes. He sat unblinking, as if caught by some vision he couldn't take his attention from.

"Nathaniel," Rachel said.

He looked right past her, as if he were looking at some uncertain place over her head. She remembered him watching her like she was his own child while she recovered at Meredith's. She swore she would watch over him now. The dog lay at his feet, staring at her, his tail thumping the floor.

"I hope you don't mind I'm here, though I guess you do." She wanted to reach out and touch him, but something in his distant gaze told her not to move. Did he even know she was still in the room? It was as if he had fallen into some deep and private part of himself where no one else existed.

"What are you doing here?" he asked.

"I've brought you some dinner."

"I don't need your pity."

"It's not pity," Rachel said. "It's scallops."

———✦———

In the morning, Rachel was wiping the front windows with vinegar and a rag when Francis Miller, the attorney, came into the restaurant. She quickly put the rag away and wiped her hands on a clean cloth.

"Mr. Miller, how can I help you?"

"I've come to talk to you about Mr. Boyd. He refuses to see me, and we have business that needs to be addressed. Land purchases that were left unfinished, tenant agreements that need to be signed. He can't let these things flounder. I know that you're his friend, and I was wondering if there was any way you might be able to convince him to come see me."

"I can try to talk to him, but he's stubborn."

"The man can't languish for the rest of his life." Francis looked hard at the girl. "Whatever you have to do, just do it."

When he was gone, Rachel went back to washing the windows, watching the boats in the harbor unload crates of fish and cargo from Boston. Men rushed by wearing waders, shirtsleeves rolled to their biceps. Life in Yarmouth Port went on, and Nathaniel Boyd needed to climb aboard.

—⁓—

When Rachel arrived the next night with fish chowder, Nathaniel didn't argue. He met her in the kitchen and sat while she spooned chowder into their bowls. She sliced bread and spread a thick layer of butter across each piece. He ate his meal in silence, dutifully lifted the spoon to his lips. He tried to listen to her talk of the restaurant, news of the people in town.

"Davey's gone. He was traveling toward New Bedford, then Worcester with a satchel full of money. He wants to start a business on his own." Rachel didn't tell him how she missed Davey, how maybe she loved him after all. She didn't tell him how she'd watched him go with the purpose of an older person. "What about you? Will you continue working the timberland? What will you do now?"

Nathaniel placed his spoon beside his bowl, then put his bowl on the floor for the dog to clean. "I don't know what I'll do," he said. "There are business matters, the tenants. It's overwhelming." Words spilled from his mouth into the room, as if she were only a witness to his wondering. Dusty evening light fell on the table and lit the wooden legs of the chairs. It glowed along the counters and lit the copper pots that hung on iron hooks over the stove. "I never imagined my father dying. He was so vital. I never imagined any of this."

Rachel placed her hand on his shoulder.

"I've brought apple crisp. You like that, don't you?"

"Sure," he said, and he received the bowl of dessert as the offering she meant it to be.

***

Two nights later, when Rachel showed up with dinner, Bea was gone. Nathaniel offered to cut up the potatoes while she boiled water and readied the fish for the fry pan. Rachel hoped working in the kitchen would distract him from whatever shard of misery had hold of him. She wanted to say something to acknowledge his grief over Meredith. The silence took on the edge of her tension.

"I'm sorry, Nathaniel. I truly am."

He stopped cutting the last potato and stood motionless at the counter. Rachel was afraid she'd said the wrong thing. She kept her eyes on the fish in the pan and waited for Nathaniel to put the potatoes in a bowl, but he didn't move. They looked at each other with a moment of pure seeing, and then the moment passed and they went back to their work. The spatter of fish frying in the pan, the crackle of the fire from the stove, and the silence beyond held them in the room together.

"I should be apologizing to you. It was my brother—"

"None of it's our faults," Rachel said.

"The whole town must think it's monstrous. I can't face the way people look at me, as if somehow I'm guilty, too."

"That's nonsense."

"It's true, I feel ashamed of this family. I'm afraid every day what I'm going to see in the newspaper. I have Bea take the papers away as soon as they're delivered."

"You need to get out and mix with people. You can't hole up here for the rest of your life. Start with a visit to your lawyer. Take care of your own business, and nobody will bother you."

"I can't."

"You must."

Rachel directed Nathaniel to sit at the table. He complied like a child. He drank the water she put in front of him and ate the bread and butter.

"You need a haircut," she said. "You can't go to the lawyer looking like that."

After dinner, Rachel found a pair of scissors in a kitchen drawer. She washed his hair in the sink, then Nathaniel sat while Rachel draped a towel around his neck. She lifted the hair from the back of his neck, feeling its weight and the shape of it against his skull.

"Cut it short," he said.

She cut swaths of hair so that it fell on the floor by her feet. She cut until the shape of his head became more apparent from beneath the tangles, and then she shaped along the edges by his ears. She cut the hairs along the back of his neck to reveal the white skin that hadn't been darkened by the sun, then lastly she did his bangs. She left them long and brushed to one side so that he looked like a cleaner version of himself.

"I think you're ready to meet the lawyer," she said.

"I don't know about that," he said.

51

FRANCIS MILLER MET NATHANIEL AT THE DOOR. "NATHANIEL, come right in. I'm so glad to see you."

"I'm sorry it's taken so long." He felt exposed as he ran his hand along the back of his neck. He wore a linen summer suit with a stiff white shirt, brown shoes with laces and matching socks, and he carried the codicil and other paperwork in his father's leather satchel.

"I'm only glad that you're here now."

Nathaniel sat in the chair before the attorney's desk. He was ready to do business, and he knew that Francis would help him. Francis was a friend of his father's and so was a friend of his. The codicil to the will turned out to be valid, and his father had been meaning to make an appointment to come in, only he'd been putting it off, as if the prospect of a will presaged death.

"I'm sorry, Nathaniel. I didn't have anything in writing from your father. It's my duty to execute the written will. I couldn't have known—"

"Still," Nathaniel said. "Why didn't you tell us what he wanted when we were here that day? You could've stopped Finn. It could've changed everything."

"He'd never—"

"How do I protect the estate from Finn?"

Francis nudged the piece of paper across his desk and watched Nathaniel slide it into his satchel. "I could never tell you to tear up the codicil. That could get me disbarred." Francis gazed out the window, then turned back to Nathaniel. "I wish I'd been able to help you boys, but it was out of my hands. I wish I'd been more firm with your father."

"He was a stubborn man," Nathaniel said.

"I'm sorry."

"It doesn't matter now. None of this matters." Nathaniel opened his satchel and dropped the old will on Francis's desk. "Elizabeth and her children," Nathaniel said. "They need to be provided for from the estate, a generous monthly stipend."

"Okay, all right," Frances said. "I'll see to that. Also, there's the business of the tenant farmers. Their leases need to be renewed, and your father wanted to raise their rents. I've got the papers drawn up. You'll just need to sign—"

"No, I don't like that arrangement. Those people will never make enough money to buy their own land. They're locked into us like indentured servants. I won't have it."

"That's a bit drastic, Nathaniel. Why don't you keep their rent as is, and think about raising it next year?"

"No, I want them to buy the land. Have their rent go to the cost of the land at a lowered price, in consideration of the rent they've already paid. I don't need the land. They do. Their families do. I'll not be a thief and keep them down like that."

"It's a significant amount of land." Francis paced behind his desk. "Your father would roll over in his grave."

"Let him roll."

"Okay then, I'll draw up new contracts."

"All this wealth," Nathaniel said. "It's too much for one man, Francis. Too much."

When Elizabeth showed up at the house with Ezra, Samantha, and Susie, Rascal herded them into the house. Providing for his family was one thing, but the noise of the children, the social demands—Nathaniel felt it beyond him. He didn't want to have to figure out how to make conversation, but he was happy to talk to the dog. He leaned back in his chair while Elizabeth brought in a chicken pot pie and a lemon cake.

"Your dog followed us up from the harbor."

"He's always on an adventure."

Elizabeth slid the food onto the counter and turned to face Nathaniel. She softened toward him in a most intimate way that made him uncomfortable. "It's very kind what you've done for us, Nathaniel."

"No need to mention it."

"Very kind," Elizabeth said.

"It's only right."

Ezra stared at him as if he were a puzzle the boy needed to figure out while the girls ran into the living room, looking for toys. Nathaniel seemed to remember that his father kept a cabinet filled with children's toys—dolls, a wooden truck, a marble game—for when they came to visit. Elizabeth looked around the house, which hadn't changed since Nathaniel Sr. died.

Nathaniel poured a bowl of water for the dog and placed it on the floor, out of the way. Ezra listened to their conversation about the fish store, which Elizabeth would sell to the Garrison brothers. When Ezra tired of their talk, he walked to the bookshelves and stared at a small tintype of Nathaniel and Finn as boys, each holding up a flounder. "Did you catch these?" the boy asked.

"We used to go out on our skiff every day in the summer and fish.

Never missed a day. Even in the rain. My father didn't want to raise any
fair-weather sailors."

"How old were you?"

"Maybe ten years old in that picture."

"I'm seven."

"Seven's good."

"Can we go fishing soon?"

"Sometime soon," Nathaniel said, but the bay felt remote to him. It
was the town that took up his time now, and meetings with surveyors,
land court, and lawyers. He felt safe away from the harbor, where he
didn't have to look at Meredith's house or his boat or the island where
the shack used to be.

Ezra put the picture back on the shelf and went to his mother where
he leaned in to her. Nathaniel felt the boy's eyes on him as he gazed over
the harbor toward the distances he didn't want to know about. The girls
had been playing, their soft voices like background music as they drew
on chalkboards—animals and letters that they now wanted to show
their mother and uncle. With the attention off himself, Nathaniel felt
relieved. He lost himself in the sounds of the children's voices until he
forgot that he didn't want company. He forgot the sound of his alone-
ness, and he played with the children until dusk, when they had to leave
and he was alone once more.

52

R ACHEL KNOCKED ON THE DOOR OF THE SMALL HOUSE ON OAKUM
Road. She didn't bring a basket of muffins or a loaf of bread—
nothing to explain why she was visiting.

"Yes?" Jane answered the door. "How can I help you?"

"I'm Rachel, Meredith's friend."

"Oh yes, she's told me about you. Come in, dear." She held the door
to let Rachel into the sitting room. She offered Rachel tea, but Rachel
was too agitated to accept any offer of tea, cookies, or cheese.

"I need to see Meredith. It's important."

"She'll be thrilled to see you. Let me get her. She's just in her room
here."

Meredith came into the sitting room and sat across from Rachel on
the small sofa. "You've come," Meredith said, fiddling with her pearl
earring, taking it from her ear and rolling it around in her palm.

"It's about Nathaniel," Rachel said. She waited for Meredith to react,
to stop her or lean in closer to hear more, but Meredith didn't flinch.
She appeared to neither care nor not care, so Rachel proceeded. "He's
changed, Meredith. This has changed him."

"That's what I feared."

"No, not like that. He's living in his father's house, managing
the estate. He's been to the lawyer and the bookkeeper. He's got
the tenant farmers on a rent-to-buy program so they can become

self-sufficient. He's staked out a parcel of land where you and he are to build a house. He's moving forward, hoping you'll come back. Hoping beyond hope and dedicating himself to creating a life that you'll want to share with him."

Meredith listened reluctantly while Rachel continued. "I miss you. I need someone right now. Davey's left. He's gone away once and for all, and Nathaniel is wonderful, but I need you."

"You don't need me. You're quite all right on your own."

"Sure, but I don't want to be on my own. I loved being at your house with you. I loved being around you and Nathaniel. I know you love him. I felt it in the room between the two of you, thick as any substance."

"So what do you want me to do?"

"I want you to give him a chance."

"I can't."

"But why, Meredith?"

"When things get hard, he runs, whether it's out to the island or out in the boat. I can't take that again."

"He's been ashore for a while now. He's watching over Ezra in Finn's absence. He's really quite committed to Elizabeth and her children. He's taken on responsibilities, like a man who's going to stay ashore for more than a little while."

Rachel could see that Meredith was slowly opening up to the possibility that what Rachel said was true. Maybe Nathaniel had come in from the island once and for all.

"I don't want him to change just for me. That won't work."

"But he's not. It's for himself that he's changing. Being back with you, loving you again, that's what's changed him. It's so obvious. Why can't you see it?"

"I'm afraid to believe it."

"Okay, I understand. But you should give him a chance."

"I don't know if I can."

"Just go see him."

"I'm not ready."

"When do you think you'll be ready?"

"You're talking to me like you're an adult, Rachel. Where did this come from?"

"From knowing you."

"My goodness."

"So will you do it?"

"We'll see," Meredith said. "Now I've got to get back to work, so you'll excuse me?"

"You'll think about what I said?"

"Yes," Meredith told her.

Rachel gathered herself and her small purse and headed for the door.

"You walked all the way here?" Meredith asked.

"Yes, it wasn't bad."

"Six miles. You're very determined."

"You ought to be, too." Rachel let the door close behind her and walked to the gate. She wasn't sure if she'd gotten through to Meredith, but she would visit Nathaniel every day until Meredith came back. She wouldn't leave Nathaniel alone, whether he liked it or not. She walked with steely determination across town, then down the wharf road to the Boyd house. She'd done all she could to bring Meredith back, and she hoped it was enough.

53

THE SKY WAS CLEAR. THERE WAS NO WIND. IT WAS A DIFFERENT KIND of day, and Nathaniel was glad to be out in it. He baited a hook for Ezra and showed him how to lower the squirming eels over the side of the boat where schools of minnows swam in familiar sweeping patterns. Hooks set, Nathaniel leaned back along the seat with his head propped on his rolled-up shirt. The boy leaned over the edge of the boat and peered into the water. He waited silently for a nibble on his hook, then the tug that meant he'd caught one.

Nathaniel saw Jacob in the boy's scrawny arms, in his silent determination to catch a fish. But he'd stopped worrying himself with questions of who was to blame for losing Jacob or what if he'd done something different or what if they hadn't taken the trip at all. The accident had settled into his being like a familiar portrait on the wall, a memory he visited every day but that didn't puncture him in the same way.

Nathaniel closed his eyes against the glare. When he turned away from the sun and looked toward his father's house on the hill, he thought he saw Meredith in the yard, a spyglass in her hand. He stood in the boat, shielded his eyes with one hand, but there was no one there. How his heart had lifted at the thought of her!

"Uncle, I had a nibble, then it was gone."

"Next time, it'll be a tug," he said, patting Ezra on the shoulder. "You'll feel it, and you'll flick the line. Then you'll catch him."

Sails swept along the horizon like fins against a deep-blue sky. Nathaniel watched the business of the bay with a sense of relief. He'd always hated the way men worked, but watching the boats now, imagining seamen hauling nets full of fish over the rail, he felt compassion for their duty. He'd never have to work, and any work he'd done so far had been perfunctory.

"I've got one. I've got one," the boy squealed.

The line grew taut, and Nathaniel helped him haul the fish in slowly. He guided Ezra's hands in his own. "You gotta feel it fight on the other end of the line," he said. "Let it tire itself out, then you slowly reel it in."

He helped Ezra pull the fish close to the boat where it swam in desperate circles, so close the rainbow sheen of the scales shone up at them, the hectic rhythm of the gills, and the dull, beautiful look of the eyes. There was life in him, Nathaniel thought. The sun burned Nathaniel's eyes, and he squinted against the glare as he cut the fish loose.

They watched the fish swim down into the murky depths.

"Let's catch it again," Ezra said.

—⁓—

Hours on the boat, and the boy grew exhausted. His skinny shoulders slumped over, and he struggled to keep his eyes open. Nathaniel placed the boat cushions in the shelter of the bow to create a makeshift bed, and he told Ezra to rest there while he rowed them in. "I'm not tired," Ezra said.

"Just for a few minutes," Nathaniel told him. Ezra, lulled by the sweep of the oars and the motion of the boat, fell sound asleep, his body curled into a fetal position on the cushions, so much like Jacob at that age, trying not to sleep while his brothers did the work.

When Ezra woke up, they were coming around the jetty into the harbor. Nathaniel threw his back into rowing them against the tide. He stayed close to the jetty where the tide didn't run as fast, and when Ezra woke, he nearly leapt up. "I don't want to miss anything," he said.

Nathaniel let him onto his lap where he could practice pulling on the oars. They rowed like this across the harbor to the thin spit of beach where Nathaniel anchored the skiff. He rowed knowing where the beach was without turning around, because he'd seen so often the row of boats that let him know he was there. When they neared the beach, he rowed hard onto the shore, and when he turned around to climb over the side of the boat, there was Meredith getting herself up from the sand. She was a little shy as she wiped her hands across the sandy bottom of her skirt, looking at him to see if her presence was welcome here.

"You made it," she said.

Nathaniel kicked the anchor in the sand and tried to think of what to say. *Are you coming back to me?* He stood before her, and she looked down at the boat, then up to his face until she met the safety of his gaze. He held his arms open for her, and she stepped into them, dropped her head onto his chest. Ezra gathered the fishing gear from the boat and stacked it against the rocks. He worked back and forth from the boat to the jetty, then he pulled the oars in and slid them under the seats, coiled the loose ropes, and pushed the boat out into the water where it could float in the tide.

"I did all the work," he said to Nathaniel.

"Yes, you did."

"So let's go," the boy said, and Meredith laughed, and they walked up the harbor road toward the Boyd house, each of them carrying a fishing pole, a bait bucket, or the canteen that had been emptied hours ago.

Epilogue

T
HE PIECE OF LAND WAS ALONG THE WATER ON FLAT GROUND WEST of his father's house. It bordered an estuary where mussels stuck to the barnacled rocks in awkward clumps, and the tide ran through the river in a rush of water that poured beneath a narrow bridge. When they were boys, they played in the cool air under the bridge, their voices echoing against the rocks, their small feet gripping the rocks as they stepped across the water, hands out to either side. It was a game, and only once in a while did someone fall in.

"It's a shame to cut down all the trees," Meredith said.

"We'll use the lumber to build the house." Nathaniel pointed toward the less wooded area in the center of the property. "Over there," he said, "in view of the water."

"Yes, and a nice barn for horses and chickens, a big garden."

"I'll need an office. I never would've thought—"

"And you'll have one." Meredith leaned against him and tilted her head back for a kiss, and they both felt themselves on the edge of something new and beyond what they had dreamed of as children. They were older now. They could draw their life around them with each action they took. Every choice and purchase and plan was theirs. All they had to do was reach toward it.

As they stood on the edge of their property, a line of men approached from the road. They were the farmers on Nathaniel's land, which would one day be their land. They carried crosscut saws and axes. As they got closer, Nathaniel could make out the friendly, open expressions on their faces. A tall, bearded man with an ax approached Nathaniel. "We're here to help with the trees," he said.

"There's no need," Nathaniel said, but the men persisted.

"Mr. Boyd, we're here to work."

For weeks, Nathaniel visited the land to watch the men work. They were grateful for his generosity, and it showed in every swing of an ax, every cut across an oak trunk with the long, bandy saw.

After the trees were cleared and the stumps removed, the men hewed long trunks of wood into solid boards. Nathaniel laid out the outline of their home with string fastened to sticks in the ground and stretched along what would be their walls. Rascal jumped back and forth over the strings as Nathaniel threw sticks for him. When Nathaniel was done laying out the house, he stood back to survey his work. He saw the stone foundation and the walls of their home that would form shelter against the heat of the sun and the weather as it rolled in off the bay. He would make it sturdy, just as he'd built the shack. A barn out back would house their animals, and there'd be a plot of land for his garden. And there would be a post by the shore to tie up a skiff for Ezra. His hope was for more than Meredith's love. It ran deeper to encompass the breadth of his life and the people he loved, including the small boy who would grow into a man, Ezra Jacob Boyd.

Nathaniel walked through the wet seagrass, flattened now as the tide receded, and in an open spot along the edge of the river, he stopped and wiggled the post he'd placed in the ground, a post where he could tie up his skiff. He imagined Ezra growing up rowing the small boat, then craving larger adventures. Until then, he would fish with the boy, take him farther and farther into the bay until he could row out there himself. He rolled up his pants and stepped into the water. It was colder than the harbor and shocking to his skin.

Without thinking about it, he pulled his shirt over his head and tossed it onto the seagrass. Then he dove into the icy chill and swam out from the shore, Rascal following him with his head held high above the water. From there, Nathaniel saw the sweep of his land and the place where he would build his house. He saw the Boyd house, *his* house, atop the hill on the other side of the marsh. He didn't feel the sense of ownership he imagined his father had felt but rather a sense of belonging to the place, as if he was responsible for the stewardship of this land.

He swam along the shore and then back to where he'd planted his post in the ground, as if to say, *Here. Here is where I'll be.* He pulled himself onto the land, shook the water from his hair. It happened in a moment. He saw the sweep of his life, from his early years with his brothers, losing Jacob, then his existence on the island, and now his future unfolding before him, as if his life were all one moment that he could hold inside him. He was at peace with it all. He pulled his shirt on and followed the dog toward the house where Meredith and Rachel were preparing Ezra's catch for their dinner. He thought, *We can go home now.*

READING GROUP GUIDE

1. How does the Boyd family cope with losing Jacob?

2. What are some of the themes in the novel?

3. What are the different ways Nathaniel and Finn respond to their father's pressure to live a life like his?

4. How does the natural environment inform the characters and the story?

5. Why does Nathaniel exile himself to the marsh, and what brings him home again? What enables him to make the transition from living on the marsh to living in his father's house?

6. In what ways do the brothers give in to their fate, and how do they resist it? Why do they respond so differently?

7. How much of the story is fate, how much is timing, and how much is the characters' volition?

8. Do you feel that the story stays true to the characters' motivations?

9. Can you imagine an alternate ending?

A CONVERSATION WITH
THE AUTHOR

How did *The Last Sailor* first come to you?

I was reading *Suttree* by Cormac McCarthy, and the main character's isolation as he rowed along the river resonated for me. The character of Nathaniel Boyd was a response to that feeling. As a kid, I grew up across the street from an expansive marsh that captured my imagination. I fantasized about living on one of the far islands by the bay. In a way, the novel is an exploration of that fantasy and of the fact of loneliness that we all share in perhaps less radical ways. The idea of someone struggling to live with an awful loss is often a fact of life, but in Nathaniel's case, the fact that the loss occurred when he was such a young man and responsible for his younger brother led to an extreme response, and this interested me as a novelist. What could bring Nathaniel in from that lonely existence on the marsh? What would have to happen to bring him home?

How much of the novel is autobiographical, and how much is invention?

So much of writing springs from the nest of experience and imagination that lies within. As I said, the marsh is real. I

lived there and dreamed about it long after I was gone. It was
a home to return to again and again, a place where I could
re-engage with that childhood fantasy through the life of
Nathaniel Boyd. I also have a strong background growing up
on the water and sailing, and I'm drawn to disasters at sea over
and over again. I'm not sure what psychic vein that impulse
is tapping, but it sure would be nice to know! As far as the
characters and situations go, those are all a product of my
imagination.

**You've done many interviews with authors, including two books of
interviews and a book on how to interview writers and creative people.
How did conducting these interviews inform your writing?**

Those many interviews were my literary training ground. I
read all the books by each author I interviewed, then read arti-
cles about them and any other interviews they did. I steeped
myself in the writing world of each author, then asked them
anything I wanted to know. It doesn't get any better than that
for a writer. I went straight to the source with any questions I
had about craft, the creative process, living the life of a writer.
You name it, I asked it. Then I transcribed the interviews, so
I was able to inhabit the authors' words in a unique way that
helped me absorb what they were saying. Additionally, con-
necting with authors and publishing the interviews put me in
touch with a literary community that went beyond my imme-
diate circle, which provided inspiration and support while I
worked on my novels.

What draws you to write novels rather than short stories?

I love the landscape of a novel and knowing that I'm going to hang around with the characters for the long haul. I'm drawn to exploring broad periods of time. I admire short story writers tremendously. They have a special set of skills that I don't have—they're able to create worlds in a few pages. I need at least three hundred pages to figure out what I'm trying to say.

Is it difficult as a woman to write male characters? How do you inhabit their experiences?

Theoretically, a writer should be able to inhabit any character's perspective. It's an act of compassion and empathy. I don't find it more or less difficult to write about men. In some ways, writing men is easier because it's purely an act of imagination and I feel freer.

This is a story set in the aftermath of trauma. What drew you to this difficult terrain?

I was interested in the ripples that such a loss would create on a family. The loss happens in a minute, but the aftereffects take place over years and even decades. I wanted to explore how characters operate around loss, how they come together and move apart, how they react in their own lives separate from the family, and how they think about what's happened. This is rich terrain that I couldn't turn away from once it found me.

What is your process like for developing a novel?

So much of writing is revising and deleting. I let myself loose on the first draft—anything goes. Then I have to get a grip and see what this book is that I'm dealing with. I have to get rid of anything that feels outside the story's characters and themes. Anything that doesn't touch a nerve has to go. Then I deal with what's left over, move things around, write to fill in the gaps, then revise, revise, revise. There is no end to the revisions, but it's all in service of the characters and telling their truest story.

Richard Ford once said that place is a character in fiction. Do you agree?

Yes, I do, and yet I don't think about it as I write. Place sets a mood and a tone for the novel and can also echo a character's reality. I find that this happens without my thinking about it— the characters and the landscape or weather work together in unfathomable ways.

How does your reading life inform your writing life, and what are you reading now?

I read for at least four hours a night. I believe that what goes in comes out, so I'm very careful about reading great literature, whether classic or contemporary. I underline passages that speak to me in terms of what I'm working on now, and I often write things down. Not everything I read inspires me to do this, but still, the language and technique get into my brain. Who knows how it plays out in what I write? I just know it does. I'm reading the novels and stories of Patricia Hensley, a biography of Frederick Douglass, and *Wild Decembers* by Edna O'Brien. I'm struck so often by the poetry of fiction that I have to stop and read passages over and over, just to take in all the nuances of language.

What are you working on now?

I'm working on a novel set in 1923 during Prohibition. One of the main characters is a rumrunner in Provincetown. I've done a lot of research, and I'm having a great time writing it. The beginning phases of revision are always daunting, but this novel has a life of its own—all I need to do is keep showing up.

I'm going to ask you the question that you end all your interviews with. What would you say to new writers working on their first novel or stories?

I think I've said this before, but read, read, read. Everything you need to know, you'll find in books. It's also critically important to keep your ass in the chair. When you think about getting up, wait fifteen minutes. Resist the cup of coffee, the mail, petting the dog—just sit. You'll be writing before the fifteen minutes is up. Trust me.

ACKNOWLEDGMENTS

I first want to thank my family for their ongoing belief in my work. My early experiences in boats on the waters off Cape Cod's shores have made all the difference in my life. Thank you to all the generous readers who offered their time and encouragement, including Ailish, Leslie, Randi, Susan, and Myra. Thank you to Shana Drehs and the team at Sourcebooks who have worked on developing this manuscript from its fledgling beginnings and dedicated themselves throughout the journey to completion. I couldn't ask for a better editor and team. To Laurie Liss, an extraordinary creative collaborator, who's read this book more times than any human should have to—thank you for your tireless dedication and friendship. To Gregg Almquist, who walked the path with me, through some often lonely terrain. And finally to my love, Leslie, for so much support and belief—*forever*.

The
LIGHTKEEPER'S
WIFE

1

NEAR DAWN A LOUD CRACK CAME, LIKE A TREE FALLING. THERE were no trees near the house. Hannah reached quickly for a pair of John's work pants. She'd never worn pants before, but he wasn't here to stop her. Out the northeast window, the fog was so dense she could run her hands through it. Pants cinched in a rope knot at her waist, she stood at the kitchen counter eating a piece of salt beef. There was no pleasure in it. Outside, the wind had made the low-lying bushes tilt with a strange bend that made them yearn in the same direction rather than lean. The light, Dangerfield Light, flashed a steady pulse. There was nothing to see but more fog. No cries or calling out from below, only canvas sails snapping in the wind.

The familiar sound of a shipwreck.

From the top of the stairs that led down to the beach, the wreck was a veiled shadow some three hundred feet out from shore. She gazed toward the road, but there was no sign of her husband. John had been gone for a couple of days up Cape for supplies. She'd missed him in their bed, missed the size of him and his arms around her, but she wasn't going to wait for him, not with sailors struggling for safety. She followed the rickety staircase, down the two hundred and some odd steps that shivered beneath her footfall, easy for her heel to miss and send her to the bottom in a heap of broken bones.

The rain on the stairs sounded like pebbles pouring down, relentless. Rain trickled down the neck of her jacket, frozen until it warmed against her skin. Nearly one hundred and fifty feet she descended to the beach, where the surf frothed at her feet. She kept her eyes on the faint impression of the stranded ship. Wind lashed the covering over the rescue skiff until she got the canvas under control and shoved it beneath the stairs.

Make sure the lines are coiled. Keep the life ring at the ready. The thrill and shiver of the storm vibrated through her as she guided the skiff on rollers toward the surf. She rolled up the bottoms of her pants and waded into the icy cold, holding the boat steady as she pulled the oars from beneath the seat and climbed onboard.

She'd promised not to go out alone, to stay ashore and keep the lights flashing, but there could be men aboard that ship about to drown. As she put her back into rowing, the beach faded in the fog behind her and the flash from the lighthouse grew dim.

Over her shoulder was the looming architecture of the ship, sunk low in the water, the foremast shorn.

She kept a safe distance to avoid any wreckage, a falling mast or topsail spar. The skiff's seams creaked, the seat sagged beneath her as the waves knocked the little boat about, but she used the oars to steady it. The wind drummed at her ears, that hard rhythm the only sound now.

She rowed closer, until the ruin took shape. The ocean had poured into the hull from below. It had dismantled hatchways, bulwarks, cupboards, everything splintered apart and drifting.

A froth of oil and something red and soupy floated across the water in a wide, reeking arc around the wreck. Seagulls dove into the slick, pecking at bits of bread and food, their cries piercing and debauched.

Hannah rowed to leeward, following the drift of debris, keeping her eyes sharp, glancing over her right shoulder, then her left, shifting her attention aft again. A clunk against the hull stopped her midstroke.

"Hello! Anyone there?"

The fog muffled her voice. Reaching into the water, she dislodged a six-foot piece of rail that rested against the skiff. She tried not to think about how many men had been onboard. Oars set and ready, she watched and searched, scanning the water in circles around the wreck. Minutes passed.

Or was it longer?

"Hello!" Hannah called. Was that an arm reaching up from the water? Right there, a man clinging to a broken spar. The life ring was attached to a long rope, which she fastened to the back of the boat. She stood and shifted her weight in rhythm to the waves. She'd never saved a drowning man, but instinct took over, and with a heave, she flung the life ring toward him. *Grab it, you can do it.*

The man kicked toward the ring, but he wouldn't let go of the wood spar that kept him afloat. He rose and then dropped behind a wave, rose up, then down again. The wind billowed her oilskin jacket and chilled her. It dried the saltwater onto her skin in a thin crust. Waves splashed the wreck in a rhythmic blast as Hannah pulled the ring in. She tossed it closer to the man this time, intoxicated with the prospect of reeling him in.

"Grab hold, man! Grab hold! You'll freeze out here." He lifted his head and slowly drifted toward the circle of bobbing cork. When he finally looped an arm through it and let go of the spar, she braced her foot against the stern seat and hauled until the sailor appeared, face-down, behind the skiff. She'd have to bring him over the transom. She pushed the life ring aside and grabbed him under the arms. His legs floated back so that she was able to use the rise of the waves to hook his elbows over the gunwale, then pull him up and tilt him into the boat. He landed in the bilge, a shrimplike curl. Frozen breath hovered by his mouth. She removed her jacket and draped it over him and pulled it to his chin to shelter him from the wind.

Hannah leaned in close to the man. "Was there anyone else? You've got to tell me now." The man groaned and pulled his arms in around his body. His eyes batted beneath the lids, thick eyebrows plastered to his skull, a blue vein marking the side of his face like a scar. She shook him hard. "Was there anyone else?" Hannah scanned the water in every direction. "Anyone out there?" She plunged the oars into the water and took another turn toward the wreck, but the debris had drifted off and there was nothing left to see.

The man didn't move or make a sound. She took notice of his gray undershirt and long johns, no other clothes. Sailors often removed layers in the water to stay afloat. *You're hardly blue at all.* Sole survivor. *That says something about a man.* She turned to get her bearings. *I'll get you ashore. You may be the first one I've rescued, but you'll not be the last.* The wind was dying off, the surf easier now, and the sailor wasn't jostled. The fog had lifted enough for her to see the beach. She ignored the ache in her arms and steered the skiff toward the lighthouse. If the sailor couldn't make it up, she'd have to haul him in the life cart. At least he was small. Some of the men John rescued were so big he had to wait while Hannah went for help to get the men up the dunes.

Blood ran from the sailor's forehead now, red streaks in the bilge water. Hannah crossed the oars in front of her and bent down for a look. A three-corner tear, but not to the bone. She quickly removed her woolen sweater, rolled it into a ball, and stuck it under his head.

When she turned to locate the lighthouse again—she wanted to land near the base of the stairs—there was Tom Atkins, John's best friend who lived next door, pacing the beach. Hannah recognized his willowy figure, one hand over his eyes to shield them from the hazy light. She didn't want to have to explain herself, or talk, or do anything but get the sailor up to the house. She'd known Tom since the day she moved to the lighthouse. The three of them—John, Hannah, and Tom—had sat around many fires and tended many half-drowned men. Once they got a man ashore, he was kept alive with heat from the fire, Hannah's chowder, and good conversation. The sound of people talking kept a fevered sailor attached to this world, Hannah was sure of it.

"Hey," Tom called, waving as if his worry could bring her in faster. Finally, he walked into the surf, boots, pants, and all. As the skiff lifted and rolled in on a breaker, he guided it onto the beach, eyeing the man in the bilge. "Hannah, Jesus Christ. You shouldn't be out in the boat alone."

"I'm not alone, am I?" she said.

"That was a brutal nor'easter, tore the corner of my barn roof off."

"Storm's over, Tom. Now, you want to help me or not?"

"It's just luck you're okay. You know that, don't you? It's pure luck." His long fingers felt along the man's neck to find a pulse. "He's alive, at least."

They lifted the sailor from the skiff and carried him up the beach. He groaned until they put him in the life cart and covered him with blankets. The life cart was nothing more than an old skiff with wheels on the bottom that John used for hauling injured survivors who couldn't climb the stairs, but it did the job.

"I went by the house to check on you after the storm, then saw the wreck and had a hunch you might be down here. This was the only one, then?"

Hannah nodded.

Blood from the sailor's forehead ran down the side of his face. Hannah wiped the blood with her shirtsleeve and took another look at the gash. "We've got to cover that," she said, "to stop the bleeding." She unsheathed the rigging knife from her belt.

"What are you doing?"

"You look at me like I'm going to kill him, Tom." She cut a strip of cotton from her shirttail, handed Tom the knife, and went to work bandaging the sailor's head, folding the strip of cotton in half and covering the wound.

Tom winced and stepped back when she tightened the bandage. "You'll need a shot of something to warm him up," he said, and searched through the gear beneath the stairs until he found the bottle. He held the man's head up and tipped the whiskey to his lips until he swallowed.

With the sailor in the cart, they worked fast to pull it onto the rollers, wooden logs shaved to be even all the way around, and then they maneuvered it back to the dunes. "He's shivering near to death," Tom said.

"So, let's hurry up."

"I'll haul him up, just give me a few minutes," Tom said, heading for the stairs.

Hannah stared across the water, wondering how many men had been aboard the ship. Over a hundred ships wrecked along this coast every year—last year, 1842, had been particularly bad. And there was nothing anyone could do. No flashing light, no navigational chart could save them—the sandbars shifted during each storm and tides carried off parts of the beach so that the coast was always changing and impossible to chart. Experienced sea captains knew to stay offshore, but in a storm, the northeast wind forced ships onto the shoals where they ran aground and fell victim to the battering surf.

"Hello down there." Tom tugged on the line, and the front of the cart lifted. Hannah guided it up the dune, over brambles and sea grass until it was closer to Tom than to the beach. Then she trudged up the stairs, the wind at her back pushing her, nearly lifting her up.